Dedicated to

my former students

ACKNOWLEDGEMENTS

Special Thanks

Shirley Tassin

Vickie Flanders

Christopher Flanders

Bret Pollard

Dodie Landry Lachney

Randy DeCuir

Just a Piece of Red String II

Rebellion and Rectitude

by

Dr. Thomas S. Smith, Sr.

"Each age tries to form its own conception of the past. Each age writes the history of the past anew with reference to the conditions uppermost in its own time."—Frederick Jackson Turner

"The past is a foreign country;
they do things differently there."—L. P. Hartley

Just a Piece of Red String II

Rebellion and Rectitude

Natchez, Mississippi—1859

In Natchez the day after Solomon had left, Sawyer went to the bank to discuss a business idea with Mr. Baxter. The banker referred him to Samuel Whitmore after they had talked of investment capital and general business financing options. Sawyer long had the idea of starting a foundry in Natchez. Baxter had told him that Samuel Whitmore was interested in a similar idea and that the two of them may want to discuss a possible partnership.

Sawyer was about to leave when Mr. Baxter said, "Did yew hear about poor old Holcumb?"

"No, what happened?"

"He was found dead in his front room this morning by a neighbor. Doc Whiddon went and looked at him. He had been dead since sometime yesterday as near as he could figure. Doc said he jist up and died. He cain't determine why. I suppose it was jist old age."

"Yeah. I guess so."

"Well, good day, Sawyer. Come back in after yew and Samuel talk. I think yew two can make some money together," said Baxter.

"And you, too, I think." Sawyer shook Baxter's hand and left the bank to call upon Samuel Whitmore.

In a few minutes Sawyer walked on the porch of the Whitmore house and knocked on the door. Cryer, the black maid, opened the door and asked, "Kin I hep yew, sur?"

"Yes. Mr. Whitmore, please. My name is Sawyer Dundee."

"Master Whitmore be out on business, but will comes back soon," Cryer said.

At that moment Eve looked down the stairs and cried out, "Sawyer, how nice to see you. Won't you come in? Daddy'll be back in a short time." She came down the stairway and extended her hand to Sawyer. "Cryer, fetch us some coffee. In the sitting room, please."

"Yus'm."

Cryer exited to the kitchen while Sawyer and Eve walked into the sitting room. "Sit down, please."

They chatted about the weather, homes in Natchez, and steamboats arriving on the river. Then Eve said, "I hope Solomon is all right. I wish he would have stayed in Natchez."

"Oh, we do, too. But I guess Solomon just had to go. He'll be fine. He's always been able to take care of himself. He'll be back with us before we know it. And I believe he'll have some stories to entertain us with," Sawyer replied.

They heard steps on the porch, and the front door opened. Mr. Whitmore was removing his hat when he saw Eve and Sawyer. "Well, well, young Mr. Dundee. Welcome," said Mr. Whitmore. They shook hands.

"Mr. Whitmore, call me Sawyer. You and I think alike. Let's talk business," Sawyer said. The two men talked for an hour and then through the mid-day meal, which was prepared by Eve and Cryer. By the end of the meal they had agreed in principle to a business partnership for a foundry in Natchez. They would meet with the banker the next day. Sawyer left convinced that the business would be profitable for all concerned and that Natchez would benefit, too.

Sawyer stayed busy working to get the foundry established and keeping his other business interests going. Days turned into weeks, and weeks turned into months. Sawyer, through his new business partnership, became fast friends of the Whitmores. He saw Eve every few days. Also, Sawyer visited the Surgets often, with and without Stelcie.

The new little foundry would be going at full capacity soon. Sawyer could slow down some now.

Miriam had to return to Memphis within a week at her father's request. She had told Stelcie and Sawyer the news one Sunday afternoon at Clifton. She would eventually return to Natchez because she had fallen in love with Clifton. The Surgets were sad because of her leaving soon but said that she was welcome to return to live with them if she wished and had her father's permission. Miriam also had to decide whether to go to further her schooling. Her father had always encouraged her to find a private, live-in tutor.

On the day Miriam was to leave for Memphis, Stelcie and Sawyer went to assist her and the Surgets and bid her farewell. It was a bright sunny day.

On the way to the steamboat landing, the older Surgets spoke little. Miriam and Stelcie chattered away to mask their sadness at the parting. Sawyer rode along beside the carriage on Country Boy, mostly silent himself. Stelcie's horse was tied to the wagon with the travel cases. At the top of the hill on Silver Street, they saw the steamboat with its tall stacks, smoke curling lazily upward.

The landing was a beehive of activity. Men were loading the steamer with large trunks and luggage of passengers. A few passengers were boarding the vessel by way of the gangplank, too. Miriam's baggage was being loaded while Mr. Surget went to the ticket office to be sure all was in order for Miriam's trip. He soon returned, and they all went aboard to settle Miriam in her cabin for the trip.

The heard the whistle blast too soon, and the announcement for all non-passengers to go ashore. The Surgets embraced and exchanged kisses on the cheek. Mrs. Surget had tears rolling down her face. The older Surgets left the cabin to disembark. Miriam came out on the upper deck. She hugged Stelcie and kissed her on the cheek. "You are my best friend," she said, stifling a tear.

Stelcie couldn't hold her tears back. "Yew're mine, too. Come back soon. We'll miss yew, Miriam."

Sawyer felt awkward standing there until Miriam turned to him and smiled. "I'll miss you, too, Saw. I've become accustomed to seeing you often." It was the first time she had ever called him Saw. It made him feel good. He was basking in the warm feeling when Miriam embraced him and kissed him on the side of this face. He returned the embrace and then stepped awkwardly back to the railing and said nothing for a long moment.

"I'll miss you, Miriam. Return to Natchez as soon as you can," Sawyer said warmly.

The whistle blasted out again. Sawyer and Stelcie left the steamboat immediately. On the bank the Surgets and Dundees waved and shouted to Miriam as the steamboat moved out onto the river. The sound of the great paddlewheel at first was loud and then diminished as the distance from the shore increased.

At the top of Silver Street the Dundees and Surgets bid each other good day and separated to go home.

Time went by. Miriam and Stelcie constantly exchanged letters. In August Miriam's letter said that now she had a private tutor, and her letters then came less often.

The little foundry prospered. Samuel Whitmore and Sawyer Dundee proved to be good business partners.

Stelcie talked Sawyer into purchasing a carriage for the family. Sawyer was against the idea at first but relented when told by Stelcie the advantages for their mother. He could not go against that reasoning.

Sawyer and Stelcie, as well as their mother often visited the Whitmores and the Surgets. Clifton was a dream world year round, but it still was not the same without Miriam there.

In January 1860 the Dundees and the Whitmores were visiting the Surgets at Clifton. The women, Mrs. Surget, Mrs. Dundee, Eve, and Stelcie, were in the sewing room working on a quilt. The men, Sawyer, Samuel, and Frank, were sitting in the study talking business.

Frank Surget said, "I was in the bank talking with Baxter Friday, and he asked me if I wanted to sell any of my acreage. He quoted a very liberal price, but I don't want to sell any of my lands. He then asked if I knew of anyone who wanted to sell. I told him I didn't know of anyone wanting to sell, but I had not been looking. He went on to say that several large tracts across the river had recently changed hands. Also, one section northwest of Natchez."

"Who's the buyer?"

"I asked him that very question. All he said was that he was brokering for someone in New Orleans, some bank there. Either he didn't know or he had been instructed not to reveal the person," answered Frank.

"I hope whoever is buying comes to live here in Natchez. The idea of an absentee landlord doesn't appeal to me, especially now with the Presidential election later this year and the uncertainty that's going to accompany it," said Sawyer.

"Couldn't agree with yew more, my boy," added Samuel.

"Land isn't the only thing sought after," Frank said.

"What else?" Samuel inquired.

"The Silver Street Hotel is being purchased. Jonathon Brock has accepted a generous price, and he'll stay on as manager, Baxter said," Frank continued. "Whoever this buyer is, he has money, plenty of it."

"I hope it's not some Yankee," injected Samuel.

"Maybe the person will come live here as I said before," Sawyer stated. "And maybe it's a Southerner."

"And maybe we can put a Southerner in the White House," muttered Frank.

At this point in the conversation the ladies walked in. Stelcie, as usual, could not refrain from jumping into the conversation, and said, "Not if them damn Yankees have their way!"

"Stelcie! Yew know it's not proper fer a young lady to speak in that manner," admonished Laura Dundee. "Now don't yew repeat that phrase."

"Yes, Mama."

"She's right, though," Frank quickly said. "She's right about them having their way. We Southerners have only the Senate to block the Yankee politicians if we don't elect a friend to the Presidency."

The men shook their heads in agreement, and the talk turned to other things. Shortly Laura Dundee asked, "Charlotte, have yew heard from Miriam lately?"

"Yes, she's still involved deeply in her private education. She wishes to visit us again this summer, she writes. We want her to come for the entire summer."

"What about Solomon?" asked Frank Surget. "Anything from

him?"

"No," replied Laura, "we haven't received a letter, not a single line. I worry about him. I pray nothing bad has happened to him."

"He's all right, Mother," Sawyer said. "You know he's doing well. He's lucky. He's probably living it up somewhere."

"I hope he comes back soon," said Eve.

"We jist want to hear from him. To know he's still alive," said Laura.

"Mother," Sawyer responded, "he's alive. He'll turn up here one day when we least expect him. And I'll bet he'll have lots more money than when he left."

"I hope yew are right," sighed Laura Dundee.

The rest of the afternoon was a happy visit with lighthearted talk. The Dundees and Whitmores remained for dinner and left shortly afterward.

Spring brought warmer weather and new green and other colors to the land. Warm days encouraged everyone to go outside. Stelcie convinced her mother to go riding in the carriage to get out of the house. Stelcie wanted to show Laura Dundee the work that was beginning on the new home of the family of Dr. Haller Nutt. Sawyer had told both of them some things about it, and Stelcie wanted to see the site herself. Gabriel drove them for a time down a dirt road shaded by trees hanging thick with Spanish moss. They rounded a curve, and there up on a small hill was the beginning of a huge house. Another carriage was there as well as many wagons loaded with lumber and other building materials.

"It's Dr. Nutt. And his wife," said Stelcie. "Stop here, Gabriel. Let's visit with them, Mama."

"If we won't interrupt," replied Laura Dundee.

The doctor and his wife looked up from where they were. Gabriel stopped the carriage. The Nutts waved and started walking toward the road and the carriages.

"Hello, Dr. Nutt and Mrs. Nutt. How are y'all today?" shouted Stelcie, who was already out of the carriage.

"Good day to yew," said Laura Dundee cheerily.

"And good day to y'all, also, Mrs. Dundee and Miss Stelcie," Dr. Nutt said.

"Laura, I haven't seen yew all winter," Mrs. Nutt said. "Isn't that shameful of me?"

"No, no, not at all," replied Mrs. Dundee. I haven't really been off our home site much. We'll catch up. Tell us about yore house yew are building."

"It's been our dream for several years now," responded Mrs. Nutt.

"Yes, it has," added the doctor. "It was designed from our ideas last year by Samuel Sloan, a Philadelphia architect. It's essentially a Muslim plan that literally stuck in my mind. It's going to be octagonal in shape, six stories, a sixteen-sided cupola, and crowned by a Byzantine onion-shaped dome."

"It sounds grand and glorious," said Stelcie dreamily.

"Yes," added Mrs. Dundee.

"We are so happy that the work has finally begun," Mrs. Nutt said.

"Yes, when everyone sees our oriental villa, the octagon shape will be the style," Dr. Nutt added with a smile.

"How many rooms will there be?" Stelcie asked.

"Thirty-two are in the plans," answered Mrs. Nutt. "And we are ordering furnishings and décor from France, Italy, England, and up north."

"It sounds as though yore house will be beautiful," said Laura Dundee. "I can hardly wait to visit yew after it is complete."

"Yew know y'all and y'all's family have a standing invitation at all times," said Dr. Nutt. "Sawyer will supply much of the wood building materials. He can keep yew informed of the progress whenever he comes around. And yew can take a carriage ride by ever so often. We might even meet as we did today."

"We're calling it Longwood," put in Mrs. Nutt.

"How lovely," said Laura Dundee.

"We'll visit and talk soon," said Mrs. Nutt. "I'll share my decorating ideas, and y'all can make suggestions."

"We'll look forward to seeing y'all," Stelcie said.

"By the way," said Dr. Nutt, "please tell Sawyer I'll be coming around to see him to order some lumber. I must talk with these workers to see their progress. Most of them are from Pennsylvania. The work boss is from there. Excuse me, please. Good day, ladies."

"Good bye," said Mrs. Nutt as they walked back up the slope.

"Bye," said the Dundees at the same time.

"I'll tell Sawyer," added Laura Dundee.

They got into the carriage and had Gabriel drive back toward Natchez and the river. "Since we're out," said Stelcie, "let's go by some of the other beautiful homes and gardens."

"That's a nice idea," said Mrs. Dundee. "Do that, Gabriel, please."

"Yus, Missus."

Gabriel drove by many beautiful homes. Stelcie and Laura Dundee enjoyed the bright, warm day while passing by the houses and stopping a few times to chat with friends.

Stelcie convinced her mother that they should go to the landing under the hill on Silver Street to have tea. She knew that a steamer would probably arrive soon, and she always loved the excitement of a steamboat coming in.

Stelcie was right. A paddle wheeler came in about half an hour after they had ordered their tea at the cafe. The usual buzz of activity happened, and Stelcie took it all in, wide-eyed and smiling.

They left Silver Street before the steamboat pulled back out onto the river. At the top of the hill, Stelcie looked back at the landing and said," I had hoped that Solomon would be on that boat, Mama."

"I know, dear, I know."

That night at the supper table, Stelcie filled Sawyer's ears with her day's activities. Sawyer was in awe of the future Longwood, too. He told them of the planned mirror system to use reflected sunlight to illuminate the inner recesses of parts of the house.

"I'm gonna marry me a rich, rich man one day and have a big house like Clifton or Longwood," Stelcie said in a dreamy tone.

"Of course yew will, Stelcie," answered her mother. "Yore knight in shining armor will come riding in on his great white steed."

"Oh, Mama."

"Oh, Stelcie" said Sawyer in a mocking tone. He patted her on the head and smiled dreamily at her as he rose from the table. "I'm going out back to the stable to check Country Boy and then to the slave quarters. I'll be back in a while."

Sawyer looked in on his horse and went back to the slave cabins the way his father had always done to check on the buildings and the slaves. He had visited the two family cabins and even stuck his head in the bunk house where the two unmarried males lived and was walking

16

back up to the house when heard a horse coming up beside the house. There was a rider on it. He was tall in the saddle. The horse snorted and then whinnied. Sawyer thought the sounds of the horse and the silhouette were familiar. "Solomon?" he questioned himself silently. "Hello," he said aloud.

"That you, Saw?" asked his cousin Solomon Witcher.

"Solomon! You're back!" shouted Sawyer. He let out a yell that brought Beulah to the kitchen door and Stelcie to her window. "It's Solomon," he shouted again as he ran to embrace his cousin, who had dismounted Midnight.

"Sawyer, what are you doing outside this time of night?" asked Solomon. "Oh, I know. You're just like Uncle Jeremiah. You've been visiting the quarters. You and that Daddy of yours. You're so much his makeover. You two actually care about your niggers."

"Massa Solomon, welcome home," said Beulah. "Comes in, and I fetch yew a drink." She held the door and motioned both young men inside.

They heard footsteps on the stairs. Stelcie shot into the kitchen in her nightclothes and robe. "Solomon! Solomon! Yore back!" She ran to him and hugged him tightly. "It's been so long."

Laura Dundee entered the kitchen and said, "Solomon, welcome home." She smiled at him and extended her arms. Solomon went to his aunt and embraced her.

"I'm glad to be back, Aunt Laura," said Solomon when he had kissed the side of her face.

"Sit down and tell us what yew've done," Laura Dundee urged.

"Yes, Solomon, did yew find the outlaw's buried treasure?" put in Stelcie.

Beulah handed Solomon a glass of tea and stepped away to prepare glasses for the others. Solomon took a long drink from his glass and looked at his aunt and cousins. Then he grinned a broad, toothy grin and said in a firm voice, "Yes. Yes. I did. I knew that I could find some of it. I had faith." He paused momentarily. "I found it after several weeks of riding and looking for a sign. I found it under a young sycamine tree."

A glass broke noisily as it hit the floor. "Sorry. Sorry," said Beulah as she stooped to pick up pieces of glass. "I fixes anuther. Jist a bit. Sorry, Missus." Beulah continued to mop up the spilled tea with a cloth rag and pick up pieces of the glass. No one heard her mumble under her breath, "Grandma Dundee. Faith. Sycamine tree. Seventh son. Sweet Jesus, hep us'n."

Solomon continued, "It was like old Holcumb remembered. I went to the start of the French settlements just south of the Red River. I searched the region around the Louisiana settlement of Marksville. I finally knew where to dig when I accidentally dropped that coin Holcumb gave me at the roots of a young sycamine tree. Grandma Dundee knew what she was talking about."

"How much silver and gold did you find?" Sawyer asked.

"Enough for a lifetime of luxury, cousin."

"Yew mean you're rich?" Stelcie asked excitedly.

"Quite so," answered Solomon firmly.

"That's wonderful," Laura Dundee said.

"What are you going to do with all your new-found wealth?" asked Sawyer.

"Are yew going to stay with us? Are yew going to stay in Natchez?" asked Stelcie quickly.

"Natchez is my home. I'll stay in Natchez," answered Solomon.

"As to your question, Sawyer, I've already done something with part of my money. Have you heard that the Silver Street Hotel changed hands? And that several tracts of land have been purchased recently on both sides of the river?"

"Why, yes, I have. I was concerned about the unknown purchaser being a Yankee," replied Sawyer.

"A damn Yankee," put in Stelcie quickly.

"Stelcie!" said Laura Dundee.

"You? You are the mystery buyer?" questioned Sawyer.

"Yes," said Solomon, smiling.

"Hallelujah," said Sawyer. "We were so worried for nothing. It's all in my family. I can't wait to tell Samuel and Frank."

"I also have interest in a steamboat company that runs the Mississippi and Ohio Rivers. It has twenty steamers plying the waters. I went to New Orleans for a while after I had found Murrell's money. I invested some there. Then I took a sailing ship to New York. I invested in some banks there, too. I explored other options for investments as well. I'll explain more later. I have had many enlightening experiences and learned much. It's good to be back home in Natchez. I'm exhausted. Midnight is, too. I pushed him hard today."

"Gabriel took care of Midnight, Massa," said Beulah from the dark side of the kitchen. "He come up when he heered Massa Sawyer yellin'."

"Good. I think I'll go upstairs and sleep for a few days," said Solomon with a chuckle.

"Yore room is jist as yew left it," said Laura. "Sleep well and as long as yew need." She smiled and stood on her tiptoes to kiss his cheek. "Welcome back home." She turned and said, "Come along, Stelcie. Good night all." She walked out. Stelcie followed, bidding all a good night.

19

The young men followed, too. Beulah blew out the candles, leaving herself in darkness. She pondered Solomon's return, his new wealth, and things said by Grandma Dundee about and to Solomon.

The next day Solomon did not stir in his room until noon. He made it downstairs for lunch with Stelcie and his aunt. They questioned him about his adventure. He elaborated on many things and told them some incidents not mentioned last night. He told them about bursting in during the thunderstorm on the French couple and the birthing of the baby and what had happened. Aunt Laura and cousin Stelcie were amazed with the story, and Beulah could be heard responding, "Sweet Jesus." He talked about many things that he had experienced while searching for the silver and some of his travel in New Orleans and New York. The business side and investments he avoided. He, also, did not tell about the New Orleans voodoo and other experiences with foreigners in New Orleans. He as well failed to mention the mysterious redheaded woman.

In mid-afternoon he asked about Miriam. The Dundees explained that Miriam had remained in Natchez with the Surgets for a long time after he had left but was now being educated by a private tutor in Memphis. They said she hoped to come to Natchez for the summer.

Solomon then asked about Eve and Mr. Whitmore. Stelcie took the lead in the conversation and filled him in about the business partnership of Sawyer and Samuel Whitmore and of the strong friendship that now existed between the Whitmores and the Dundees. Solomon said that he would call on Eve that same afternoon and went to dress for the outing.

Laura Dundee was going to send word inviting the Whitmores to the Dundee home for a celebration in honor of Solomon's return, but Solomon suggested instead that the Dundees, the Whitmores, and the Surgets all go to the Silver Street Hotel's dining accommodations for the meal. It was agreed. Solomon would invite the Whitmores, and Stelcie would go to Clifton to invite the Surgets.

At seven the families assembled at the private dining room at the hotel and were enjoying the meal and the company. Solomon retold his treasure-seeking adventure, and then the men started talking business. Solomon explained his investments and said that he was now looking to get slaves to work his newly acquired land that he would soon be clearing.

Frank Surget said, "Yew should be able to purchase several good field hands here in Natchez.

"I want to get started as soon as I can," answered Solomon.

Frank Surget now said, "Solomon, yew can start looking for the slaves yew want at the Forks of the Road. It is not an auction. It is more like a general store where yew can find exactly what yew want and then haggle with the owner for the price yew are willing to pay at the moment. Yew remember the Forks, don't yew? It is still in the same location as when yew left Natchez to seek yore fortune. I'll tell yew what. I will accompany yew there tomorrow if that fits yore schedule. What do yew say?"

"That is what we will do tomorrow, sir," replied Solomon.

Mr. Surget spoke, "Had yew visited the Forks of the Road with yore Uncle Jerimiah?"

"Only once—when I was 13 or 14, I think. My uncle did not like that place. He avoided it like the plague. I remember him commenting about humans and animals being sold side by side in the same place. He did not like that place at all."

"Yes, I inferred the same thoughts the few times he and I had the Forks enter our conversations. However, yore poor uncle is now deceased, and life must continue. I have not ridden my horse in a while; so, why don't we meet out front of Monmouth near the Forks of the Road at ten o'clock in the morning and ride into the Forks together?" said Frank

Surget.

"Yes. Yes. That will be fine. I will meet you then," replied Solomon.

The next morning at ten the two met, greeted one another, and rode the short distance to the Forks of the Road. Frank Surget told Solomon that before 1833 slaves were bought and sold everywhere in Natchez on various street corners on the hill and under the hill. They were housed in the city until then. In that year the city of Natchez, fearing the influx of cholera brought in by interstate slave traders, prohibited the housing of slaves in the city proper by slave traders. The Forks was mostly outside the city limits and thus was not included in the city ordinance prohibiting the practice in the city.

They approached the intersection of Washington Road and Liberty Road about a mile or so from the center of Natchez. "See that knoll that begins thereabouts," said Frank Surget, pointing. "The Forks site is right on the line for the city. They attempt to keep most activities on the outside of the line I am told confidentially, particularly the housing of the newly-bought in slaves," he laughed as he spoke those words.

Solomon did not remember much about his prior trip here at the Forks of the Road. What was here now was a bunch of rough-hewn wooden buildings clustered together in the angle of the two roads. Already hitched or held by young black boys were individual horses and several wagons or carriages. A handful of other young black boys was anticipating holding on to the horses of Solomon and Frank for a tip. "These boys are being put to work by the slave market owners," said Frank, "while waiting to be sold." They dismounted their horses, and Frank motioned to two boys to attend to the horses until they returned. Frank gave each boy a coin, and Solomon indicated that he would give another coin to each upon the finish of their business. Frank pointed to a rear building to indicate where the two of them were going.

22

They entered the area through a rather wide gate and walked into a narrow courtyard partly surrounded by other low drab-looking wooden buildings. Immediately both Frank and Solomon saw a line of Negroes almost completely around the courtyard. Solomon quickly counted between 70 and 80 of the slaves. Frank noted to Solomon, "These must be some from the walking coffle from Virginia that was expected within the last few days."

"These slaves walked from Virginia? Isn't that a thousand miles or so?"

"Yes. I believe they did so. The men were more than likely chained. The women and children could have ridden in wagons for a time or two each day. Sick ones rode, too. Look. They are being inspected. Let's watch. Yew may learn something here, young man," put in Frank Surget.

The two men walked over to an open vantage point to see what went on at an inspection. They watched as one of the Forks administrators systematically went down the line of newly-arrived slaves. He began on the side with the men and young boys. He yelled for all of them to remove their shirts. They still wore their coffle traveling shirts. Some of the shirts were but old rags, just barely hanging on the shoulders of the men and boys. All of the slaves obeyed the direction, and some dropped their shirts while others held them with one hand by their sides. The grizzled-looking white man was six feet or so tall, barrel-chested, and rather muscular himself. He barked out orders to each slave as he went through his inspection routine. He rubbed their heads and made them open their mouths wide for him to reach inside to inspect their teeth and tongues. When finished with each one, he slapped the side of the slave's face. He next grabbed their ears and gazed into them, and then he looked at their eyes momentarily. He make them hold out their hands and extend their fingers. He had each slave remove whatever shoes or boots worn in order

23

for him to look at their feet and toes. He made each one turn around for a look at their backs. It was at this point in the inspection that he would call out to one of his assistants to take this particular slave away for some reason or another that he said in a low voice to his man. One of the male slaves seemed defiant and reluctant to obey the commands. Solomon could see fire in his eyes across the wide area. When this one turned around for the inspection of his back, everyone could see scars from the lash. Solomon could just barely hear the white man say in a low but vicious voice, "Here be a troublemaker. Pull him to the back pen." His assistant took the slave away.

When he had finished inspecting the males on one side, the white man went over to the line of women, young girls, and other children. Now he began the inspection of this line. He barked out "Remove yore shirt or blouse!" He looked over at his assistants and grinned as the women, young girls, and other children took off shirts and blouses or lowered dress tops. "A fine lookin' bunch of mammies here, eh?" he shouted. Then he began individual inspections, not lingering long over the smaller boys and girls. He, too, had his assistants take several out of line to other areas of the slave pens. He did, however, hover over two of the more comely young women. He leered at them more than he did for the others. He would get in each one's face, grin a grin with several missing and rotten teeth, and move even closer to breath in each woman's face. He moved his face so close to the second of the two slave women to brush her face with his scraggly beard; she instinctively flinched and moved slightly backward. He yelled at her, "What's the matter, nigger; yew ain't got no 'preciation of yore betters?" She glared at him with a hateful grimace on her face. He saw and sensed her defiance of him, spit on her breasts, and laughed scornfully at her while she stood perfectly still and straight upright. "Save this one for a more personal inspection. Pull her on the way out." He glanced at one of his assistants to ask, "What's her name?"

"Thomajia," came the reply.

He moved on down the short line and then shouted to all of the slaves, "Out that way over there!" He and his assistants pointed the way as one of them led the way and the others herded the slaves out like sheep or cows.

As they watched the slaves move out of the courtyard, Frank Surget shook his head and looked downward at the ground. Solomon did not notice because he was observing how the white man goaded the slaves along. Frank Surget said to Solomon, "Yew know that this place used to be called Niggerville, don't yew?"

"No. Never heard my folks say that name," replied Solomon.

"I, for one, am pleased that it is now called the Forks of the Road," added Surget.

"What does it matter?"

Now the two men moved to another section of the courtyard and went into one of the dank rough-hewn wooden buildings. "Here is where yew can personally look at the slaves and bargain for the one or two that yew want. Haggling is quite an art. I hope that yew can be persuasive in yore dealings with these people. Remember they are dealing and haggling all day and every day. It is their business to make as much money as they can on each and every slave they sell."

Solomon replied to Frank's commentary by saying, "I can take care of myself, sir. I can take care of myself." Solomon had a smug look on his face as he replied to Frank. "I can be very persuasive if I need to be, my friend." He immediately thought of old man Holcumb, that bartender in New Orleans, and a couple of the pretty young women that he had charmed.

"What do yew wish to do now, young man?" asked Mr. Surget.

"Let's walk about the whole place for me to observe what happens here and to gauge these non-auction proceedings," answered Solomon. "I need to learn more about this business."

They walked through areas where new arrivals were washed and cleaned up and given other clothes for a better appearance for the selling. Now he saw slaves with coarse corduroy trousers, cotton shirts, better shoes, cotton and gingham dresses, and new kerchiefs for the women's hair. Some of the men had good hats and rather new boots. At one point in their rounds of the Forks, Solomon noticed a black man examining some slaves as if he were going to purchase a slave or two.

"Is that black man a free man? Is he really going to buy a slave for himself?" asked Solomon of Frank Surget.

"Most certainly, Solomon. I think that man is one of the sons of William Johnson, who had a barber shop in Natchez and owned fifteen or so slaves and worked them on his landholdings nearby. But now that I see his face clearly, I think not. Sometimes someone from the Metoyer family, a black family with a large plantation near Natchitoches, Louisiana, journeys here to Natchez to purchase or to arrange purchase of some slaves ever so often.

"Who is this black barber? I remember, I think, that he was murdered not too long after I came to stay with Aunt Laura and Uncle Jerimiah. Am I remembering the story?" spoke Solomon.

"Yes. Yes, yew are. The barber's name was William Johnson, a half-breed. He was born a slave but freed by his owner—most probably his father and worked in the role of an apprentice in a barber shop that belonged to his brother-in-law, also a freed slave. Eventually he, being ambitious, purchased that barber shop and made his fortune. He owned some commercial buildings and a plantation south of town. He knew that wealth around here was measured in land and slaves, and he was a shrewd businessman who took advantage of opportunities that presented themselves to him. He worked and became a prominent free black man here in Natchez. He performed the job of a barber, and it is said that he

26

even loaned petty sums of money to white people that needed to borrow small amounts when they were in a bit of a financial bind. He had an uptown barber shop on Main Street that served some of the richest and fanciest clientele and a shop under the hill that served some of the worst outlaws and low-class men ever. Johnson often worked at both locations himself and made connections with men in all levels of society. He furnished and outfitted his barber shops like some of the mansions around here. In all of his business enterprises he hired free blacks and used his slaves to further his business ventures as well as his personal fortune."

Frank Surget added, "William Johnson even came out here to the Forks of the Road to buy a slave or two—so the story goes. And he was well received here as he was in town or under the hill. That was one thing he had in common with white slave owners. He disciplined his own slaves and had the local patrol whip his slaves when he deemed that appropriate. Johnson even helped train mulatto children of some of the leading planters in skills that would enable them to live in the sub-community of free blacks in their adult lives. Indeed, he was one of those rare Negroes that Natchez seems to have had several of."

All the while they talked, they walked the buildings and grounds of the Forks of the Road. At one point in one of the drab buildings the two men were prevented from going into the back part of that building. It was off limits to the public they were instructed. It was where obstinate slaves were held and rehabilitated. Solomon thought he caught a glimpse of Thomajia through a doorway. She had intrigued him with her defiance of the white overseer in front of everyone in the courtyard. He wondered if, indeed, she could be a real test of his subconscious abilities to convince or coerce people to do his will. He wanted to confront this defiant young black woman slave merely to prove something to himself. He would return tomorrow to see if he could buy her.

They finished their visit to the Forks of the Road at the livestock area where cattle, hogs, and horses were the major sellers. Both of the men agreed that it was time to go. Solomon mentioned that he may return tomorrow to view and perhaps purchase a slave or two. Frank Surget said that he had other business tomorrow and would not accompany Solomon. Solomon thought to himself, "All the better for what I intend." The two men rode together for a time and then parted ways to go to their residences.

The next morning Solomon went to the bank just after it opened to confirm recent financial transactions from New Orleans and New York banks. Everything was in order. He felt financially secure. He would soon achieve his goal of becoming one of the elite in Natchez by increasing his landholdings on both sides of the river. Today he had donned his best, most expensive, gentleman's outfit, including fancy vest and fancy hat to match. He decided today to take a hack out to the Forks of the Road after he walked a while to think. Today would be a day for him to feel good about himself and his life that was now on the avenue to success. He strode to the livery near the road from under to the top of the hill. He remembered the hack service begun by a free black man by the name of Robert D. Smith and now run by his widow. He passed near their house. It was beautiful. It was named Bontura. He wondered how the former slave gained the wealth and success he had.

He remembered a bit of the man's story from when he lived with his aunt and uncle before he and Sawyer went off to college in the North. Then, too, he recalled meeting Smith, whom the local citizens dubbed "the Hackman," once with his uncle and Sawyer in town when the boys were in their early teens. Uncle Jeremiah asked, "Mr. Smith, would yew be interested in hiring a couple of young, strapping boys to pull one of yore hacks? The two of 'em would make for a fair team I suppose." Uncle Jeremiah laughed loudly, and so did Smith.

But Smith replied, "I be thinkin' dat des two eat too many buckets of oats a day fer me to be makin' much of any kind of profit on dem. I pass on dat deal, Mr. Dundee!" Both Jeremiah Dundee and Robert Smith laughed out loud once more. But Smith put a hand on the head of each of the boys and tousled their hair and said, "If'n yew gets tired of that there sawmill, boys, yew kin always comes heah and works fer me drivin' a hack or evens shovelins de stable!"

"Mr. Smith is a good man to work for, and a good man in general. Better than most whites hereabouts yew'll find out when yew git grown," added Uncle Jeremiah. "Never judge a man or a woman by skin color. It's what's inside a person that counts. Always remember that. I hope my words come back to yew often—even after I'm gone from this place. When yew hear that name 'Smith,' may my words come back to yew both." Robert D. Smith smiled graciously, knowing Jeremiah Dundee was genuine in his thoughts and words about him.

Solomon thought to himself that his uncle's words did come back to him. To Solomon it was rather a haunting memory considering he was a slave trader and owned several slaves himself. But Solomon dismissed his uncle's words as he came back to reality in the moment.

Before Solomon realized it, the hack pulled up in the Forks of the Road. He paid the driver and with an extra generous tip asked him to remain for the time it would take to complete his business. Solomon was feeling on top of the world. He anticipated success in focusing his attention and abilities on the defiant black slave woman. If he could soften her, he thought it would prove to himself what he could do in influencing others—it would prove that he had strong abilities in persuasion. Now he thought about Egiap and her seemingly supernatural powers and abilities. He knew she had power to heal, and he recollected the incident with the Guillot's new-born infant. He recalled removing the caul from the baby's head and the infant being rather rigid and still, and his yelling for the lifeless baby to breathe. Now he wanted confirmation of what he could do in difficult conditions. After handing the money to the hack driver, Solomon walked confidently to the gateway to the courtyard. He ambled through the courtyard where slaves were lining up around its perimeter. He saw the same white men—the overseer and his assistants—talking near the opposite entrance, seemingly almost ready to start the day's inspection of newly-arrived slaves. He noticed four other well-dressed men who must be rich planters from the area. He did not recognize any of them.

Solomon strode over to the men in charge and addressed the overseer, "My good man, could you direct me to the slave named Thomajia who arrived yesterday?" That name got the overseer's quick attention, and he turned around to see who had asked the question. But he looked at Solomon quizzically. "Good day, sir. My name is Solomon Witcher."

"Yew interested in buying that bitch?" The overseer grinned profusely, but the grin did not hide the big bump on the right side of the man's forehead. The swollen place on the man's forehead was a bit bloody and purple in color. He reached up and touched the bulbous area. Two of the other men exchanged glances and laughed quietly, but not quietly enough for their boss to fail to overhear. He glared at the two helpers and said in a mean voice, "Yew got nothin' to laugh at. Ain't yew got some work to do to line up them niggers?"

"My good fellow," said Solomon, trying to gain the overseer's attention again. "That slave woman Thomajia?"

The overseer turned back to Solomon. "My name's Moab. Yeah, she still here. Nobody'll buy that wench. She be crazy, crazy. Don't know why neither. No whip marks on her back. A bad demeanor on her part. But I be the one to tame that shrewish bitch! Give me some time when no new niggers comin' in next week." He stopped his talking and looked coldly at Solomon.

30

"Maybe I want to purchase her today," advanced Solomon, smiling at the man.

"Can't sell her to yew de way she be. She mad!" said Moab.

"If I buy her, it will be today," stated Solomon matter-of-factly. "Where is she?"

"Mister, we here at Forks of the Road don't sell no-good slaves. That woman won't work until she be broken and tamed down," said the overseer.

"Where is she? Let's see if she is tamed or not, Mr. Moab," pursued Solomon. "Perhaps she just doesn't cotton to you."

The overseer laughed out loud at Solomon's last remark. "I saw last night that this bitch is a crazed wildcat. See here where she walloped me with a big rock she found in her pen. I be tryin' to teach her some manners, and she done throwed that stone and knocked me out cold afore I could git my hands on her," said Moab as he pointed to his forehead. "Yew be crazed as her if'n yew buy her in her condition."

"Let me be the judge of that, my good man," said Solomon politely, as he walked past the overseer toward the rear pens of the complex.

"Wait. Wait, Mister!" said Moab. "I'll go wit yew. I want yew to see her and how she acts. Yew won't want this bitch I know. But if'n yew does, I kin set a fair price fer yew to take advantage of."

Solomon continued his walk toward the rear pens with the overseer struggling to keep pace with him. They reached the rear pens. What Solomon encountered shocked him.

They were at the last cell in the darkest part of the slave pen. The smell from human excrement, urine, and blood from open sores and whip marks overwhelmed Solomon's breathing, and with every breath he took

31

it was carried deep into his lungs, causing him to stifle a cough and at first cover his mouth and nose with his hand. They walked past individual cells on each side of them as they approached the one that held Thomajia. One of the cells held the defiant male slave that Solomon had seen yesterday in the courtyard. He was lying face-up in the back corner of the cell. His right eye was swollen closed, and his face was covered in dried blood. Bloody whip marks showed from his side. He moaned in pain as he drew shallow breaths but otherwise remained still. A smaller cell on the other side provided a dank, dark space for a couple of large rats. That cell contained no one at this time. Its dirt floor, covered here and there by a bit of straw, revealed recent occupancy.

Heavy chains restrained Thomajia. One chain came down from a ceiling rafter in the low building. Its manacle pulled her right arm and hand up above her head. The other chain that held her affixed itself to her left ankle and pulled it to the side as it attached itself to a heavy beam at the bottom of the outside wall of the cell. The old rusty chain pulled and stretched her slight frame into an uncomfortable and painful position at her slightest movement in the restraints.

Solomon really had not paid attention to the size of the female slave but now noticed her slight build and height of only five feet at the most. He could see no blood on her or her clothes except for her left ankle and her right wrist that had been caused by the action of the heavy, rusty manacles rubbing against her flesh to restrain her. Her eyes were closed as her limp body rested as much as possible on her right leg and foot. Her right foot, not covered by a shoe, seemed to dig into the coarse dark dirt in an effort to steady her body in the restraints of the chains. Her clothes were the same as she had worn the day before.

"I did not have her whupped as warranted by her behavior. I had her put in chains to teach her what lesson she needs. If'n she'd been nice to me, I'd be good to her. But she done got violent wit me when I jist go in," said Moab.

When Thomajia heard his voice, she opened her eyes really wide so that the whites of her eyes were lily-white teacups holding coals of fire in her head. She remained silent, but her eyes spoke hatred and anger. Her rather limp body tightened as Moab unlocked the cell door and walked in. Her eyes followed him as far as they could as he went behind her. Her breathing increased dramatically as she began to take quick but deep breaths. The white man said nothing when behind her, but he looked at Solomon, waiting for him to say or do something.

Solomon paused for a moment to look at the slave woman and then at Moab. He walked to the entrance of the cell and said in a voice that only the slave woman Thomajia and Moab could hear, "You just do not know how to treat a woman." Then he stared directly and deeply into Thomajia's eyes.

"This here ain't no real woman. She be jist a nigger slave wench," said Moab.

Solomon continued in his rather low voice, "That is where you are dead wrong."

Now Thomajia looked only at Solomon and heard only his voice it seemed. Her labored breathing continued but now not with hatred and anger but with anxiety and apprehension about this new white man at the cell doorway. Her eyes remained on Solomon but now harbored bewilderment and something akin to fear. Solomon took a couple of steps up to her, still staring deeply into her eyes. Thomajia felt only Solomon's presence in the cell, and the rest of the world was non-existent. She desired him to speak to her—only to her. Her mind blocked out everything else in her miserable situation at the moment.

She did not hear Moab say to Solomon, "If'n yew wants to buy this bitch, I name yew a most fair price."

33

Solomon did not let up on his hold on Thomajia's vision and inner thoughts. He did say to Moab, "One hundred dollars?" His eyes and Thomajia's eyes continued to be locked in visual and mental bonds.

"Mr. Witcher, one hunerd dollars be less dan she be worth! I meant a good and fair price for us both."

"One hundred dollars!" said Solomon as he took his eyes away from Thomajia and now looked intensely at Moab, who recognized the powerful look aimed at him.

Moab grimaced and grunted, "Sold for one hunerd dollars to Mr. Witcher." He himself now breathed heavily. He looked at Solomon with disbelief at the transaction that just occurred. "But I ain't hepin' yew git this heah demon woman out of this heah holdin' box. Once I unchain her, she yore problem, not mines."

Looking at Moab, Solomon said, "Just a minute or two. Let me talk to her before you release her. It will be in your best interest."

Moab nodded in acknowledgement and stepped from behind the slave woman to the side of the cell. He spat on the bottom of the near wall.

Solomon took a step to be closer to Thomajia to capture her eyes with his eyes, to focus intently on her, and to whisper in her ear, "Thomajia, I will have Moab release you in a few minutes after I speak to you. Please listen carefully to what I say to you, and things will get better sooner than you think."

He stepped back and gazed into her once defiant eyes as they softened. He concentrated on her with his eyes and his mind. Her face now softened from the grimace it had held since the men entered the holding cell. Now he winked at her. He moved closer once more to whisper to her, "Let's see what kind of fool that Moab is. You know I am purchasing you because I understand your anger and resentment and

34

because I think you can be valuable to me. I will treat you well as my slave. You will not want for anything if you do as I expect. Be calm and watch Moab with eyes of polite kindness."

"Yes, Master Witcher."

Solomon moved back from her and smiled, first at her and then at Moab. "Moab, release her now."

Moab moved and reached up to release the manacle and chain on her wrist and arm. Then he did the same for the ankle. All the while Thomajia was quiet and calm. At one point she said in a low voice, "Thank you, Master Moab."

Moab took a step back and looked at Solomon. Upon Moab's face waxed a perplexed look, and he said, "What ya tole her?"

Solomon remained silent, but Thomajia quietly murmured, "He be a voodoo man." Solomon turned to walk out of the cell with Thomajia following him slowly. She turned to look at Moab and smiled ever so faintly, just enough for him to see. Moab's perplexed look turned to a resigned indignation, but he said nothing.

At this time Solomon did an abrupt about face and looked at Moab with a determined expression on his face and said, "One other item of business, Mr. Moab. I want to purchase this male slave for a hundred dollars as well." Solomon now pointed to the defiant male from the day before. He heard Thomajia gasp.

Moab had a quizzical look on his face. "Mr. Witcher, yew mean that one?" He pointed at the male slave that had been whipped and beaten and was still lying in the straw on the dirt floor.

"For a hunerd dollars, too?"

Solomon looked strongly at Moab, directly into his eyes. Moab developed another funny look on his face and stammered, "He ain't worth

. . ." Moab stopped abruptly what he was about to say. He returned Solomon's look and said, "Sold."

Solomon now addressed Thomajia, "Go in. Help him up and walk him out of this place."

"Yes, sur, Master Witcher, yes sur."

Outside the low buildings Solomon motioned for his waiting hack. The driver brought the hack over to where the two slaves and Solomon were standing. "Five dollars extra for you for driving the three of us back into Natchez. Another dollar if you have a shirt or coat for this male slave. And two more dollars to help you clean the seat if we stain it or soil it as we ride."

The hack man agreed. The three climbed up and sat. Solomon directed the driver to his house. There Solomon instructed Thomajia to tend to the male slave. He told them to locate him in the small room off the kitchen, assess his injuries there, and inform him if a doctor would be needed. "Oh, Thomajia, what is his name?"

Thomajia replied, "His name be Charon."

"Let's meet for supper in the dining area at six. Bread and some smoked meat are in the cupboard," instructed Solomon as he pointed. "I will be going out tonight after that." Solomon left the room to go upstairs as Thomajia turned to go to Charon.

The next week found Solomon and Sawyer talking with one another at the small foundry. Mr. Whitmore rode up on his horse and dismounted, expressing greetings to the two cousins. He informed the two that the Dundee women's carriage was only a few minutes behind him on the road. He then inquired of Solomon, "Have yew purchased all the slaves yew need fer yore properties?"

Solomon, about to speak, was interrupted by the sound of the Dundee carriage nearing. He simply told Mr. Whitmore that they would talk later. Stelcie yelled out, "Hey, y'all, the Surgets invited all of us out to Clifton this evening. We are on our way there now. Please come out theah when yore work day is done! Yew, too, Mr. Whitmore. And Eve!" Gabriel goaded the horses to resume their pace after slowing here momentarily.

At Clifton the men had grouped to talk and the women had grouped in the quilting room. Stelcie and Eve broke away from the older women and walked into where the men were talking. A few minutes later Laura Dundee and Charlotte Surget joined them. The women, silent, listened to the men's conversation.

"But it may take yew several months to buy what yew really need. Buying slaves is an investment in itself. Acquiring a passel of slaves requires a passel of money. Yew must select with care the coloreds yew buy."

"A slave is a slave so long as he's in good health. You can make them work," answered Solomon.

"You can't beat them all the time," responded Sawyer.

"If one doesn't work, I can," came back Solomon emphatically.

The ladies all looked at Solomon.

"The whip can get results. It's a mighty motivator," remarked Solomon.

"How do you know that?" asked Sawyer.

"Because one of my investments had taught me much about nigger slaves while I was in New Orleans. I am a slave broker. In fact I have several shipments due to arrive in Natchez within the next several weeks. Most I will keep as my own to put in my fields. Others I will put on the block for auction. I intend to have a direct hand in weekly auctions and other sales at the Forks of the Road here, and I will travel to New Orleans and other areas of the South for acquisition purposes."

Shocked, Laura Dundee spoke, "Solomon, don't say yew are involved in that awful business of buying and selling humanity."

"Yes, Aunt Laura, I am. It is an excellent investment, and I'll make much money. In fact, I already have. In New York I found out that many investment firms in that city and others in the northeast are heavily involved in the slave trade because of the great profits it produces. I don't apologize for making money any more than those Yankee businessmen do. Slavery is our peculiar institution in the South, and I will help keep it strong for the South's sake."

Laura Dundee sat in silence. She knew that saying anything else would only antagonize her nephew. For once Stelcie was silent, also.

Samuel Whitmore spoke next. "If that Republican Party gets stronger and in control in Washington, the entire South, including yew, will have greater worries than jist slavery."

"Yes, but let us speak of more pleasant matters this night. Enough of politics. Tonight we celebrate the return home of Solomon Witcher. Young Solomon has embarked upon a new stage of his life," said Frank Surget. He raised his glass of wine and continued, "We toast yew, your return, and your future as a businessman here in Natchez." Everyone raised a glass to Solomon. The remainder of the evening was pleasant discourse on future prospects and past family memories.

The next afternoon found Solomon Witcher sitting on the cafe porch of his Silver Street Hotel waiting for a steamboat to arrive. It was a dreary, rainy day. For a few minutes the rain came down heavily, and then it slackened. It had rained heavily with much thunder and lightning for several hours. Silver Street itself presented a quagmire of mud, and traffic on it was almost nil because of the rain. Only once in a while did Solomon even see a worker venture from under shelter to perform some brief task under the rainy sky.

Finally he, after hearing a subdued steamboat whistle in the diminishing rain, did make out the shape of a steamboat in the distance on the river. He sipped his last bit of brandy, settled back comfortably in the wooden chair, and watched the steamer come through the rain to the landing.

A few landing workers appeared out in the rain when the steamer neared the landing. When the gangplank was lowered, only one passenger emerged from the boat to cross the gangplank. He ran through the rain to the hotel porch.

"Popalowski," said Solomon as the man nimbly came up the steps to get out of the rain.

"Mr. Witcher," growled the burly man who was six feet tall and weighed over 300 pounds. He was dressed in wet, drab-looking, rough work clothes. He had a scar, about an inch in length, leading upward from the right corner of his mouth. "The shipment is aboard. It's thirty of 'em. My two boys is bringing the niggers out now. Where do we take 'em?"

"Up the hill. Then to the outskirts of town. Here's a map I drew of the streets and the road out of town to the holding barn. Look at it. Can you follow it?"

"Yeah. Shore," said Popalowski as he studied the map.

Solomon had his eyes on the steamer and the figures that had emerged onto the foredeck. He could hear gruff voices through the rain. He watched the slaves shuffle off the boat. They were chained together at the ankles. There were six groups of five blacks. They came down off the ramp to the boat and huddled together in the rain, waiting for the second white man to touch ground. He came off the steamboat after talking momentarily with one of the steamboat crew. "Git going, yew lazy sons of bitches," he yelled as he gesticulated with a short whip.

They moved in their huddled group and were herded toward the hotel. Popalowski yelled to his two subordinates, "Line 'em niggers up fer Mr. Witcher to take a look-see."

The white men, grubbily dressed and rough-looking, dutifully lined up the slaves in the rain in front of the hotel porch. The rain slacked up for a time. A slight mist continued. Solomon Witcher stood tall and looked at his human property.

Popalowski lumbered off the porch and stood in the rain in front of the blacks. "All good'ns, Mr. Witcher, straight from New Orleans. Five young Negresses fer household domestic duties and twenty-five young bucks fer field duties. Ought to bring a good price. Each one of 'em."

Solomon looked down the line. He stared intently at each one. Only one male looked him in the eye. This one wasn't the biggest or tallest or most muscular. But Solomon could see a spirit of defiance in his eyes. He may have to deal personally with this one he thought. Solomon pointed to him and asked, "What's his name?"

"That buck?" said Popalowski, pointing to the one Solomon meant. "Name. What's yore name, boy?" asked Popalowski, poking him on the arm with his finger. The black flinched a bit and answered "Mancil" in a loud voice after a moment's silence.

"Mancil," echoed Solomon Witcher, "I shall remember you." He looked down the line at the women. He pointed to the last one in the group. "Her name?"

"The comely one, Mr. Witcher?" answered the white man standing by her. He held a rifle in one hand. With the other hand he reached for her chin to hold her face. She jerked her face from his slippery fingers. His hand slipped downward and caught her dress neckline and ripped the fabric, exposing one of her breasts. She squealed but did not move, not even her hands to cover her partial nakedness. The white man laughed and said, "Her name is Ruth. Ain't she a purty Negress? Bet she'd be nice to her master fer a new dress." He laughed again and pointed his rifle at her head.

"Ruth," said Solomon. She looked up at him when he said her name. He locked his eyes with hers and stared intensely. She let out a small gasp, and Solomon blinked his eyes to look at Popalowski. "Move them up the hill."

"Yes, sir, Mr. Witcher," replied Popalowski as a loud clap of thunder sounded, and the heavy rain resumed. "Git goin' up the hill," he yelled. The Negroes began moving up the street in the rain and mud. Solomon watched them slosh slowly away, hearing the sounds of the leg irons and chains muffled clinking in the wet weather and on the muddy street.

The next afternoon Solomon went to the holding area he had purchased outside of town to look over the additional shipment of slaves that had been transported into Natchez by steamer. It was late afternoon when he was riding up to the barn. He was thinking about other business that he had transacted during the day and about his long-range goals. He had eaten lunch with Eve and her father and had discussed the politics of the day with Mr. Whitmore. Solomon was musing over the leading contenders for the Presidency. As he rode up to the barn, Popalowski walked out of the little house next to it and greeted him, "Good afternoon, Mr. Witcher. Yew come to see today's shipment of niggers?"

"Yes. I did. I want a look at them. There may be a few I want to keep myself. I just completed the transaction to buy a house on the south side of Natchez. It's a temporary home for me until I can build. I need two domestics to take care of it and me. I also need three more field hands for my acreage across the river." He got down off his horse. "I want that Ruth I saw yesterday under the hill. What other one you got that would be good at my house?

"Come on in the barn, Mr. Witcher. The new niggers are inside. Let's look at 'em. I think I know one that'll suit yore needs." He strode into the barn ahead of Solomon and yelled, "Stand up, all of yew! Stand up! Yew hear me!"

The slaves, still chained together in their little groups stood for inspection. Popalowski moved quickly to one black female. "Yew the one who cooks and done maid duties afore, ain't yew?"

The black woman, who was in her thirties and slightly stocky and average in height, looked up at Popalowski and shook her head, saying, "Yus, sur, Massa, I's done dat fur a fine family down in New Orleans until the Missus Duhor up and died."

"She's the other one I want," said Solomon. "Now fetch me Ruth while I look for some field hands among these males." He began walking about, looking at the male slaves.

"I'll do jist that, Mr. Witcher," said Popalowski. He turned sharply toward the barn door and took a step. A voice from outside the barn called loudly, "Popalowski! Popalowski! One of the niggers escaped! He's done run away! We gotta git the hounds to run him!" Into the barn came one of Popalowski's men that Solomon had seen yesterday. He was out of breath and had trouble saying the last few words.

"Which'un was it?" growled Popalowski

"Mancil."

"That figers. I had him pegged fer trouble. Git me my shotgun and whip. Go git John. I'll fetch Bobby Joe and the dogs. We'll plain larn that nigger to run away from us. Don't worry, Mr. Witcher, we'll ketch that runaway," Popalowski said harshly as he ran from the barn.

Solomon didn't worry. He knew that if anyone could recapture the fugitive slave it was Popalowski. Solomon continued looking at the field hands slowly and methodically.

42

Several hours later Gabriel was working some leather harness in the back of the Dundee stable when he heard hurried footsteps and labored breathing outside. Then a black man stumbled into the stable and leaned against the wall. He closed his eyes and rested his head back against the board. His chest heaved, pulling in air and pushing it back out. Sweat had drenched his clothes, and huge drops of it ran off his face and head.

The Dundee slave stood and dropped the harness. The noise made the runaway Mancil start with surprise. Mancil looked at Gabriel in silence. Gabriel asked, "Yew a runaway?"

"Yeah. From the auction. Popalowski ain't selling me if'n I's kin hep it."

They stood there silently for what seemed like several minutes. Both of the black men realized at the same moment they faintly heard the barking of dogs in the distance.

"Bloodhounds," said Gabriel. "Aint' no way yew 'scaping dem dogs. Dey done gots yew in dem noses."

"I kin hide," said Mancil desperately.

"Yew cain't hide, boy!" came a harsh voice. "Yew cain't hide from Popalowski." Popalowski cocked his shotgun. "Git out here. Both of yew boys afore I blast a hole in yore bellies. Move out heah now!"

Mancil stood straight but hesitated. Gabriel walked forward to Popalowski and stood. Mancil moved by Gabriel.

"Yew boys done earned yorselfs a whuppin' for running away and hepin' a runaway," said Popalowski as he looked at Mancil and then Gabriel. He cracked his whip.

"I's ain't done nuthin' wrong, Mister," said Gabriel. "My missus be up in de house."

"Shut up, boy. I knowed what I seed. Yew were afixin' to hep this

43

nigger," shouted Popalowski. The hounds and the other white men came up. "I done caught our nigger and found one ready to hep him if I hadn't come along."

By this time other slaves and workers of the Dundees were gathering about to see what was happening. Most of the sawmill workers and field hands had not come in yet, but a child, two women, and an old male were there, gawking at the situation.

"I's ain't done nuthin' wrong, Mister," repeated Gabriel.

"Shut up, boy," shouted Popalowski. At the same time his hand moved quickly, and the whip lashed around Gabriel's back, cutting his shirt and his flesh. "Don't talk back to me!" Popalowski's face was crimson red, and the blood vessels in his temples pumped furiously. "Shut up!"

"I be fetchin' the Missus," said one of the Dundee slave women as she started running to the house.

"Tie 'em to the trees there and there," Popalowski said as he pointed at two nearby small oaks that were about twelve feet apart.

The white men quickly tied Mancil and Gabriel to the indicated trees and ripped off the slaves' shirts. Popalowski spit on the ground and swung his arms over his head. "The whip'll larn yew to not run away." The whip uncoiled, and with a motion of Popalowski's arm, lashed out across Mancil's back. The slave winced in pain. "And yew, boy, don't hep a runaway and don't sass Popalowski," he shouted in a mean tone. The whip lashed across Gabriel's back, and Gabriel flinched and ground his teeth together.

Popalowski turned his full attention on Mancil for a time, striking him repeatedly with the whip. As he was about to deliver another lash to Gabriel, a loud and determined female voice said, "Yew strike my Gabriel again, and it'll be the last time yew whip anybody."

He dropped his arm and turned to look at the source of the voice. Laura Dundee leveled her husband's double-barreled shotgun at him and said, "Cut Gabriel loose now!" She cocked both hammers and raised the weapon to her shoulder.

Popalowski looked at Laura Dundee in the eyes. He grinned and then laughed. "Do what the lady says." His men quickly cut Gabriel's bonds.

"Git behind me, Gabriel! Beulah, Stelcie, git something on those lash burns," she ordered. Beulah and Stelcie ran to the house for medicine.

"Now. Who are yew? And what are yew doing on Dundee property?" she demanded of Popalowski as she lowered the shotgun a little.

Popalowski grinned again. "This here's an escaped slave. He belongs to Mr. Solomon Witcher."

"Solomon?" Laura Dundee said as she lowered the shotgun and eased the hammers down.

"Yes, ma'am," replied Popalowski, grinning still. He relaxed himself. "Know him?"

"Yes. Yes. He's my nephew," replied Mrs. Dundee. "He's my nephew."

A rider came around the corner of the house. It was Sawyer. He hurried his horse to where the gathering was. "What's going on here? Mama, are you all right?"

"Yes, son. That slave over there is a runaway. He belongs to Solomon."

"And that slave of yourn done been hepin' this no-good runaway. I was larnin' 'em a lesson when yore mama aims that scattergun at me like

I was doin' wrong. I'm jist doin' my job. My name is Popalowski, and I'm responsible fer Mr. Witcher's slaves fer auction tomorrow. I have to make shore they know to not run away. Now if yew would jist move back, I'll finish this heah one's lesson." He limbered his arm by swinging it around and over his head. He grasped his whip handle tightly and made it crack the air beside him. He grinned and struck Mancil across the back once more.

"Don't do that again on Dundee property, Popalowski!" said Sawyer. "You're not going to whip any slave here on our property."

"He'll just move him off your grounds and whip him worse later," came another voice. It was Solomon's. He had ridden around the corner of the house unnoticed, dismounted, and walked to the group. "Runaway slaves must be dealt with. You know that. If not, they're not good for anything. It's better gotten over with here and now," he said. He nodded to Popalowski to continue.

Popalowski let the whip cut another line across Mancil's back. The slave let out a low moan.

"No! Stop it!" yelled Sawyer.

"Stop it?" asked Solomon. "Would you want to buy this nigger? That's how you can stop it."

All eyes turned to Sawyer. He saw Popalowski grin and move his arm back to use the whip.

"Yes, I'll buy him," replied Sawyer. "What price?"

"Fifteen hundred dollars," said Solomon in a strictly business voice.

"Cut him down. I'll get you the money tomorrow," Sawyer said.

"No hurry. I trust you," said Solomon. "I'm not worried that you won't pay."

The Dundee women began to cry. Beulah, who was back from the house and tending Gabriel, started weeping. She went up to Sawyer and said," Thank yew, Massa Sawyer, thank yew."

When Beulah moved, Solomon saw Gabriel and went over to him. "What happened to you?" He saw the whip marks on Gabriel's back.

"Yore man Popalowski said Gabriel was helpin' the other slave escape," said Stelcie indignantly. "And he and yore other henchmen had started whipping him. Jist look at those marks. Mama saved Gabriel from worse."

"Popalowski! Leave here at once. Cut Mancil down. I'll see you later. Get moving!" said Solomon in an angry voice.

Mancil was cut loose from the tree and collapsed in a heap. Popalowski and his men left quickly. Solomon looked more closely at Gabriel's back and traced the whip burns with his fingers. Gabriel flinched. "I am sorry you were hurt," said Solomon earnestly.

Then Solomon went over to Mancil and stood over him, looking down on him. "Beulah, bring that salve over here." Mancil opened his eyes and looked at Solomon. "There's still defiance in your eyes, isn't there?" Solomon whispered to the slave. "Even though your back is on fire with pain." He paused and then said, "Beulah will tend to you." Solomon looked him in the eyes and in a low voice said, "Your pain will lessen." He squatted down and put his hand on Mancil's back. Mancil's body flinched as had Gabriel's when Solomon touched him.

Beulah was standing over Solomon and Mancil. She heard the last thing Solomon said. Gabriel came over. Solomon rose, went toward the house, and entered it without looking back.

The Dundees walked over to Mancil, Gabriel, and Beulah. "I be tendin' them, Missus. It be all right. Thank yew. Thank yew." The Dundees followed Solomon into the house.

47

Gabriel looked at Beulah and said, "My marks ain't burnin' no mo, only stingin' a bit after Massa Solomon touch me." He looked at Beulah for an explanation. She looked at him and then at Mancil.

Mancil gave both of them a perplexed look and said, "I be whipped afore. My back only stings now. That Witcher man put his hand on dis back and drawed de hurt out. He be a doctor man?" Mancil looked at Beulah for an explanation, too.

She looked back at both Gabriel and Mancil. "Massa Witcher be no doctor man," she answered Mancil. "Buts, Gabriel, yew 'member Grandma Dundee?"

"Yus. I duz."

"She done tole me one time about Massa Solomon. She tole me he . . . "

"Old Missus Dundee tole yew what, Beulah woman?" said Gabriel.

"Swear to sweet Jesus dat both of yew never tell nary a soul. Promise Jesus and me!" said Beulah sternly.

"Jesus, I promises," said Gabriel.

"I's swears to Jesus," said Mancil.

As she stood, she said firmly and calmly in a low voice, "Seventh son of seventh son."

Solomon had gone directly to his room upstairs and did not come downstairs until early the next morning. Sawyer was eating breakfast, and Solomon joined him at the small table in the kitchen. Without talking, Beulah quickly supplied him with coffee and food.

Sawyer, too, was silent. It was Solomon who spoke, "Saw, I want to tell you that I never thought that Gabriel would be harmed. That a situation like what had happened yesterday would have ever happened here. Please extend my apologies to Aunt Laura and Stelcie. Tell Gabriel again for me that I regret his experience with Popalowski. I would tell Aunt Laura myself, but I don't think I can face her right now."

"But Solomon."

"No, I can't do it now. I had other news I was going to tell last evening, too. But this unfortunate thing came about. I have purchased a house of my own. I'm moving there today. What happened last evening has no bearing on my move. I was going to move, anyway. The house is a temporary residence for a year or so. I plan to build a home much larger. I want something that will rival or surpass Clifton and Rosalie and all the other magnificent homes here in Natchez. I am in the process of accumulating the means to achieve my ambition. My investments are already reaping rich dividends, but I must reinvest some of my gains and redirect some of my other financial matters. I will send for my belongings during the day. I can't face Aunt Laura with this announcement now."

"Solomon, let me say—"

"You don't have to say anything. I know all of you love me and care for me. I love all of you. You are my family. I have no one else. One day I'll marry, and then I'll have another family. Saw, I—I just don't want to see Aunt Laura upset again. Yesterday was enough. Too much. I'll visit soon." He stood. "I must go now." He walked to the kitchen door and turned to face Sawyer. "Goodbye, cousin. I'll be right here in Natchez. I hope we stay close." He opened the door and walked through it, leaving it open. He turned once more. "Saw, I'll always remember Grandma Dundee sitting on the front porch with us at her feet. She told us about the sycamine tree and faith and the grain of mustard seed. I believe what she said helped me to do what I have done. The sycamine in the front is special to me, too. Ask Aunt Laura if I can dig up a root or a young sapling from its seed scattering for my house's yard, will you?"

Sawyer shook his head and replied, "I will. She will do that for you."

"Thanks. And, Saw, do you have a grain of mustard seed of faith within your soul, within your very being?" Solomon turned and strode to the stable. Minutes later Sawyer, who was still sitting at the table thinking, heard Midnight with Solomon astride him gallop by the corner of the house on his way into Natchez.

Solomon waited at his house all morning until the two female slaves were delivered. "Ruth, I know your name," said Solomon as he smiled at them both. "But what is your name?" He looked at the other woman as he posed the question.

"Esther, Massa."

"Ruth and Esther," mused Solomon. "Follow me. I'll show you where your room is. You two will share it with Thomajia." He began walking to the rear of the first floor of the house with the slave women following. "Esther, you'll do the cooking and be in charge of the kitchen and dining room. I'll entertain guests often. You'll have plenty to do," he said as he walked through the dining room.

"Yes, Massa Witcher."

They went into the kitchen. It was practically bare of furniture and foodstuffs. But standing there awaiting Solomon were Thomajia and Charon. They were silent. Solomon told the four slaves the names of one another and cautioned them to get along well with each other. As he said this advice, he looked intently at each one of them when he said their names.

"I have established accounts at several local merchants here in Natchez," related Solomon. "In a few minutes, Esther, you will accompany me to these business establishments. I will take you in and introduce you as my slave so the people will know you are buying for me on a regular basis." He continued to look at Esther as they all stood in the kitchen. "You have cooked before. You know what basics we will need here. I'll let you decide what to prepare after I tell you some of my likes and dislikes. On special occasions, I'll tell you what to cook and have ready." He paused. "You are a good cook, aren't you?"

"Oh, yus, sur, Massa Witcher. I kin cooks real good foods. Yew'll see."

He turned to face Ruth. "You, girl, will be in charge of the rest of the household. I'll hold you responsible for everything upstairs and downstairs except for the kitchen and cooking. Of course, you'll assist Esther whenever she needs you or if she is ill. And she can help you when you are ill. You will wash and care for my clothes as well as the clothing of the three of you. I expect the house to be kept neat and clean. Everything must be in its place. Do you understand me?"

Ruth looked at him and nodded. "Yes, Massa Witcher. I's understand. Yore household be kept nice for yew."

Now Solomon issued job duties to Thomajia and Charon. He said, while looking at both of them, "Charon, you will take care of my horse and general maintenance of the house. First, you will help build a small horse barn with a room attached for you. You are to be my right-hand man for many tasks. I will purchase new clothing for you. Do you understand?"

"Yus, Massa Witcher," said Charon, hardly believing what he had just heard. "Yus, sur."

Thomajia looked at her new owner with disbelief as well. Solomon now addressed her directly, "Thomajia, your duties will be oversee the other three and the general household and land. While we are in this house, your tasks will be light; but when we move into a bigger house, there will be more demands on your time. Is that understood?"

51

"It be understood. Thank yew." Thomajia smiled at Solomon Witcher.

Solomon turned back to Esther. "Let's go into town after I show Ruth the bedding and linens that were delivered earlier. She can sort and place things while we are gone. Wait here, Esther. I'll be back. Come along, Ruth." He turned and started toward the staircase in the hall and then slowly ascended the stairs.

In a few minutes, Solomon was back downstairs, and he and Esther were soon out the front door on their way to their first stop at several stores.

Charon and Thomajia decided to look at the house from the outside and to view the grounds. The two walked around the house, observing what needed to be mended and thinking about the small barn and room to be built.

In the house, Ruth began her work as directed. She unpacked the materials that Solomon had already purchased, sorted them, and took what belonged downstairs to the room where the three slave women would sleep. She made the beds, dusted, and swept away a few cobwebs. Then she began sweeping and dusting the parlor and hall. Next she went upstairs to the master's room and gave it a sweeping and a dusting.

Ruth just finished making the bed and stood up straight. She wiped her forehead with her arm and turned toward the door to walk to the guest bedroom.

She was startled by a figure in the doorway. "Oh!"

"Ruth, no need to be afraid. It's only me," said Solomon in a calm yet authoritative voice. He took a step toward her and removed his coat. He loosened and removed his tie. He threw them on a chair near the door.

Ruth just stood there.

"What's the matter, girl?" he said in a voice that sent shivers up and down Ruth's spine.

Ruth did not speak. He walked past her and sat on the edge of the bed. He removed his boots and tossed them into the corner. Ruth took a step toward the door without looking back at her master. She was stopped abruptly by his voice, "I didn't say you could leave, girl."

She was motionless.

"Turn to look at me."

Ruth turned slowly. Solomon Witcher had moved from the bed and was standing right in front of her when she had turned around. Ruth looked up at her master and trembled.

"What are you shaking for? There's nothing to fear."

She looked at his eyes and was stilled by the look he gave her. She froze, completely under his influence.

"Massa, I—"

"Don't talk," he said as his hands unbuttoned her blouse. Her eyes were locked onto his. Her will became his will. She spoke no other words as now Solomon removed the rest of her clothes and stood back to look at her naked body. She stood perfectly still and smiled weakly. Solomon backed himself to the bed and sat once more. He removed his shirt while Ruth stood there.

"Come to me," he said, as he held out his arms. Ruth obeyed her master.

When Esther came back into the house, Solomon had already left. Ruth was busy in the guest bedroom and didn't go downstairs until Esther called her and the others for supper.

Solomon stayed at his hotel on the river that night. The next day he went about his business activities in the morning and went to his house for the noon meal prepared by Esther.

After he ate, he instructed Thomajia, Esther, Charon, and Ruth to mind the household because he was leaving on a business trip of a few days on the afternoon steamer. He said to all four of them in the kitchen as he focused his attention on them, "I trust that all of you will be here when I return—that not one of you will run away." He looked each one intently and directly in the eyes. The four slaves gave their word as he shook their hands while seemingly gazing into the soul of each. "I will have packages delivered, and someone will be by some days to see if you require anything. A carpenter will be here tomorrow for you to help, Charon." Charon nodded at his master. Solomon added that a longer business trip was in the near future a few days after he would return from the shorter trip.

Solomon Witcher went upstairs to complete packing his bags for the trip. Then he left to take care of other business before departing Natchez. Solomon went by the foundry to inform Sawyer and Mr. Whitmore. He told them he would be away for days, and he was not sure when he would return.

While Solomon was taking care of his other business before leaving Natchez that evening on a riverboat for a business trip of a few days, his four slaves talked among themselves about their new master and recent instructions from him. They were in disbelief that they had promised not to run away and to tend to the household while their master was gone. Each professed that no thought of leaving was ever on their minds. Thomajia ended their conversation with these words, "Massa Witcher bes sum kin' of voodoo man. I's knowed it frum de time he furst comes in de slave market. I's felt it like my ole mammy tole me whens I be little. He be not a massa to mess 'round wit. I be stayin', and all y'all be rat heer when de Massa comes back!" Charon, Ruth, and Esther all nodded in agreement.

That night on the steamboat to Memphis Solomon talked with several other Southerners about national politics over a friendly game of cards. When Solomon excused himself from the table, he was in a happy mood because of his winnings; but in the back of his mind was a nagging thought of the future. It was an anxious, unnerving thought. That night he dreamed of a war within the United States. He dreamed of Miriam. In his dream he saw her at Clifton dancing with gray-clad soldiers in the grand ballroom. He watched her from a distance. She was beautiful in a lovely pearl white dress with full skirt and an off-the-shoulder bodice. She wore a string of creamy white pearls about her neck. Her smile was radiant. She smiled at everyone there, it seemed. Solomon walked toward her on the dance floor, but she didn't notice him. He walked slowly yet deliberately toward where the flow of the dancing would take her and her partner. He smiled, wanting for her to see him and return his smile with her own. Abruptly she stopped her partner when she cast her glance upon Solomon. Solomon's smile now became loaded with charm. "Hello, Miriam," he said softly.

Her smile transformed into an ugly grimace. "Traitor!" she yelled. The music stopped, and all there turned their eyes on Solomon Witcher.

"Miriam. Miriam. What are you saying?"

"I'm saying for you to leave Clifton at once!" Her voice was angry.

Solomon jerked upward to a sitting position in his bed in his room on the boat. His face and body were beaded with sweat. "What kind of dream was that?" He wiped his forehead. The first morning light was coming in the window. He brushed his hair back from his eyes with both hands. He shook his head and said aloud, "A dream to be soon forgotten." He rose from the bed, put on his clothes, shaved, and went for breakfast. He thought about trying to see Miriam while he was in Tennessee, but he knew that his business matters required him to make the mid-morning steamboat leaving Memphis for the north. He would come back through Memphis. He would attempt to see her then.

It was hot in the late summer of 1860 in Natchez, Mississippi. The politics of a presidential election year made things even hotter. Tempers flared into angry remarks about Yankees and the Republican party in general and the Republican candidate Abraham Lincoln in particular. The Democratic party had split at its convention, and the Southern Democrats had nominated their own candidate, a Southerner from Kentucky, a few weeks later.

The Dundees were coming out of church and chatting with friends. The ladies, Laura and Stelcie, lost Sawyer in the crowd of people when he drifted over to a group of men talking politics. Stelcie was ready to go because she had been promised a carriage ride about Natchez to look at homes and specifically to see the progress at Longwood. Sunday dinner would be later in the afternoon. Stelcie got her mother by the hand when the couple she was speaking with turned away to leave.

"Mama, let's find Saw and go carriage riding about Natchez."

"Yes, dear. We promised. We'll do so."

"Come on, Mama. There's Saw."

Mrs. Dundee and Stelcie walked quickly over to a shaded area where the gentlemen were talking.

"If that ape man Lincoln is elected, the North will have hell to pay. We'll show them Yankees. We'll secede from the United States and have our own country with the right to own slaves guaranteed ironclad," said one of the men angrily.

Another chimed in, "Them damn Yankees don't understand us and our slaves. The Bible tells of slaves and slave-owning. It's meant to be. It always has been so."

56

Then Sawyer spoke, "Gentlemen, let's don't get heated up over what may not happen. Lincoln is not President yet. We would still have the Senate to block northern political moves no matter who is President. We just came out of church. Let's not forget our faith in the Lord. He will take care of things."

"But Sawyer, don't yew remember how them Yankees talked when yew was at school up north?" asked another man.

"Yes, but I—"

"Saw. Saw. It's time to go," interrupted Stelcie. "Yew promised we'd go out by Longwood. Remember?"

"Oh, yes. Yes. Pardon me, gentlemen. Little sister calls. Excuse me. Good day. Have faith," Sawyer said as Stelcie grabbed his arm and tugged. Mother followed them as they walked gingerly toward the carriage.

Stelcie leaned over closer to Sawyer and whispered, "Y'all were talkin' 'bout them damn Yankees agin, weren't y'all." She beamed a naughty smile up at her older brother.

Sawyer returned her smile and whispered back, "Now, little sister, watch your language."

Laura Dundee saw her children whispering and smiled. She hoped they would always have a close relationship, one of mutual, re-enforcing family love.

The women got into the carriage, and Sawyer mounted Country Boy. Gabriel was given the nod to drive out of the churchyard onto the street.

Sawyer said to Gabriel. "Miss Stelcie will tell you where to go. It's her ride today."

"Yus, sur, Massa Saw."

"Let's go by Dunleith first," exclaimed Stelcie.

"Git up, hoss!" shouted Gabriel. The carriage lurched forward, causing Stelcie to giggle. Laura Dundee just smiled.

They rode by Dunleith, which looked as imposing as a Greek Revival temple. It had colonnaded galleries all around.

Next they went by Magnolia Hall. It was another example of Greek Revival architecture in Natchez. It had been completed only two years ago in 1858. It was a house that Stelcie had always pleaded to pass by on carriage rides on Sunday after church.

Stanton Hall was next driven by. "Oh, they are all so beautiful, so magnificent!" exclaimed Stelcie to her mother. "I wish . . . "

"Stelcie, dear, remember how your daddy always felt about mansions and what he always said," reminded Laura Dundee.

"Yes, Mama, but one day. One day, yew'll see."

"Mother, I think I'll go by Connelly Tavern to see if there is any news I need to know. Somebody there always knows the latest," said Sawyer.

"Yew know Beulah will have dinner waitin' within an hour. Be home then, Saw," replied Mrs. Dundee.

"Yes, Mother, I'll be there," said Sawyer as he trotted Country Boy away.

"Longwood. Gabriel, let's go to Longwood, please," Stelcie quickly said.

"Yus, Miss Stelcie."

Gabriel turned the carriage to go to Longwood. After a leisurely ride under moss-covered trees, they came to the site of Longwood. Doctor Nutt and his wife were there, walking around the initial stages of the planned Oriental villa. They waved the Dundees over, and all talked for a while. The ground floor was to have nine rooms. Dr. Nutt elaborated on the octagonal shape and design. Dr. Nutt expressed fear of a political strife nationally and of hotheads in the North and South preventing the building of his home.

The Dundees left Longwood in time to reach home for Beulah's meal. Sawyer galloped in just as Laura and Stelcie were getting down from the carriage. And just as Sawyer was dismounting from his horse, they all heard the noise of another horse and rider coming up to the house. It was Solomon.

"Is dinner ready?" Solomon asked politely.

"Yew are right on time," replied Laura Dundee, delighted to see her nephew. "Where have yew been? We haven't seen yew for more than a week."

"I've been busy, Aunt Laura," answered Solomon. "Business. You understand. You won't be seeing me for a longer time after. Business is taking me to Washington, D.C., and New York City. But let's discuss my journey over food." He dismounted.

Laura and Stelcie went into the house. Beulah, who was waiting at the door, began talking to them about the food. Sawyer and Solomon, following behind the carriage as it moved, walked their horses toward the stables to unsaddle them and talk business and politics.

"Watch your money. This is a risky time for investments. Don't venture into anything new. Hold on to cash money when you can," advised Solomon.

"Why? What concerns are there? All the talk about secession? A fight for states' rights?" asked Sawyer. "All that is just talk, loud talk."

"I don't think so, Cousin," answered Solomon. "I think there will be a big fight, a war between the North and the South. I feel it. I know it. I can sense a terrible time in the near future. I wake often from nightmares in the middle of the night. There's fighting, war all around me. Men are dying. Destruction is all around us. And there's nothing I can do about it." He was strangely silent for a moment. "And Lincoln will be President."

"You really think it will come to a war, Solomon?" asked Sawyer unbelievingly.

"Yes."

Solomon turned and strode toward the house. Sawyer walked briskly to catch up with his cousin. They went stride for stride for a time before either of them spoke.

Sawyer broke the verbal silence. "Let's not mention a possible war in front of the women, Solomon."

"I agree. It would only alarm Stelcie and Aunt Laura. They don't need that kind of speculation about the future."

"When do you leave?" asked Sawyer as they entered the kitchen.

"I leave for New Orleans Thursday," replied Solomon as they went through the kitchen and turned toward the dining room, where Laura and Stelcie had just been seated. Beulah directed the young men to their places at the large oak table and began hovering around each person, serving them their food and cool drinks of sweet tea.

Solomon informed the Dundees that he would first go to New Orleans on a short trip and return to Natchez. A longer journey to New York was to be next on his agenda. After he finished his business there, he would travel overland to Washington, D. C. He planned to return to Natchez in late October before the national elections.

The meal was enjoyed by all, and Beulah was pleased. As Solomon got up from the table, he inquired about Miriam. Stelcie stated that they had not received a letter from her in a while, and that one was long overdue.

Solomon told his aunt and his cousin goodbye in the parlor.

"I'll go out to the stables with you, Solomon," said Sawyer.

"Good," Solomon answered and went through the kitchen. There he thanked Beulah and went on with Sawyer following.

"Saw," said Solomon as they walked, "Remember the war dreams I told you I was having?"

"Yes."

"I've had other dreams, too. In one I am at Clifton, and Miriam calls me a traitor. Another one I vividly remember is that of a stranger lurking in the darkness around me. I can never see his face. But I know it's an old man. I feel that I know him, but I don't know him. It's really strange. I've had this same dream twice now. Once was last night. I almost saw the old man's face, but I woke suddenly. This has been in my consciousness all day. It has troubled me. That's why I'm telling you." He stopped and turned to look his cousin straight in the eye. "I think the old man is Death itself. I'm afraid someone close to me is going to die soon. I just feel it. I just feel that way. And you know these feelings I get."

"Yes, Solomon, I know."

"But who? Who can it be?"

"Shake off that morbid feeling, Solomon," said Sawyer, feeling uneasy himself.

"I'm trying, Saw." Solomon put his hand on his cousin's shoulder and said, "Be careful at the sawmill. Watch Aunt Laura and Stelcie."

"Everything will be all right, Solomon. I'll be careful. You, too," replied Sawyer.

In silence Sawyer watched as Solomon saddled Midnight, mounted, waved, and rode past the house. Sawyer did not see Solomon stop momentarily by the sycamine tree to strip some leaves off it into his hand. Solomon held the leaves up to the moon in the late afternoon sky and let them flutter downward. "I have faith, Grandma Dundee. I have faith." Solomon patted Midnight on the rump to encourage him forward toward Natchez.

After his return from New Orleans Solomon stopped to rest and reflect on his business dealings at his hotel on Silver Street. He went to a corner table in the dining room and had a bottle of bourbon whiskey brought to him along with two shot glasses. He sat for several hours alone, nursing the bottle, drinking from one glass with the other one empty sitting directly across the table from him. He sat brooding on his thoughts, only looking beyond the table a few times when asked something by one of his employees.

Finally Solomon Witcher poured a drink into the empty glass, raised it to his lips, and drank its contents down. He smiled, picked up the half-empty bottle, walked over to the bar, and said to the bartender, "Send the remainder of this bottle to the card game in the back." He walked out, found Midnight, and rode up the hill to his house. There he went immediately to his room and soon was fast asleep.

It was well past midnight at the Dundee house when Beulah from her room off the kitchen heard a knock on the back door. She awoke but didn't move. She hadn't heard the hounds bark or a horse outside. The knock came once more. It was louder this time. "Who dat?" she asked in a loud voice.

A voice from outside the door mumbled something she couldn't understand.

"Who dat?" Beulah asked again. She picked up a skillet from the kitchen rack. "Who dat?"

She heard the sound of someone falling or collapsing against the door. "Who dat?" She edged closed to the door. No sound except for labored breathing. "Dat yew, Gabriel? Youse jokin' Beulah at dis late sleep time? Gabriel? Dat yew boy?"

Only a breathing sound could be heard. She lit a candle and crept to the door. She put her ear to it. Only labored breathing. Putting the candleholder down, she unlatched the door slowly while holding the skillet back over her head ready to deliver a blow to the unknown visitor.

There was pressure on the door. The latch was hard to undo. But when Beulah released it, the door was slowly pushed open by the weight of a man, an old man dressed in raggedy clothes. The body sprawled itself out over the floor, face downward. The man's long gray hair swept over his face and covered the identity of the stranger from the night. Beulah's curiosity was stronger than her fear. She bent down after she picked up the candleholder once more. She put the candle down on the floor so it would illuminate the man's bearded face when she would brush his hair back. She still held the skillet cocked back in her hand. Timidly, she reached her other hand to brush the locks of gray hair from the man's face. Gently, easily, she did so. She stared intently at the old man's face. "Who dat?"

The man's eyes jerked open and scared Beulah backward. "Sweet Jesus!" she exclaimed. The man attempted a feeble smile, and then his eyes slowly closed.

In that single instance of the old man's eyes opening, Beulah knew who the strange was. The skillet dropped from her hand to the floor with a heavy thud. Beulah's eyes still bulged from her scare when the old man had opened his eyes, but now they bulged even more in disbelief as she said out loud, "Mr. Cain. Lawdy mercy. It's Mr. Cain, Solomon's pappy!"

Beulah's eyes rolled back in her head, and she fainted, collapsing on the floor beside the old man.

Sawyer was awakened by the thud of the skillet Beulah had dropped. He heard a voice and got up to investigate. He pulled on some pants and bounded down the stairs to find Beulah.

He found the strange sight on the kitchen floor. A single candle burning on the floor, along with a strange old man and Beulah collapsed there.

He first picked up the candle and used it to light two others nearby. He then poured some water on his hand and patted Beulah's face until she came around. "Beulah, what happened? Who's this? You look as though you've seen a ghost."

"I's taught I's done seed one fer true, Massa Saw," said Beulah breathlessly. "Dat's Mr. Cain. Solomon's pappy. Lawdy mercy, Massa Saw. Sweet Jesus, hep me."

Sawyer helped Beulah to her feet as Laura Dundee entered the kitchen. "What is going on here, Saw?"

"We have a visitor, Mother. It's Solomon's dad, Uncle Cain."

"What? Saw, give me yore arm. Help me sit over there. Yew say it's Cain? It's Cain Witcher?"

"Yes, Mother. Beulah says it's so."

"By sweet Jesus, it be him, Missus Laura," added Beulah.

Laura got up from her chair and bent over the old man. She looked at his bearded face and confirmed, "It is. It is Cain Witcher. Well, I do declare. It's yore Uncle Cain." She stood. "Sawyer, git him to the guest bedroom. We must find out what is wrong with Cain." She paused. "And we must send for Solomon at once."

Gabriel was immediately dispatched to Solomon's house in Natchez. The slave was instructed to tell Solomon to come to the Dundee homestead as soon as he could, not to say why. Gabriel was not to mention the name of Cain Witcher or that there was a visitor.

Solomon had been sleeping soundly and restfully for the first night in quite a while. He was not troubled by dreams or nightmares. He was in a dead sleep.

Even Gabriel's loud knocking on the front door did not rouse Solomon, but it did awaken Ruth, Thomajia, and Esther. They went to the door together, each holding a candle. After they realized that it was Gabriel outside, they admitted him; and all three went upstairs to awaken Solomon. It was difficult to get him to open his eyes and chase the sleep away.

Ruth kept saying, "Massa Solomon, yew must wake up, wake up. Yew be needed at the Dundee house." She had her hands on his shoulders and shook gently but firmly.

Solomon, finally coming out of his deep slumber, said in a gutteral voice, "What? What do you want? I'm resting at last? What?"

Ruth explained that Gabriel had come for him to go to the Dundee house. Gabriel left to help Charon saddle Midnight and then to return home with the news that Solomon had been informed and would soon be there. Ruth and Esther excused themselves from the room while Solomon got dressed to go. Ruth began to light candles on the first floor. Esther went into the kitchen to make some coffee, while Thomajia went out back to see if Gabriel and Charon had readied Solomon's horse.

"Be anyone ailing at the Dundees?" asked Ruth.

Gabriel, having been instructed not to reveal anything, brushed aside the question with his brief answer, "The Dundees be well." Midnight was then taken to the back door by Charon, who handed the reigns to Thomajia and went around the house to his horse that was tied to the hitching post there. Gabriel galloped into the darkness to return home.

Minutes later Solomon, his mind wondering why he had been summoned in the middle of the night, followed on Midnight. His mind could not focus on a single thought, but his heart seemed to well up in his chest and cause a heaviness of breathing. He took deep, labored breaths.

Solomon and Midnight caught Gabriel and his old horse at the sycamine tree in the Dundee yard. Solomon looked at the sycamine in the moonlight as he passed. "There's somebody else here," he said loud enough for Gabriel to hear.

"How Massa Solomon knowed dat?"

"Take Midnight for me, Gabriel," said Solomon as he dismounted and headed for the kitchen door that was ajar with light shining through the slight opening.

"Yus, sur," answered Gabriel, climbing down from his brown horse.

The kitchen door opened before Solomon reached the step, thrusting more light outward. Laura Dundee stood there and said, "Solomon. It's Cain. Yore father. He's here."

Solomon halted. "What? Who?"

Laura Dundee explained, "Cain's in the guest bedroom. He came knocking on Beulah's kitchen door and nearly scared her out of her wits. She thought he had died right here on her kitchen floor. Saw found her passed out on the floor next to Cain. We couldn't get him to wake up, so we moved him where he is now. We sent for Doctor Whiddon. He should be here soon. Yew want to see yore daddy now?" She looked at Solomon intently.

Solomon stood there with a perplexed expression on his face. "Yes. Please," he said slowly. "Take me to him."

Laura Dundee, Stelcie, Sawyer, and Solomon left the kitchen and made their way to the downstairs guest bedroom. At the doorway, Mrs. Dundee motioned to Solomon to enter first. In he went. There he saw Beulah, bathing Cain Witcher's face with a wet cloth. Beulah stopped what she was doing and cast a weak smile at Solomon. She got up from her tender task and walked away from the bedside. Just before Solomon was to move next to his father, Sawyer said quietly, "Doctor Whiddon is here."

The noise of the doctor coming into the house and the guest room froze everyone in place. Solomon gazed upon the man who was his father, the man he had not seen in more than thirteen years. He thought to himself, "This is the stranger in the dream. This is the stranger I know but don't really know. My father, Cain Witcher, has come back to Mississippi, to Natchez, to die."

Everyone watched the doctor put down his black bag on the bed, open it, and then take a quick look at Cain. Doctor Whiddon then said, "Folks, please leave the room for a few minutes."

All except Solomon turned to exit the room and were going out. Doctor Whiddon looked at Solomon. Solomon uttered, "I'm staying, if you don't mind."

Dr. Whiddon was about to say something when Laura Dundee moved and whispered something into his ear. The doctor, looking surprised, said to Solomon, "Stay if yew will. It's quite all right."

Solomon's thoughts ran wild. Why had his father come back now? Where had he been all this time? What had he done? Why?

The doctor attempted to rouse Cain from his slumbering condition. At first it seemed that he was to prove unsuccessful in his actions, but in

67

a few minutes Cain Witcher was moving his head and his body. His eyes had not opened, but his lips wanted to form some words to speak it seemed. Only the doctor could hear what Cain Witcher said. His first words came out, "What? What do you want? I'm resting at last? What?" Now Solomon moved closer.

Without opening his eyes, Cain said loudly, "Where, where is my son? Where is Solomon?"

Before the doctor could respond, Solomon pressed closer and said in a firm voice, "Here. I am here with you, Father."

Cain Witcher opened his eyes wide and looked upon Solomon. "Come closer, boy." He held out his hand. Dr. Whiddon moved back from the bed, and Solomon filled the place.

Solomon grasped his father's frail hand firmly. "Come closer, Solomon. My voice is weak. I need to tell yew somethin'." His voice broke on the last word. Solomon leaned closer to his father's face. Cain mumbled a few syllables, paused, cleared his throat with great difficulty, and spoke again in a low volume. "Solomon, I am sorry for not bein' with yew, but yew are like me so I know yew'll understand. I know I am dying. I've known for a while." He coughed. "Yew are like me. Yew are different from the others. I sensed it all along. But when yew were the onlyest one of all my boys to live through the fever, I knew that everything I had been told about yew was true. Yew see, Solomon, yew had six older brothers. Yew are a seventh son. Yew can do thangs others cain't. Yew can sense things." He paused and swallowed painfully. "Yew knew I was comin' back, didn't yew?"

"Yes."

"Yew have a destiny unlike others. I know that a great war is comin'. It's nearer than most folk want to admit. Yew know it, too. Don't yew, Son?"

"Yes."

"Solomon, I had to see yew agin, one more time. I had to tell yew this. Now that yew know, yew can use yore power to do better than yore pappy. Yew didn't know' but I'm a seventh son myself. I done said it. Now I'm at peace. Remember me kindly, Solomon." With those words his eyes closed, and his hand went completely limp. He let out his last breath.

Solomon said, "Doc." His grip on his father's hand slackened, and Cain Witcher's hand and arm fell on the bed. Dr. Whiddon quickly moved to Cain, and Solomon slipped back from the bed quietly.

Dr. Whiddon examined Cain for a few minutes and turned to Solomon saying, "I'm sorry. There's nothing I could do." But Solomon was already at the closed door of the room. He turned the knob and slowly pulled open the door.

Everyone waiting outside saw a single tear trickle down Solomon's cheek. He stood there for a brief moment until Dr. Whiddon ushered him completely out of the doorway. "I'm sorry," said the doctor.

A chorus of wailing cries went up from Laura, Stelcie, and Beulah. Solomon walked slowly and sadly into the parlor and sat in his Uncle Jerimiah's big rocking chair. He stared out the window into the front yard. Tears clouded his eyes. He blinked them away and stared out the window, fixing his gaze upon the sycamine in the pale moonlight.

Cain Witcher was buried two days later. Solomon told no one his father's last words to him.

The night before Solomon was to leave Natchez found Solomon and Eve Whitmore dining alone at Solomon's residence. The slaves had been dismissed for the evening, sent to the Dundee homestead to help in a quilting bee celebration in the slave quarters until the next afternoon. Eve and Solomon were discussing his journey up north and his return to

69

Natchez.

It was a cool evening, unusual for the time of year. It was actually pleasant.

"We are all going to miss you," said Eve. "I will miss you, Solomon, very much."

Solomon looked at her with a generous smile and returned her remark with, "I shall miss you, too, Eve." He said nothing else but looked at her with a beguiling eye. She smiled again and blew out one of the three candles lighting the room. Solomon placed his dinner napkin on the table and settled back onto his chair. He gave Eve another generous smile. She rose to blow out the second candle. Solomon was even more handsome in the weak, flickering light to Eve. "Father is away on business. I can go home whenever I want," Eve stated bluntly.

Solomon smiled a sly grin. He stood, moved close to the third candle, and pinched out the flame with his thumb and index finger. In the moment of temporary adjustment of his eyes to the absence of candlelight, Eve moved next to him and pressed her body against him. She put her arms around him, and he felt her small hand on his face.

"You'll be gone for such a long time," she sweetly said. "Such a long time," she repeated huskily. "Solomon."

"Yes, Eve. It will be a while, but I'll return."

She pulled his head downward so that she could trace his lips with hers. She kissed him passionately, and he responded in kind.

"Solomon," said Eve when their lips finally parted. "I love you."

"I know. I know," he said quietly and patronizingly. He swept her off her feet and carried her to the stairway. There he kissed her again and put her down. She quickly went halfway up the stairs, stopped, and turned to look at him in the dim light. He stood silently at the bottom of the stairs, in control as he knew he would be. He flashed her another sexy smile, removed his coat, and said, "Go on up. I'm right behind you." He slowly ascended the stairway.

Eve had already disappeared into the bedroom when he had reached the top of the stairs. She stood in front of the mirror and played with a ringlet of her hair. She turned sharply to face Solomon when he entered the room.

"My dear Eve," he said, "Fix me a drink of that bourbon there in the decanter. Pour me a glass half full."

She did as he directed and brought the glass over to him. He took the glass from her, allowing his hand to linger on hers. She stood in front of him as he took a swallow of the drink. His eyes sparkled. They mesmerized her. She was his. He was in total control. But she cared not. She was exactly where she wanted to be. Her mind had no reservations or doubts. She melted into his arms.

He embraced her. His mouth pressed hers relentlessly. Her heart raced and pounded in her ears. His embrace was crushing. Her ribs ached. Her very being ached, but she was in love. Nothing else mattered.

He released her for the moment and put the glass to her lips, which were already on fire. The liquor seared her lips and burned its way over her tongue and down her throat. He kissed her again, and the burning spread over her body, into her very soul.

Their lips parted. Solomon unbuttoned his shirt. She unbuckled his belt.

"Solomon, I love you."

He kissed her once more. He then began helping her remove her dress, and soon she stood before him naked and shivering. He stepped back and smiled at her. He embraced her after taking a single step. They kissed. He ran his hands down from her shoulders to her hips. She

71

moaned as the kiss ended. He guided her over to the bed and gently but firmly pushed her downward, first to sit there and then to lie there. He took a few seconds to undress and then pressed himself upon her.

"Solomon, I love you," she said again. He did not answer again.

The next morning when Eve awoke, Solomon was not there. When she left his house with Solomon on her mind, he was on board a steamboat traveling to New Orleans and beyond with business on his mind.

Time passed with national politics the dominant talk everywhere in the North and the South.

In Natchez, Mississippi, every steamboat brought fresh news and new gossip about the future. The day before the Presidential election had the Dundees and the Whitmores wondering about Solomon's return as well as wondering about the election. They did not have to wonder long that day about Solomon. He showed up in the morning first at the foundry where he encountered Mr. Whitmore and Sawyer in the office.

"Solomon! How are yew? When did you get into Natchez?" asked Mr. Whitmore, rising from his chair when Solomon walked through the open doorway. They shook hands.

"I just got off the steamboat, sir. I'm fine," answered Solomon. "Sawyer, it's good to see you."

They exchanged a handshake, and all were seated.

"You said you would make it back in time for the voting," said Sawyer. "And you did."

"Yes, I did."

"What's the news from Yankee land?" asked Mr. Whitmore.

"All is not good. Northerners want Lincoln and the Republicans,

72

it seems. They don't understand us, our ways. And they don't want to. Lincoln's going to be elected. I just know it," said Solomon. As he said his last words, he looked at Sawyer and nodded his head. "I know it," he repeated. "And when that happens, all hell will break loose because the South has been taunted and mistreated and misunderstood for years. Damn Yankees don't understand slavery and how intrinsically it's woven through our cotton economy and everything else that is Southern."

"Yes, slaves are needed to work our plantations and farms. The Yankees like our cotton in their textile mills. If they abolish slavery, why then they won't have cotton for their mills. Then what?" stated Mr. Whitmore. "They'll be sorry; that's what!"

"Maybe Lincoln and his party will leave us be," suggested Sawyer.

"I don't think so, Saw," said Solomon. "We may have to force him and his cohorts to come over to our side of the fence."

"What do you mean?" Sawyer asked.

"We can withhold our cotton from their looms, no doubt," said Mr. Whitmore. "And other crops from them."

Solomon, very serious, said, "It may take more than that. It may take a show of force. We may have to get our backbone up and get mean with them."

"You mean a fight?" asked Sawyer.

"You and I have talked about that before, Saw," replied Solomon. "Remember what I said I felt would happen."

"Yes."

"There's some talk of up and leaving the Union if we cain't get some guarantees of our property rights," added Mr. Whitmore.

"Secession is the talk in many Southern households from what I heard in my travels," said Solomon.

"Let's hope it'll never come to that," replied Sawyer. "Anyway, there are others in the family who would like to see you, Solomon. Come to the house for dinner."

"Good. I will. Let me go to my house to check on things," said Solomon.

"Eve would be glad to see you. Why don't you drop by on your way to your place?" suggested Mr. Whitmore.

"Good idea. I'll do just that," said Solomon. "Good day, gentlemen."

Soon Solomon was on the porch of the Whitmore's house and was knocking on the door. The door was opened by Cryer, the black maid. She was surprised that Solomon was there. "Massa Solomon, comes in. Comes in dis minute. Miss Eve done gonna be happy to see yew. She be frettin' herself ever day yew done be gone."

Cryer ushered him inside and motioned him into the parlor. "I's git Miss Eve. She still be's dressin'." Cryer bustled out of the room quicker than a wink. Solomon could hear her going up the stairs and loudly calling her mistress. He heard his name.

He sat in the parlor and looked about. The room was a nice size. It had a large sofa against one wall with a small table at its left end. Opposite it were two stuffed chairs, one on each side of the window on the street. He sat in one of two rocking chairs, the one he usually sat in when he was visiting the Whitmores. Both chairs had blue seat cushions. That was something new since he had been there. He noticed that the room was decorated in a pale blue and white, restful colors it seemed to him at the moment. He had just apparently taken it for granted before. There was a new blue patterned Oriental rug on the floor in the middle of the room. A portrait of Eve, something else new, adorned the wall opposite the window. It had arrested his attention when he first entered the room and sat in the rocker. He moved his eyes off the portrait to look out the window, but they soon were back on the likeness of Eve. Solomon got up from the rocking chair and walked over to the window to look out. With his left hand he pulled back the lace panel next to the glass. He gazed outward at a wagon with a tired old horse pulling it and with a tired old black man half-heartedly urging the horse onward. He let the lace panel drop back into place and turned to look at Eve's portrait again.

"Do you like it?" asked Eve.

"Oh, yes. It's good. It's just like you. Beautiful."

Eve went to Solomon and embraced him. He returned the hug with feeling. He kissed her on the side of her face.

"Let's sit and talk," Eve suggested. They did so for almost an hour.

Later that day after he had checked on his house and his four slaves, Solomon had a happy reunion with the Dundees over a hearty meal. They discussed politics and picnics and parties and people.

Election day, November 6, 1860, came at last. Talk was that possibly the actual election of the President could be thrown into the House of Representatives if no candidate had a majority of the votes from the Electoral College. A sense of apprehension precluded all other emotions of the day.

Within several days everyone knew that Lincoln had been elected the next President of the United States. He had garnered 180 electoral votes, a clear majority, but had polled less than a majority of the popular vote. In ten of the southern states, he had not received any popular votes. The South was shocked at the outcome of the election.

Talk in Natchez was that the Mississippi governor had indicated back in October to Governor Gist of South Carolina that if any other state should secede, Mississippi would go with that state. People in Natchez

75

were concerned about the future of the state and themselves as individuals.

State and national events were on everyone's mind. News came to Natchez little by little.

On December 20, 1860, by way of a popularly elected convention, the state of South Carolina passed an ordinance of secession. Secessionist fever, already in existence in the other slave states, began spreading like a plague. Talk abounded about a possible Southern confederacy.

Mississippians felt no different than their Southern brothers. There was some hesitation and some argument for slowing the pace of events, but the convention held at Jackson passed an ordinance of secession on January 9, 1861, by the vote of eighty-four for and fifteen against. Mississippi had left the Union.

Louisiana followed its neighbor state on January 26.

More than a month before Abraham Lincoln would take office as President still existed, and seven Southern states had left the Union.

President Buchanan seemed to hope his policy of being friendly with the South and of being non-aggressive was the answer to the problem of the time. He did not want to start a war with an overt act of violence or aggression. Buchanan did not want war, even though he thought secession was not valid.

Natchez had been in an uproar ever since the news of Lincoln's election. The course of events that had brought secession to the state of Mississippi caught the Dundees and all other families up in confusion, anxiety, and excitement.

Laura Dundee prayed for no war. Stelcie was glad to be rid of them "damn Yankees." Sawyer was apprehensive about his businesses and investments as far as the family was concerned.

The Whitmores were nervous. The Surgets were fearful and

alarmed.

Solomon was the only one who seemed in any way calm about the tide of events. But he seemed preoccupied with something. He was aloof when surrounded by people and didn't visit the Dundees or Whitmores as often as before.

In February, 1861, Mississippi was one of six secessionist states that sent delegates to organize a Southern government, a confederacy. A provisional government was set up in Montgomery, Alabama. Jefferson Davis, a Mississippi planter and politician, was elected provisional President of the Confederate States of America.

On March 4, 1861, Abraham Lincoln assumed the office of President of the United States. On this day Solomon Witcher left Natchez. One hour before he left on the steamboat, he had met with Sawyer Dundee. No one else knew he had gone.

More than six weeks of uneasiness and anxiety passed with little news of any great consequence. But by the middle of April, news came of the firing on Fort Sumter in Charleston harbor. Lincoln had issued a call for 75,000 volunteers to serve the Union, to fight the South as all true die-hard Southerners viewed it, to put down the insurrection. Northerners responded to Lincoln's appeal to arms readily.

Southerners knew a war was at hand. They had been preparing for just such a situation. Natchez was no different than the rest of the South.

At the Dundee homestead the evening meal's conversation centered on the issue of war.

Stelcie said, "I thought we had got rid of them damn Yankees."

Laura Dundee cast a disapproving look at her daughter but said nothing. In her heart she realized what the war might do to her family.

"Are yew joining the regiment, Saw, to go fight them damn

Yankees?" quizzed Stelcie. Before he could answer, she kept on, "Yew will be handsome in a military uniform. I'll be so proud of yew."

"Yes, I'll join. It'll be a few days before I can make the arrangements for our businesses. You and Mother can look after some, and Mr. Whitmore can handle the remainder. The regiment won't leave until next week. It's awaiting orders."

Laura Dundee had tears run down her face. Sawyer saw this and gently admonished her, "Mother, we've been through this before. You know I must go. You know how I feel."

"Yes, Saw, but a mother still has her feelings. Yew are my only son."

Sawyer grasped her hand. "I'll be all right, Mother. You'll see. I'll be back as often as I can."

"And that Solomon. He left Natchez without tellin' us goodbye, without tellin' us nothing. I don't know what to think of him," said Laura Dundee, still crying. She looked at her son.

Sawyer averted his eyes, put a blank expression on his face, and said nothing.

"He's terrible for not tellin' us before he left," added Stelcie. "What am I to say to Miriam when she arrives and asks of him? She comes in on the steamer from Memphis tomorrow."

"Yes, I had forgotten when Miriam was to arrive," said Sawyer. "I'm glad I'll be able to see her.

Laura Dundee spoke now, "I'm happy her father is sending her to the Surgets' to get her farther away from possible danger. He made a good decision in anticipation of what might happen. She'll be safer here in Natchez with all of us until all this war business is settled in a few months."

"Yew're right, Mama," added Stelcie. "None of them damn Yankee soldiers will ever set foot in Natchez."

"Stelcie," said Laura sternly. "Yew're a lady, I hope."

"But Solomon? Where is he? What is he doing?" asked Stelcie.

"It's time for me to check the quarters," said Sawyer quickly. "I have to talk with Gabriel and others back there." Sawyer got up from the table and went through the kitchen to the outside.

"Mama, do yew think more states will secede?"

"Probably so, dear, but that's business and politics of the menfolk. Other states out of the Union won't change the course of events for us now." Laura Dundee paused momentarily and then took a deep breath. "Beulah," she said loudly. "We are done."

The next day found Stelcie and the Surgets waiting at the Silver Street Hotel for the steamboat to arrive. They didn't wait long. The steamer was right on time. Miriam was one of the first to appear on the deck to get off the boat. She was greeted with warm embraces and kisses from the Surgets and Stelcie. Before her trunks were unloaded from the steamer, all four got into the Surgets' fine black carriage and went up the hill and then toward Clifton. Two slaves were left to fetch home the baggage in a small wagon. Stelcie told Miriam that it was planned that she stay the night with Miriam at Clifton at the Surgets' request. Miriam was delighted with the idea. On the way to Clifton, they discussed Miriam's journey from Memphis. Miriam told them that her father insisted she remain with the Surgets until all possible danger had passed. The Surgets were happy to have Miriam.

Upon sighting Clifton in the distance, Miriam exclaimed, "Clifton is so lovely! I feel it's my second home."

"It is yore home," insisted Frank Surget.

The slaves, from the ones that greeted her at the front of the house to the maids, were all pleased that Miriam had returned. They were all smiles.

"The domestics love when yew are here, Miriam," said her uncle. "They all say yew add the sunshine of youth to Clifton. They say that yore aunt and I are too set in our ways, even though we entertain guests regularly. All were anxious for yore return, especially Nazlee." He paused and looked up the long stairway. "And here she comes now." They all looked up at the bustling figure descending the stairs.

"Miss Miriam! Miss Miriam! I be too glad to sees ya! Lordy," exclaimed Nazlee as she came on down the stairs.

Miriam went up to Nazlee and hugged her. "I'm glad to be back at Clifton. To see all of you."

"Miss Stelcie," said Nazlee, "I's done through layin' out yore things in the guest room next to Miss Miriam's. Does ya wants me to puts dem away?"

"No, thank yew, Nazlee. I can do that while Miriam freshens up from her trip. We can talk through the opened French doors just the way we did when we were younger and I would spend the night."

"Cool water be in the pitcher and basin fer ya, Miss Miriam," added Nazlee.

"Let's go up. Excuse us, Uncle Frank and Aunt Charlotte," said Miriam. She and Stelcie started up the stairs quickly. Frank and Charlotte smiled at each other. "She does bring sunshine to Clifton," he commented.

By the next day Miriam was settled in at Clifton, and Stelcie was ready to show her Natchez again. They had the Surgets' fine carriage at their disposal and were driven up and down the Natchez streets. They went out to Longwood. There they saw the unfinished structure. The northern workers that had been used had heeded Lincoln's call and went

80

north as soon as they could. Only the ground floor's nine rooms had been finished. The structure had only a little more work done on it since the Yankee carpenters had gone. Longwood looked somewhat ghastly and eerie.

"Dr. Nutt is in a dither about all this. He had such great plans for the home," Stelcie told Miriam.

"Perhaps all this strife will soon end, and everything will return to normal," Miriam said optimistically.

"I hope so," added Stelcie. "I'll miss Saw."

"Can we go to your house now" asked Miriam. "Sawyer is there now?"

"He probably is. He was finishing his business before having to leave. Mother is finishing his uniform, and she needs him there."

"Driver, please take us to the Dundee home now," directed Miriam.

"Yus, Miss."

The driver turned the carriage toward the Dundee homestead and urged the horses to quicken their pace.

"Sawyer's leaving by the end of the week, you say. And other young men are, also," said Miriam.

"Many other menfolk have already left for New Orleans, Jackson, and points north," Stelcie added.

"Stelcie, what about Solomon? You haven't said a word about him. Is he in Natchez presently?"

Stelcie didn't answer immediately. "Solomon slipped away, out of Natchez. No one knows exactly when he left or why or where he went. We'll all so distressed. We don't know what to think."

"He didn't tell anyone goodbye?"

"No, we know nothing. He jist up and left."

"That's too bad. I would like to see him again. He... he..." Miriam paused reflectively. "He always intrigued me. Why, he could make my little heart palpitate without even trying, it seems."

"He is handsome," added Stelcie, "even if he is my cousin." She grinned and giggled.

"Why, yes, he is so handsome. His eyes just seem to penetrate to my very soul. He makes me feel like a damp washcloth when he smiles at me in his certain way," admitted Miriam. "I wish he were here," she added, blushing in front of her best friend.

"Miriam, are yew carrying on about Solomon or not? Is there something between yew two I don't know about?" asked Stelcie, leaning toward her friend. "Why, Miriam, yew're turning pure crimson." It was true. Miriam was blushing a deep red.

"Oh, Stel, it's the heat, the hot sun, the ride," said Miriam, defending herself.

"Well," Stelcie said, "Eve Whitmore thinks much of Solomon, too. She was fit to be tied when she learned of Solomon's absence. I visited her not too many days ago, and all she could do was to hold back her tears when Solomon's name was mentioned."

Now the blood drained rapidly from Miriam's face, and she grew quiet for a few minutes. Stelcie chattered away about the heat and lack of rain in the last few days and didn't seem to notice Miriam's sudden quietness.

Soon they turned into the Dundee place, and polite conversation resumed until they pulled to a stop. Miriam was welcomed back to Natchez by everyone, including Sawyer, who was there and seemed especially glad to see her. When he grasped both of her hands with his and leaned to kiss her cheek, only Miriam noted that his kiss was not just a peck, but it lingered a brief second longer than the usual polite kiss of greeting. She gave him a smile when he straightened back up. It pleased him.

Three days later Sawyer Dundee and scores of other young men marched out of Natchez toward Jackson, the state capital. Smiles and tears and well wishes went with them.

By early August, news had gotten back to Natchez of the great victory by the Confederates over the Yankees at Manassas Junction in northern Virginia. There was euphoria, and everyone knew the fighting would soon be over.

But the fighting proved itself a war, and the time dragged onward. Sawyer at first sent a letter every week to his mother and sister. He had remained in Mississippi as an aide to senior officers in Jackson. At one time he had been sent up to Corinth. Almost a year later, he had been sent to Vicksburg to help erect fortifications there. Sawyer had made captain when he came home in the summer of 1862 for a week's furlough.

Mrs. Dundee and sister Stelcie were so happy to see Sawyer and so proud of their handsome soldier. All three visited Clifton one afternoon. Frank Surget and Sawyer spoke of the war and the importance of Vicksburg and denying control of the Mississippi River to the Yankees. Sawyer commented on the unfortified city of Natchez and his worries about his family and friends. The Dundees stayed for the evening meal, and afterward Stelcie suggested that the young people take an evening stroll through Clifton's gardens on the bluff overlooking the river. Sawyer and Miriam agreed, and the three young adults went out on the veranda. The ladies got on each side of the young captain, took an arm, and walked him down the steps.

"Any news from Solomon?" asked Miriam.

"Nothing. Still nothing," said Stelcie hastily.

"I haven't heard from him where I have been," Sawyer said.

"It's a strange thing," Miriam said. "A very strange thing."

The trio stepped from the bright lights of Clifton into the moonlight. "Tell us about yore soldiering. Have yew shot any damn Yankees yet, Saw?" asked Stelcie, tugging his left arm.

"Well, no, I haven't. I haven't even seen a Yankee soldier as of yet," replied Sawyer. He was just about to say something else when Laura Dundee's voice called from the house.

"Stelcie! Stelcie! Yew had wanted to show Mrs. Surget how yew sewed those hidden seams on yore dress. Now is the time before we forgit again. Come back in for a few minutes!"

"Oh, sawdust! I forgot again," exlaimed Stelcie. "I must go back in to tell Mrs. Charlotte about how Mama and I did the seams."

Miriam and Sawyer turned toward the house as Stelcie dropped her hand from her brother's arm. "Oh, no, y'all two don't have to go back in because of me. Y'all stroll along the bluff and visit." The couple paused. "Well, go on, shoo! What's the matter? Y'all afraid of each other? Shoo!" With these words, Stelcie grinned and giggled and went toward the house. Sawyer and Miriam watched as she joined her mother on the porch and went inside.

"I guess we can't argue with my little sister, can we? It is nice out here. It's so peaceful. So quiet. So relaxing," said Sawyer. "It's so different from our headquarters. There's always hurried activity there. Soldiers in and out. Fresh war news from Virginia and Tennessee." He was quiet, just walking arm in arm with Miriam. Neither said anything for several minutes.

"Sawyer," said Miriam quietly, "are you afraid of the war? I mean, of being in a battle and being killed?"

"Every man is afraid. But each man must overcome his fear in order to do his duty," he replied.

They walked on in silence. Both were pondering the war and its possible effect on their families and way of life. They reached the high point of the bluffs overlooking the Mississippi.

Sawyer broke the silence. "I fear that soon y'all will see Yankee gunboats there on the river. I pray not, but I fear it." They looked out across the shimmering, flowing waters.

Miriam turned to Sawyer and grasped his other hand. She put her head down.

"Why, Miriam, yew're shaking." Sawyer pulled her to him and hugged.

"I'm afraid of the war. Of when it gets here."

"Yew must be brave, girl."

She just melted within his embrace. His strong arms gave her comfort.

"Oh, Sawyer, that's easy for you to say. You're a man. Big. Strong. Anxious to fight."

"Not anxious to fight. Ready to defend my home, my family, my friends like yew, Miriam."

She looked up at Sawyer and smiled. "My hero," she said as she closed her eyes. Sawyer looked at her lovely face in the moonlight, particularly her slightly parted, moist lips. He kissed her gently on those lips. Her arms pulled him closer.

"Saw! Saw! Miriam! Miriam!" yelled Stelcie. "Where are y'all?"

Sawyer and Miriam jerked apart and let their hands drop to their sides. Then Sawyer hollered, "Over here, Stel. Over here." He waved his right hand over his head.

Stelcie walked daintily over to them. "I hurried as much as I could. I hope I didn't keep y'all waiting too long. Y'all did find something to talk about, didn't y'all? Come on, Saw, tell us about yore soldiering. Did yew see the governor in Jackson? Did yew go into Tennessee?"

"Hold on, little sister," answered Sawyer. "One question at a time. Right, Miriam?" He looked at her with a grin.

"Right, Saw."

The trio walked and talked on the avenues and through the lighted gardens for another hour. Each was lighthearted, and concerns were brushed away for the night.

Sawyer saw Miriam one more time before he left again for duty. This time in the polite goodbyes, she kissed his cheek and then she brushed her lips on his as she pulled back. She smiled at him innocently.

"It's September second, and we haven't got a letter from Saw since he was here," said Laura Dundee. "I wish he would write."

"He's busy, Mama. Yew know that. He'll write when he can," said Stelcie.

Beulah came in to the breakfast table with more food. "Mo' coffee?" she asked both of the Dundee women. She held the pot.

"No, thanks, not me," replied Stelcie.

"I'll have a little more," said Mrs. Dundee. Beulah poured.

Then Beulah said, "Oh, Missus, Gabriel tole me dat dem Silva Grays done made a round outs here dis mornin'."

"Good," said Laura Dundee. "I feel safer knowin' they come by

86

ever so often."

"Mama, what can those old men and young boys do with their old guns against some damn Yankee soldiers if they come marching through Natchez?"

"Well, Stelcie, they can fight. A little, at least. And they can shoot some of the outlaw plunderers we hear about in the countryside. I think I'm more frightened of them than I am of the Yankee soldiers."

"If'n one of dem plunderers a'comes in dis kitchen I be done plunder his head with dis heer skillet," said Beulah, bravely bristling up.

"I'm not afraid, Mama."

"I'm still glad the older men and boys formed the Silver Grays to help defend Natchez. We'll never know when we need them," said Mrs. Dundee. "I thank them for coming out this far to see about us. They don't really have to. We're not really in Natchez itself."

"Mama, they know that Saw is gone, and that we're jist womenfolk with our slaves. And besides, we're just a few minutes outside of Natchez itself. We'd be the last ones to know if soldiers came up off boats from the river." Stelcie finished her last bite of the late breakfast. "I'll be in the sewing room, Mama." She rose from the table and left the room.

Later that afternoon one of the slave children came running up to the kitchen door. He pounded on it and shouted, "Beulah! Missus Dundee!"

Beulah was at the door. "What's yew wants, boy?"

"Lissen," he said. "Hear dat?"

Beulah was quiet and cocked her head. "What dat noise be?"

Mrs. Dundee came through the kitchen to the back door.

"Missus, lissen," said the child.

"What?"

"Missus, what dem noises?" asked Beulah.

"Oh, my God!" shouted Laura Dundee. "That's cannon fire! Yankee gunboats must be on the river! May God have mercy on us."

Stelcie came up just in time to hear her mother's remarks. "Damn Yankees!" she exclaimed

Laura Dundee said loudly, "Get everyone inside the buildings. Stelcie, git our guns. Load them and prop your daddy's doublebarrel at the stairs. Is Gabriel on the place?"

"Nome," said Beulah. "He be at de mill."

"If that's the trouble I think is, Gabriel will come to us as soon as he can. When he gits here, we'll see what he knows, and then we'll send him for news. Everybody inside!"

They waited for almost an hour, listening to the sounds of war from Natchez in the distance. Twenty minutes later Gabriel came in fast on a harnessed horse cut from a wagon. He was breathless and anxious.

"All be all rat heer?" he asked as he came into the kitchen.

"Yes," answered Mrs. Dundee. "Do yew know what has happened?"

"Yes'm. I be in Natchez. I was for to git some tings for de sawmill. Dere be a call for the Silva Grays. Folks say a Federal boat with guns was on the river. Dere was shootin' at some blue jackets under de hill. Den big guns fired. And bombs up on de hill. Below it, too. It be horrors. Riderless horses wuz runnin' 'round, scared. Peoples wuz rushing heer an dere. Little children be crying. I seed a li'l white child runnin' and fall. Her pappy plucked her body up after she say she kilt. It be horrors, Missus. I comes as fastest I kin to the homestead." He was nervous.

"Yew did the right thing, Gabriel. We needed yew. Sit here and calm down for a bit," said Mrs. Dundee.

"Did yew see any soldiers?"

"Nome."

"We must know if Yankee soldiers are in Natchez now. We'll check in a while. Can yew take me?"

"Yus, ma'am. I kin."

"Good," said Mrs. Dundee. "Beulah, send word to ready the carriage. Stelcie, bring me yore daddy's shotgun."

In half an hour Laura Dundee and Gabriel were entering Natchez to survey what had happened and what was happening. Laura Dundee had the shotgun concealed by her side under a light-colored piece of cotton fabric. They heard that a Yankee gunboat was at the landing under the hill. It was getting dark. They heard comments that the gunboat was leaving about this time. Laura Dundee told Gabriel to drive to the top of Silver Street so they could take a look. When they got there, Gabriel pointed out on the river and said, "Look, Missus Laura, de boat."

Laura Dundee, who had been looking at smoke from burning buildings under the hill, switched her eyes to the open river. There, paddling upstream, was a Yankee ironclad gunboat. Smoke from its twin stacks puffed upward into the late evening sky. She could see deck hands scurrying to and fro over the boat. They watched in silence as the boat flying the Yankee flag disappeared from sight.

"Let's go home, Gabriel," said Laura Dundee crisply.

At home they reported what they had observed, Gabriel to the slaves in the back and Mrs. Dundee to all in the house.

In October of 1862, Lt. General John C. Pemberton took command of the Confederate soldiers defending the Mississippi River against the

Union armies. Captain Sawyer Dundee was ordered to Vicksburg once more. This time he was told he would remain there for a while.

It was a dreary and dismal winter in Natchez and Vicksburg. Sawyer was able to send several letters to his family to let them know the news. Spring brought renewed hope to Mississippians, but it was not long in duration. Union General Grant had cut his army loose from the river and its supply line and had engaged the Confederates at Port Gibson, Raymond, Jackson, Champion Hill, and Big Black River Bridge, and had pushed the Southern soldiers into a siege at Vicksburg by late May of 1863.

In Natchez the news of every Confederate setback only increased the dread of the impending Yankee occupation of the town. Almost daily Union ironclads would pass on the river. The few people under the hill would jeer and curse them as they went by. With river traffic cut off, little activity took place at the landing except for transporting military supplies and food across the river from Vidalia on the Louisiana side. Most activity was at night because of Union gunboats going up and down the Mississippi River.

When news of the Emancipation Proclamation filtered into Natchez and the surrounding areas coupled with news of Yankee victories, may slaves deserted their white owners and their plantation and farm homes and went to Natchez. They were homeless and hungry. Natchez itself became a tense, frightening place for both whites and blacks. The white manpower had been eroded away by the war effort so there was hardly anyone to keep law and order. Women barricaded themselves in their homes and carried butcher knives with them for a feeling of safety.

Only two of the Dundee slaves left for their freedom, even though Laura Dundee told them all that she would harbor no hard feelings to any who left. The two who left had some family members across the river in Louisiana.

In Solomon's house Thomajia, Ruth, and Charon remained. Esther had slipped away, enticed by a handsome young slave who was running away. Charon, on a trip to his master's hotel, suffered mortal knife wounds in a fight in front of the hotel.

At the Whitmore's home, Cryer stayed with Miss Eve. At Clifton most slaves remained with the Surgets. However, Frank Surget's field hands on his cotton lands did not stay.

The Surgets and Miriam decided that it would be safer for Miriam to go stay with the Dundees. She would be farther away from the river and the Union gunboats, and most of the Dundee slaves had remained loyal. Miriam would also be farther away from Natchez-Under-the-Hill, which had turned into a lawless, wicked, seething place with the influx of runaway slaves. All the Dundees and the Surgets agreed that when Yankee soldiers came to Natchez, Miriam was to continue to stay with the Dundees.

On the last day of May Miriam and Stelcie sat on the front porch of the Dundee house. Stelcie looked at the sycamine tree and told Miriam about Grandma Dundee and the younguns. It was afternoon.

"We used to play around that sycamine," said Stelcie.

"Let's walk out to it," suggested Miriam.

Miriam was off the porch first. Stelcie followed. "It's hot, Miriam."

"We'll get in the shade of the sycamine," said Miriam.

They walked slowly in the hot sun. Stelcie went on the opposite side of the tree from the house to get the best shade. Miriam walked around the tree and then stood by Stelcie. They faced the tree and could see the front porch. Stelcie pointed to a rocking chair on the porch. "That's where Grandma would sit and read us the Bible and tell us what it meant."

"Look at this old tree. I wonder how old it is," Miriam said as she backed out of the shade to get a better look. Stelcie stepped backward besides Miriam.

"It's old. Grandma Dundee had Daddy plant it for her when the house was first built," said Stelcie. "That was before I was born."

They heard a noise behind them and turned to look at the same time. They were shocked to see two men in dirty, blue uniforms rush across the road toward them. The men had pistols and were almost on top of them when Stelcie regained her senses enough to holler "Mama! Mama!!" Miriam shrieked as the two men each grabbed a young woman. Miriam's voice was muted by the dirty hand of her captor. Stelcie was quieted when a pistol was pointed at her head, and the soldier firmly told her to stop yelling.

Miriam was being dragged back across the road by the soldier that held her. She struggled feebly against the much stronger, much larger man. The man was already tearing at her dress. He had dropped his pistol on the dirt road in order to get a better grip on her twisted arm. Miriam was crying and let out a muffled scream. Her dress was torn off her shoulder, and the man drooled at her creamy white skin.

Stelcie was having more success at preventing her attacker from dragging her back across the road into the trees. Her assailant was a smaller man, somewhat older than the other one. His left hand was across her mouth, but one of his fingers slipped in between her teeth, and she bit down hard. He jerked his hand away in pain. She tasted his blood and yelled out, "Damn Yankee!"

He put his hand back at her mouth to mute her words. With his other hand, he yanked her hair and said, "Come on, my pretty young Southern gal. See what a real man kin do for yew." Stelcie still tasted his blood in her mouth. He pulled her hair and made her head go backward. She felt his hot, hostile breath on the side of her face. His whiskers were

92

sharp on her soft skin. He let go of her hair to claw at the front of her dress. He ripped buttons and tore cloth. He clawed again, this time at her exposed undergarment. It tore, and he turned her around to face him. Both her breasts were exposed. The soldier laughed and pushed her down at the edge of the far side of the road.

"This is real Southern hospitality," he sneered as he towered over her.

Boom! Boom! Two blasts came from beside the sycamine tree. The man fell forward as his hands clutched at his back. He fell dead beside Stelcie, who stood and pulled her torn clothes over her heaving bosom. She spat on him.

Miriam's attacker at the sound of the shotgun blasts looked up from his assault on Miriam and realized he no longer had his weapon. He ran through the trees.

"Stay down, Miriam!" yelled Laura Dundee. A split second later the shotgun emitted two more blasts of buckshot.

Stelcie stood, looking at her mother. Miriam raised up and looked at Laura Dundee.

"Damn Yankees!" said Laura Dundee. She dropped the shotgun as Gabriel and other slaves ran up.

"Load the shotgun for me again like I showed yew, Gabriel," said Mrs. Dundee. He picked up the gun. She lobbed him two shells from her sewing apron pocket.

Mrs. Dundee hugged Stelcie, and they both went over to Miriam.

"Are yew all right, Miriam?" asked Mrs. Dundee. They helped Miriam up. She was shaking. Now all three women began crying.

"I'm scared. I'm bruised a bit, but I'm just nervous now. You stopped him just in time. He was choking me into submission when you shot his companion," said Miriam. Beulah was there, helping her with her clothes.

"Gabriel, yous tote Missus Laura's scattergun and goes into dat wood dere for a bit to hunt that blue jacket. We's don't need yore eyes seein' de ladyfolks undergarments. Now git!" ordered Beulah. "Git goin'!"

Mrs. Dundee added, "And Gabriel, when yew come back, git rid of this soldier's body. He's a deserter, a scavenger, not a real soldier."

The young women were helped inside to recover from their attack. The night proved to be a long one of crying and praying for the war to end quickly.

Vicksburg, Mississippi 1863

The night was long for Captain Sawyer Dundee in Vicksburg, also. Union General Grant's army besieged the Confederate stronghold and had, for a couple of weeks, been tightening forces around Pemberton's defenses. The Confederate lines had been assaulted at several key points. The Yankees had been repulsed with heavy losses. The Federal gunboat *Cincinnati* had been sunk on May twenty-seventh. A Yankee general assault on the Confederate lines had been denied also with heavy losses to the Union soldiers. The Yankee attempt to work their way through the swampy marshes and bayous north of the town had proven unproductive, too. But Captain Dundee and the Confederates, even though they had been successful in stymying the Yankee advance, had other problems—problems that would prove to be the determining factors in the siege for Vicksburg. Grant's plan was that of a formal siege. He would deny the Confederates food and supplies while almost constantly bombarding their fortified positions with batteries of artillery on the land and Admiral Porter's naval gunboats on the river. Yankee soldiers dug tunnels and detonated explosives near and under Confederate defensive lines. The soldiers and civilians in Vicksburg suffered through the bombardments, already short rations, and constant anxiety and fear.

As June first dawned, the Federal cannon announced the new day with the morning's first barrage. It lasted over an hour. Sawyer, who had gotten only an hour's sleep, quickly shaved with his last bit of soap, and reported to Pemberton's headquarters for the daily officers' meeting. Very little was new. Short rations and other dwindling supplies were the already known report information. Medical supplies were almost nonexistent. A few men who had probably already realized the hopelessness of the situation had not made morning muster and had probably deserted only to be captured by the enemy.

"Times will get tougher," stated Pemberton matter-of-factly. "But we must hold Vicksburg. It is the key to the Mississippi River." He turned and stared at the map of his defenses that had been pinned to the wall. "Captain Dundee, did any medical supplies get by the Yankees into our hands last night?"

"No, sir, nothing last night. Not even a single bandage. Our contacts either were intercepted or did not make the attempt. The Yankees fired their artillery more last night than usual, it seemed," answered Sawyer.

"Major Stroud, your munitions report, please."

"Shortage, sir," replied Major Stroud. He began a more detailed listing of information. Sawyer listened with one ear and pondered the Confederate situation. It seemed an impossibility to hold Vicksburg for long.

Pemberton interrupted Major Stroud, "Thank you, Major. Should there be another assault at any point in the lines, follow our established policy of getting what we have to that point."

"Yes, sir."

"I have had no communication from General Johnston. We are operating our defenses here with no knowledge of what relief forces may become available to us. We must stand our ground. We must hold on until we can no longer do so and then hold on longer," stated Pemberton emphatically.

The Yankee artillery began its second bombardment of the day. This time all the gunboats joined in the attack.

"Dismissed, gentlemen. To your posts!"

Everyone saluted and turned to leave. "Captain Dundee," called Pemberton. "Hold a minute."

Sawyer waited until everyone else had left. He faced General

Pemberton. "Go out on the frontal defenses tonight to see what the morale of the men is like. I need to know."

"Yes, sir, I shall do so."

"I'm sending you because I trust your judgment. I believe you to be an astute young officer."

"Thank yew, General."

"You are from around here, aren't you?"

"From Natchez, sir, down the river a bit."

"Then you truly are defending your home, aren't you, son?"

"Yes, sir."

Pemberton looked at Dundee intently for a moment. "Carry on, Captain," he said crisply.

"Yes, sir." Sawyer saluted and turned sharply. He heard the Yankee cannons once again as he left the general's chamber. But this time the Union cannonading resulted in a reply by the Confederate batteries. He knew because of the closer sounds of the artillery firing and especially the unique sound of one of the Rebel cannons nicknamed "Whistling Dick." This Confederate cannon was not really a huge gun; but the unique sound its projectiles produced as they flew out of besieged Vicksburg and toward the Union batteries was readily recognized by soldiers on both sides. The odd whistling sound accompanying the flying cannonballs set this gun apart from all the others. The rifled barrel of Whistling Dick yielded a high-pitched whirring whistle that was comforting to the Rebel soldiers and civilians in the city and anathema to Yankees in the targeted areas. The sound emitted by the twirling cannonballs was both eerie and mesmerizing. Sawyer felt that comforting, that consoling, that heartening feeling. He pondered momentarily how that whistling sound would affect him psychologically even if the projectile did not explode near him. His experiences with incoming barrages from Union cannon seemed bad enough.

That night Captain Dundee made his way along the frontal defense works along the eastern side of the town. He talked with men resting and eating their skimpy rations. He was guided into forward rifle pits and earthen embankments to talk with grizzled veterans and young boys. At one spot he listened to soldiers from both sides talk unseen by one another and call each other Johnny Reb and Billy Yank in their conversation. Sawyer, going back inside the main mass of defensive earthworks, leaned for a minute or two against a stack of fascines before he moved again out to a smaller forward area that was still well behind the ring of forward rifle pits. He abruptly halted behind a group of gabions along the lower earthworks, stood without thinking, and focused his eyes out toward the darkness.

At this point the corporal with him said sharply, "Git down, Captain!" He obeyed and lay flat behind the protection of the earthworks with huge embedded logs. The corporal whispered, "It may be a Yankee sniper movin' out there to git in a better position in that line of trees. Our pickets may be able to pluck him out if he shows hisself too much."

About thirty yards out in front of the earth and log embankment they had dropped behind was the most forward rifle pit with two Confederate soldiers lying in it. Both cocked their rifles and stared intensely into the dark line of trees about two hundred yards away.

"The actual Yank line is some hundred yards out beyond them trees," said the corporal. "There is several deep ravines jist after them trees. It's not terrain fit fer much 'cept to look over. A sniper positions there ever few days."

Captain Dundee strained his eyes looking through the crack between the top log and the next one. The two soldiers in the rifle pit were still sweeping the tree line with their straining eyes. There was a sharp crack of a dry branch breaking. The soldiers sighted their rifles at where the sound came from.

From the darkness at the tree line, they could see something obviously white. It looked to be a white cloth on a branch, fashioned like a flag of truce. A figure dressed in black emerged from the trees. It held the branch with a white handkerchief tied on it.

"Don't shoot. I'm a friend. I'm alone. I'm a friend." The words floated across the open space toward the Confederate lines.

"Hold yore fire," ordered the corporal. "Yore orders, sir?" He looked at Captain Dundee.

"One of yew go meet him," said Sawyer. "The other hold him in yore sights. Corporal, alert men up and down this line."

"Yas, sir." The corporal moved away.

The intruder walked slowly toward the Rebel line, holding the homemade flag of truce up high. By this time the Confederate soldier had reached him and was quickly marshaling him toward the rifle pit.

"I'm a friend. I'm alone," repeated the man from the Union lines. "I have morphine and coffee. It's in my coat pockets."

Sawyer could hear the man clearly now, but he still could not see his face. The man's hat was pulled so the brim was low over his eyes. Sawyer stood and then scrambled over the embankment.

The other Confederate soldier now was standing, holding his gun on the stranger and waiting for the two men to reach the rifle pit.

"I am a friend," repeated the man.

Sawyer started to draw his pistol as he closed on the stranger but didn't because he wasn't afraid of him. He trusted that voice. He recognized that voice. And now he recognized the bearded face.

99

Sawyer yelled out, "Solomon!"

"How do you know my—? Sawyer, is that you?" asked Solomon Witcher as he looked his cousin in the eye. The two cousins, who had not seen one another in more than two years, embraced each other.

"Captain Dundee, yew are standin' out where yew can git shot, sur," said the corporal as he returned.

Sawyer, now realizing that fact, put his hand on Solomon's left shoulder and said, "Let's move to safety." He looked at the two soldiers from the rifle pit. "Good work, men. Carry on. I have this man." The two men took their positions in the rifle pit again.

Sawyer and Solomon hurried over the embankment to where the corporal was. "Corporal, lead me to the nearest road to the hospital."

"Yes, sur, this way."

A few minutes later Captain Dundee and Solomon were walking briskly down the road toward a hospital area in Vicksburg. When the corporal parted ways with them, Solomon handed him a bag with coffee in it. "Thankee, sur," he said.

"How did yew slip through the lines without being shot?" asked Sawyer.

"Luck and fast talking and planning. And a little focused persuasion of the unit commander. I must go back at or near the same point in three nights."

"Isn't it amazing that yew came across at the exact place where I was?" asked Sawyer. "Is that luck, too?"

"Maybe," answered Solomon. "But I had sensed that where I crossed was the place. I didn't come over at the first point I had thought about. And this is not the first night I anticipated crossing over. Something told me this was the time and place tonight. I knew you were in Vicksburg, but I didn't realize you would greet me."

"It's quiet tonight. The Yankees must be short on munitions. They haven't bombarded us yet tonight. It's strange. This is the first time in many nights that the sky has not been lit up by bombs. It's as though they wanted yew to—"

"I'm lucky. You know that, Sawyer," interrupted Solomon. "Is the hospital close by? We should have gotten your horse." He laughed. "I'm tired after climbing up and down those steep ravines."

They were halted twice by sentries before they reached the hospital. There Sawyer asked to see the surgeon in charge for the night. Captain Dundee told the surgeon about Solomon's slipping through the lines with morphine, and Solomon handed over to the doctor three packets of the drug and one bag of coffee. The Confederate doctor thanked the two cousins, especially Solomon. He said that the morphine would ease the suffering of surgery for several of the most badly wounded soldiers.

Captain Dundee saw that the packets had been stamped with "U.S." The doctor saw, also. He commented that Yankee medicine worked well on Confederate soldiers and that the coffee was welcomed by him for the long nights of observing the wounded. The doctor did not ask how Solomon had gotten the coffee and morphine.

As the cousins were leaving the hospital, the Federal cannon began firing. "I wonder what time it is," said Sawyer aloud.

"Four o'clock," replied Solomon without checking his pocket watch. Sawyer had not noticed this peculiar fact.

Bombshells exploded in the night sky in the distance all around them. They walked.

"We kin git to my quarters in a short time if we walk quickly," Sawyer told his cousin.

"You aren't afraid of the bombardment?"

"Of course, I am," answered Sawyer. "If shells start dropping closer, we'll find a ditch or a hole somewhere." He grinned at Solomon as they walked briskly. "Besides I'm with yew, my lucky cousin. Should I be afraid?" He laughed.

So did Solomon. They kept walking. They didn't talk much, except when Sawyer would indicate a turn or both would be startled by a bomb bursting closer and would joke or yell like a kid in a game.

They reached Sawyer's quarters, a tent drawn over the opening to a dug-out cave in the side of a hill. Other officers were in nearby similar protected enclaves. Most were trying to sleep. Some were just blankly staring at nothing.

Sawyer sat on a stool and said, "Sit on the cot, Solomon. It's the best I can offer yew."

Solomon sat on the cot and then tossed his cousin a fist-sized bag. "That's the last bag of coffee I got. That's the best I can offer you, Saw. Unless . . ."

"Unless what?"

"Unless you want to get out of Vicksburg before Grant pounds it and you into nothingness," said Solomon in a low voice. "You can go through the lines with me three nights from now, same time, same place. No questions asked."

"Solomon, yew know I can't leave here. It's my duty. It would be deserting my—"

"I knew you wouldn't go. I knew what you would say," interrupted Solomon. "Don't get yourself in an uproar. I just had to make the offer. For Aunt Laura. For Stelcie."

"What do yew know about Grant's plan for Vicksburg?"

102

"Don't ask."

"Where did yew get the coffee and morphine?"

"Don't ask that, either."

"Solomon, yew—"

"Sawyer," interrupted Solomon again. "Let me talk. You must arrange for me to see General Pemberton as soon as possible this morning. I came through the lines for dual purposes. You have turned me down on one. Now I must see the general for his time. It is of the utmost importance that I talk with him."

"Solomon, I—"

"You can get me in to talk with General Pemberton, can't you?"

"Yes. Yes, I can."

"Trust me, Saw. Remember what we spoke of just before I left Natchez for the last time?" Sawyer nodded affirmatively. "Just get me in to see the general today, this morning."

Sawyer nodded. He could only trust his cousin, especially when Solomon looked at him so seriously and sternly. "Let's try to get an hour or so of sleep. It's been a night."

"I agree," returned Solomon, who put his legs up on the cot and pulled his hat down over his face.

About mid-morning Solomon Witcher was ushered into General Pemberton's chamber. Sawyer provided the introductions, but just before he was about to say that he and Solomon were related, Solomon abruptly cut him off with a remark that he had a business in Natchez before the war and knew Captain Dundee from then. Sawyer lapsed into silence.

Solomon Witcher looked at the general and stated, "I must speak to you alone, General."

"You are dismissed, Captain Dundee. However, wait in the next room for when I may need you."

Sawyer hesitated, then saluted, and left the room.

Solomon Witcher and Confederate General Pemberton talked in the closed room for half an hour. Sawyer could hear their low voices but could not understand what was said. At last the door opened. Sawyer rose from his chair, anticipating an order from his general. The door had not opened wide, only six to eight inches. Sawyer heard General Pemberton's voice, "I shall not surrender Vicksburg."

The door opened wider. Sawyer saw Solomon in the doorway. "I shall remain with Captain Dundee for the duration of my stay. I am available to you for two days," said Solomon.

The general's voice blared out, "Captain Dundee."

"Yes, sir."

"Accompany Mr. Witcher while he is here with us in Vicksburg for the remainder of his time. Be available to him. Show him our artillery on the bluffs and have a gun crew demonstrate our command of the loop in the river. Then take him through the town to show him what the Yankee gunboats are doing to innocent civilians. On the night he indicates to you, escort him to the point in our front lines that you met him last night. Give him safe passage through the forward enemy lines. Then tell him 'goodbye.'"

"Yes, sir, General."

Out into the open air they went. "What did yew say to General Pemberton?"

"Basically just what I said to you about the Federals and their cannon. It's a matter of time before Grant breaks through at any given point, the bombardment gets you, the sickness gets you, or you starve to death," replied Solomon. "Saw, you look so thin now."

After a sparse and rather tasteless noon meal, Captain Dundee got horses and took Solomon up on the bluffs overlooking the hairpin curve of the river. The Union guns were silent, and no gunboats were in range on the river. Sawyer and Solomon rode up to one artillery battery. Sawyer dismounted and went to speak with the officer in charge. Solomon remained astride the horse and surveyed the area from this vantage point.

He looked back at Sawyer, who was motioning him to dismount. He did so. Sawyer led the officer in charge over to Solomon.

"Captain McSparrin, this is Mr. Witcher. He is the gentlemen that Pemberton wishes yew to demonstrate for," said Sawyer.

Captain McSparrin and Solomon shook hands. "Here, Mr. Witcher, use my field glasses, please," said Captain McSparrin as he took his binoculars from a case and handed them to Solomon.

"Thank you, Captain."

McSparrin continued, "Mr. Witcher, look across both expanses of river water. Look from here about twenty degrees to yore right. Yew'll see some Yankee artillerymen putting finishing touches on a five-cannon battery. They are rolling up the first of the field pieces as I speak."

Solomon looked through the glasses as McSparrin talked. "The second one, Captain McSparrin."

"Keep watching, Mr. Witcher. We will put several flies in their ointment." McSparrin turned toward his artillerymen and barked, "Load guns and prepare to fire."

Three gun crews immediately got busy preparing the cannons for firing. They were loaded and readied for action. One soldier at each cannon held a burning taper.

"At three second intervals," shouted Captain McSparrin, "fire!'

The nearest cannon belched fire and smoke, roared, and jerked back and up slightly. Then the middle one. Then the farthest one. Solomon Witcher kept the field glasses to his eyes, watching the Yankee battery. The first shot hit slightly behind the battery but destroyed a caisson. Yankee soldiers dashed for cover. The second shot hit one artillery piece and obliterated it. The third shot created a gaping hole in the earthworks created for another cannon.

The Confederate artillerymen stood at their positions, awaiting orders. Captain McSparrin asked Solomon, "May I borrow the glasses, Mr. Witcher." He held out his hand. Solomon handled them over. McSparrin looked through them and smiled. "Captain Dundee, would yew care for a look?" He held the binoculars out to Sawyer, who took them and looked.

"Very good, Captain McSparrin. Compliment yore men. Thank yew for the demonstration," said Sawyer. "Come on, Mr. Witcher. Those Yankees are liable to start shooting back. Let's go into town." Sawyer saluted Captain McSparrin and went back to the horses with Solomon following silently.

They reached the town in a few minutes. Most buildings had been hit by cannonballs or exploding shells. Many were partially burned. Several were only charred shells of the former structures. They rode past churches with steeples that had been knocked down. Here and there could be seen where a cannonball had entered a building or house on one side. Once beautiful homes had walls broken down or shrapnel splinters defacing them. A house was still burning with small flames licking up the last standing wall. The collapsed roof was smoldering.

The two men rode past grim men, women, and children walking slowly or hurriedly scurrying about during this time of no Yankee bombardment. They saw people, young and old, digging caves in the sides of hills

"That's what most of the town people have done and are doing for protection from the Union cannonading," said Sawyer tersely. Solomon said nothing. They rode on. They saw one well-dressed older white lady digging a hole in the backyard of her house. "She's burying some of her valuables." She noticed them and scurried out of sight with an apron full of something in her hands. Solomon Witcher said little the rest of the ride, but he was very attentive to all he saw and heard.

After the cannonade demonstration, Sawyer and Solomon rode back to the center of the town. They slowed their horses and stopped. "Let's talk with the doctor we gave the supplies to last night," said Solomon. "Do you think he is in this area? I don't remember exactly where the hospital building is."

Sawyer said rather solemnly to his cousin, "The hospital is not jist one or two buildings. Almost all of the public buildings and many private residences are hospitals that house the wounded and others that are ill due to lack of food and water and disease. That building over there happens to be the one in which the doctor who yew gave the medicine to is housed and works. The smaller building next to it holds the wounded that need nursing and other help. When men have recovered enough not to require nursing, they are moved to a house down the street." The two men dismounted their horses and went to search for the physician in the larger building. Sawyer spied him first and then motioned to Solomon for him to follow.

Sawyer and Solomon caught the doctor's attention as he was making rounds among the wounded soldiers. The doctor came over to them and said, "Thank yew, Mister, for the medicine and coffee yew gave me. I have already used some of both. I am Major Herrington." The doctor pointed over to a small table with several chairs about it. "Let's sit fur a spell. It is a lull time fur me at the moment. But who knows when them Yankee batteries will begin firin' once more on this area of the town.

107

I don't really know why the Yankee land guns and river gunboats have ceased their relentless bombardment of us since last night and now are seemingly only shelling sections of the town. I really do appreciate what yew brought to us. Did yew actually slip through the siege lines? How did yew do that? Where did yew come from? Did yew float across the Mississippi River at night the way Major Lamar Fontaine is rumored to done?"

Solomon, about to speak, was forestalled by Sawyer saying, "Solomon here is my cousin. We both hail from Natchez. And Solomon is the luckiest man I have ever known."

"That Major Fontaine had to be lucky like yew. That big river has some treacherous currents. And at night!" exclaimed Doctor Herrington. "But yew did not swim the river. Yew slipped through the siege lines?"

Solomon nodded his head affirmatively and simply said, "Luck. But I had to get through with a message for General Pemberton. It was imperative."

"Those Yankees are as thick as thieves all along the siege lines. I do not know how yew infiltrated the lines. Both sides could have put a bullet through yore skull. I even heard one soldier say that a cat could not slip through the lines without being seen and caught or shot by them Yankee sentries. Or one of those right friendly cottonmouths could have bitten yew by chance in one of them ravines. Yew are indeed a fortunate man. I don't know whether to tell yew to risk the cannonading and starvation here, attempt to go through the lines to escape, or merely to surrender to the Yanks at the perimeter," said the doctor, shaking his head.

"Well, Doc, you see, I will have some dispatches from General Pemberton to deliver outside of the siege lines. I will go out again in a couple of nights or so. I will need luck again the way I see it," answered Solomon.

"I pray yew make it through then," added the doctor. "That is, if yew don't get yoreself killed in the bombardment before then."

"Doc," began Solomon, "what might you want me to tell other people about this siege that you, the other soldiers, and the citizens of Vicksburg are enduring?"

"My greatest concern is, of course, the wounded and ill soldiers since I, too, am a soldier myself. I am concerned about the citizens of the town as well, but I have only limited contact with them. I suggest that yew visit some of the cave dwellers and other town inhabitants before yew leave to understand their plight in this horrible, horrible war," the doctor paused. He wrinkled his forehead as if he were in pain as were many of the soldiers nearby. He began once more, "These wounded and sick soldiers. I can only offer limited procedures, mostly amputations to those who have grave wounds to limbs. I cain't do much for those sick with malaria or other maladies either." The major talked a bit more about the citizens and their problems enduring the siege. "So many civilians and soldiers have died jist of disease." He shook his head in dismay. "Surgical amputation is mostly what I do when there's been some real fighting at the outer works. The last Yankee assault saw me do a couple of dozen amputations in jist about four hours here in my little hospital area. I wuz outside with my sharpest surgical knife and saw over to them sawhorses in the open area on the side of this building. I always use them doors propped up against the sawhorses to lay 'cross them sawhorses. We put the wooden tubs underneath to catch as much of the blood as possible. But yew kin see the stain on the ground if yew look close enough. At night we hang some cloaked lanterns to hep me see better. We run out of anesthetic some days ago. But the sooner the amputation is done, the greater the success rate, even here without much of anything medicinal to curb infections and gangrene. Our poultices ain't too strong any more since the siege corralled us in here." Doctor Herrington sighed and paused in his talking.

After the conversation with the old doctor, Sawyer and Solomon walked slowly through a large room in which the wounded were bedded on cots and make-shift beds. Some of the beds were doors covered with blankets and quilts. Hardly enough space existed between the cots for a person to get through to give attention to a soldier who needed it. At one point Solomon abruptly stopped and looked about him at the wounded men, lying there quietly or sleeping sporadically. Over to his left were more wounded, but they were those in pain who moaned and groaned in despair. When Solomon turned to look at his cousin, Sawyer said quietly as he gestured to that group, "Most of these probably won't see the morning sunrise."

"Yeah, they look bad, feverish and sweating more than the others. Too bad there is not much here for pain. I'm sure the doctors do the best they can," replied Solomon. As he surveyed the wounded once more, his face became more somber and sad-looking. He paused again for a moment and then started walking again. Sawyer followed silently. The two men entered an adjacent room.

The two cousins slowly walked through more wounded, but these men in this room were recovering from arm and leg amputations. Most were propped up in the cots, and some were seated in old-looking chairs and on small stools. Solomon began to pick up his pace to leave the make-shift hospital building. But suddenly he stopped abruptly and said to Sawyer, "Listen."

Two of the amputees—one sitting in a chair and one lying on a cot—could be heard talking about being wounded in the fighting. The one with double amputations of his legs in the cot said, " . . . yeah, but cain't no red string be put on my ankle now 'cause I ain't got no ankle to tie it 'round. I still wish that theah redheaded woman healer be heah the way she wuz fer that friend of mine when I went see him at the Windsor hospital afore this heah siege tighted around Vicksburg by them Yankees and their General Grant."

Solomon now motioned for his cousin to follow him over to the two wounded soldiers. Solomon stood by the two soldiers and said directly to the one in the cot, "Soldier, you said a redheaded woman tied a red string?"

Both the soldiers were surprised at Solomon's approach and his question. Each attempted to salute Captain Dundee. The one with the amputated right arm completed an awkward salute with his left arm and hand. The one on the cot saluted the best he could with his right hand. Then the one on the cot replied to Solomon's question, "Yas, sur, I wuz talkin' 'bout this woman healer that them two doctors theah at the grounds of the Windsor mansion allowed to nurse the wounded theah after them doctors done wat they cud. She wuz some sort of healer. Some even hinted she was a witch, a white witch, from down theah in Nawlins. My wounded friend wuz recoverin' frum a shot in his rat lag. He say that redheaded woman applied some sort of poultice on his lag's wound, and it drawed all the pain out it. Some soldiers swore that a single touch of her'n hand relieved some of the pain. My friend wuz theah jist temporarily afore being moved to a more permanent hospital site."

"Go on," encouraged Solomon. "Tell me all you know about that woman."

Sawyer looked and listened with rapt attention.

"Do you know where the woman is?" inquired Solomon.

"Naw, sur," answered the soldier. "My friend say she dropped out of sight as the Yankees took the Windsor mansion. Rumor is that those Yanks now use the house for a hospital. Ourn main purpose fer it wuz a observation and signal station atop that big house. Why, we could see the river plainly and spotted Yank movement on the river."

"You said your friend had a red string tied around his ankle?"

111

asked Solomon, steering the conversation back to the topic he wanted information about.

"He shore did. It wuz a bright red, like that red in the flag, yew know. My friend said that she tied a red string on each soldier she he'ped—on the ankle. She tole each soldier it was a token of good luck for 'em," continued the wounded man. "I jist wish she wuz he'pin' the wounded men heah. If she cud take away some of the awful pain . . . "

Solomon now said, "So you don't know where that woman is?"

"Naw, sur."

"What else can you tell me about her? Was there anyone with her?"

"Well, sur, my friend did mention somethin' bout a big ole tall nigger slave of her'n that wuz always close by and watchin' her like a chicken hawk flyin' circles over a hen house. My friend said that the young buck had a big ole knife to match him in size. It must have been some mighty big pig sticker! It wuz no kind of knife he never seed!" The man laughed. He paused for a moment and said, "That is the first time I laughed since I wuz wounded. That woman have some power—even when she jist bein' thought 'bout."

"Thank you, soldiers. Thanks for the information. Good luck. At least you will get to go home if the siege is ever lifted," said Solomon.

Sawyer added his thanks to the men and then said in a low voice to Solomon that only he could hear, "If there is a home to go back to."

"Come on, Saw, I will answer all of your questions when we leave these hospital buildings right here. Let's go!" uttered Solomon. The cousins walked swiftly out of the home serving as hospital and its immediate area to the middle of the street where no one else was near at the time.

"Solomon, before yew tell me about the red string and the redheaded woman, let me inform yew as to why I have us in the middle of the street. It is because of the artillery shelling of the town. Vicksburg citizens have learned to walk in the middle of the street or other open areas so they can see if the projectiles are comin' at 'em. Of course, if they think a shell is about to hit near them, they will run to seek shelter or get as far away from that spot as possible. If they can tell the shell is going over their heads, they continue their walk in the opposite direction because they know that most exploding shell fragments and shrapnel go forward at the point of impact. That is something yew should remember as long as yew are here—even if yew are the luckiest person I know."

"I thank you for that bit of knowledge, and I will heed it while here." Solomon now related his adventures in New Orleans and the story of the redheaded woman to his cousin. "All those around her called her Egypt," Solomon said at last in his explanation to Sawyer. Then he added with a sigh, "I had a red string once."

Before Sawyer could question Solomon about his comment concerning the red string, a loud explosive boom brought the men's attention back to Vicksburg in time and place. They looked up to see which direction the artillery rounds were coming in from and moved from the open area. Now explosions were occurring all about them. They picked a somewhat sheltered spot and crouched until the barrage spent itself. No other shells had exploded near them. Solomon looked at Sawyer and said, "The accompanying assault is a major one. Focused on the Louisiana Redan."

Sawyer looked quizzically at his cousin and asked in a low whisper, "How do yew know about an assault?"

"I just know."

Sawyer yelled to Solomon, "Let me report in and check my men first, and then I will meet yew at the hospital. Please go there. I figure some of the rounds landed on those buildings where we jist were. I fear the worst. They may need some extra help. Can yew git there?"

"Yes. I may be of some help there myself," answered Solomon. With those words Solomon walked briskly back toward the hospital area and then began to run. He could tell that buildings were on fire and thought that Sawyer might be right about where the bomb blasts struck. At the buildings he saw one of them ablaze and heard screams of wounded soldiers inside being literally roasted alive. He imagined what the double amputee they had talked with about the redheaded woman and the red string felt when he realized that he could not escape the burning hospital building. Solomon exclaimed aloud, "Lord, how horrible this war is!" He stood, frozen with sadness and fiery with anger. "How can I help it end?

Flames consumed the building where the soldiers were. Soldiers and citizens of the town were throwing water on the other adjacent buildings not on fire. The fire had a life of its own it seemed. Now the humans left in the building were silent, and the fire spoke on its own, popping and crackling and hissing as it consumed the wood of the building. Its heat intensified, driving back some of the nearby soldiers and citizens. Solomon stood there, frozen to the spot that was blistering with heat. He thought to himself, "This fire, like the war, consumes all within its immediate reach. But it will not consume me!" Solomon watched the wooden structure burn with more intensity.

Sawyer ran up to his cousin and pulled him back away from the flames. "Sol, yew feel like yew are on fire. The heat is so intense. Yore skin is baking!" Sawyer next said, "Let's check the other building. Is the doctor all right?" Both men looked to see what damage had been done to the building where they had spoken with the old doctor. The doctor was being assisted out of the structure by one of the townspeople. The old doctor, dazed and disoriented, mumbled to himself as Sawyer and Solomon led the doctor and his helper from the building. They placed the doctor on the other side of the street and went back into the building, seeking other survivors. As they exited the building with another victim, they heard explosions in another part of Vicksburg. The booming of the cannon from the Union gunboats and the batteries on the opposite side of the river continued for a few more minutes. When the bombardment ceased, everyone there fighting the fire and helping victims could hear the distant din of the Union assault Solomon had told Sawyer about.

When the hospital building was cleared and the burning building was no longer a danger to adjacent houses, Sawyer and Solomon sat on the opposite side of the street for a short time. They could hear the continued noises of the battle at the Louisiana Redan in the distance. Sawyer now asked Solomon if he wished to see some of the caves the civilians were living in. "No better time exists," replied Solomon. "Lead the way, Cousin."

Along the way, Solomon commented to Sawyer, "I don't see or hear any dogs or cats. Are they hiding from the cannons the way the humans are?"

Sawyer looked at Solomon and said candidly, "No, what few that are still alive are hiding from the humans. People got to eat. This is a siege in war. Rations for soldiers and citizens cut in half and cut in half again. Some civilians are starving to death. At the first of the siege, yew could hear dogs howling all night and cats screeching, seemingly in answer to the screaming of the artillery rounds coming in overhead; but now rations are in short supply. Observe tonight that yew won't spot too many rats either out in the open. Their population is dwindling for the same reason. At first in some places, especially at night, rats would swarm over a person's feet. But now they only mass around the corpses that are unclaimed at the outer works or between the siege lines. And those unreachable corpses and wounded! There's the story of one wounded fellow after an assault that was out there during the time of no truce who raised his arms and legs and moaned for help for a couple of days. And then he didn't. The soldiers on each side could only glance ever so often at the area where he was and not help him because they would be shot by someone on the other side. They did not know whether he was a Yank or a Reb."

"What a horrible fate to be here in Vicksburg at this moment in time and history!" exclaimed Solomon.

"Fate it may be, but it is a calculated chosen fate for many of the population and most of the soldiers. Courage is in abundance here among the soldiers and the citizens. Most nearly everyone here resents the Yankee invasion of their homes and their homeland. Then, to add more anger, there are the ever-circulating stories of the Union soldiers stealing everything from foodstuffs to personal belongings every location they go. They say that war is no longer 'mannered' as it had been. This war can't be romanticized as other wars in history. Those damn Yankees are a scourge. Their war may not have women and children in their gun sights, but they kill them without regret, without a second thought, without Christian charity. But the people and the soldiers possess a loyalty to their cause and their Southern way of life that most of the Yankees can not fathom. That love and loyalty makes them stand up for what they believe in, for what they cherish. They kneel for no one. This war will be a long one. It will not end here at Vicksburg—no matter which side wins. So the people and soldiers here embrace their fate." Sawyer went silent. He looked toward the courthouse and its flag rippling in the brisk wind. The two cousins continued to walk in silence.

Atop one of the hills near the outer edge of town, Sawyer said to his cousin, "Here is where I let yew explore on yore own. Look down from here. Yew see a couple of trails leading to the side of the hill away from the river. Take one and talk with the citizens of Vicksburg. Most folks are real friendly. Yew can find me later. I must go back." Sawyer quickly took his leave of Solomon.

Solomon took the path on the right, carefully stepping with each stride downward. He could still hear the din of the battle in the distance. He wondered if many persons would be in the caves at this time of day or not. He decided to check as many of the caves as possible and talk with as many citizens in the time he had. Some people were in the caves, but most inhabitants were sitting at the entrances or were atop the hill and shouted down at Solomon. The Vicksburg citizens, glad to talk about the siege, their sacrifices, and their ingenuity told him many things. He learned that cave-digging was a good business to be in these days; however, not so much since Yankees used mortars to reach the opposite sides of the hills from the river. He soon realized that Sky Parlor Hill was a gathering place for the upper-class hiatus to view the Union bombardment and survey the city and the Union fleet as well as Yankees across the river and across the siege lines opposite the river. Many told him of the awful experience of cave-living: the heavy, smothering, musty smell of the underground dwellings; lack of clean drinking water; the problems of cooking the scarce food available; clothes infested with all sorts of vermin because of not being washed; and trying, in general, to fashion an underground home.

Solomon carefully moved across the steep incline of the hill to the next hand-dug cave. It was sheltering a middle-aged gaunt woman and her two skinny children—a boy about fifteen and a girl about thirteen. The woman spied Solomon at the cave entrance and cautioned him in a weak yet grating voice, "Mister, we ain't got no money. Nuthin' of value. Yew don't want to come in here anyways becuz all us be infected with that there contagious skin disease named e-rye-sip-a-los or somethin' lack 'at. I cain't never say it rat. But if'n yew don't want it, stay out there." The weary woman explained she was told that erysipelas was a skin inflammation that was very contagious. The small girl now moaned and turned over on the old blanket on the dirt floor of the dank cave. Solomon could hardly see her in the dim light of that area of the cave. He noticed that she scratched her arm and bellowed out crying.

The woman hurried over to her, picked her up, and took several steps toward the cave entrance where Solomon had stopped. The girl, limp in her mother's arms, continued to cry softly. Solomon could see the young girl and her skin in the light. Her skin was so red that it seemed she must be on fire. The child's flesh was raw and reddish, except for the pustules that had not burst and the greenish discharge from several that had burst and oozed over the reddened skin. The girl's mother had the same skin conditions but not as bad because somehow she had refrained from scratching as much as the child had done. The thin girl clawed an area of her arm, and Solomon watched pustules pop and drain over more red skin.

Solomon winced in reaction to the girl's scratching. He thought that the girl had done nothing in the war, had done nothing to the Union forces besieging the city, had done nothing to deserve what she was experiencing. His emotions swelled, and his heart beat harder and faster in his chest—so hard and so fast he could feel it. His breathing became labored for a brief moment. Then he took steps toward the woman, still holding her child. The woman said, "Mister, yew don't want to catch this heer infection!"

"I won't," said Solomon firmly as he reached out to take the girl from her mother's arms. The woman did not resist Solomon's reach. Instead she collapsed to the cave floor and wept. Solomon heard her boy turn over and moan farther back in the cave where it was too dark to see.

The woman weakly said to Solomon, "I think both is gonna die. They so weak. They not eating none of this heah pea meal bread or nuthin'. I cain't save 'em. Gangrene could set in their irritated fingers. These two could lose them fingers. And den they die!" Now she sobbed as she struggled to sit upright herself.

Solomon felt his eyes well up with tears, and a single tear slid down his cheek from his right eye. Now he stifled other potential tears and concentrated on the frail girl he held gently but firmly in his arms. He looked at her mother, sitting upright on the dirt floor. "What is her name?"

"Her name be Dodie."

He hugged her close and said in a low voice that only she could hear, "You will recover from this infection. You will, Dodie. I know you will!" He focused all his attention on her for a few moments, held her so that he breathed in her exhaled breath and she inhaled his outward breathing, and then placed her back in her mother's arms. He looked at her face and into her big brown, sad, sick eyes. He smiled at her as her eyes fluttered open and shut.

He then dug in his pockets, seeking coins to give the poor woman. He fished out three coins and without looking at them put them in the woman's weak hand and folded her fingers around them. "Use this money to buy food and medicine for the children and you."

"But this here be Yankee money," said the woman, looking at what Solomon had placed in her hand.

"It will spend here. I am sure."

"Thank yew, Mister. Thank yew." The woman began crying once more. Solomon reached into another pocket and pulled out one of the two Slotter & Co. derringers he had purchased in Baton Rouge years ago. He handed it to the woman and said curtly, "Use this to protect Dodie, your son, and yourself."

Solomon turned to walk out of the cave. At the entrance he looked back and uttered, "Remember, Dodie, that you are beautiful now and in the future. I hope to see you after this damned war is over. I want to dance at your wedding! Remember my name, Solomon Witcher!"

119

He went outside into the full sunlight. He looked at his hands and his clothes. His clothes had soaked up much of the pustule discharge from his holding the young girl. His hands were spotted with the sick ooze, too. He examined his hands with his eyes and said to himself, "I won't get sick." He leaned down to wipe his hands on some tufts of grass. He stood tall now and looked up the side of the hill riddled with caves. He picked his way upward toward the apex.

Solomon slowly climbed back to the top of the hill. He decided to walk some of the streets to talk with people to learn how it was to be above ground and still in houses during the siege. Above ground in the city proper Solomon also learned much about endurance in the siege. Citizens informed him that dead livestock was thrown into the river; that clothes became infested with lice above ground as well as those of cave-dwellers; that measles struck with epidemic force, hitting the children and Negroes; and that malnutrition hit inhabitants above and below ground. One woman told him she was glad to stay in the cave, not just to escape the artillery and mortar boats, but also to avoid the open graves caused by wagon and horse traffic and bomb explosions that allowed the dead to look out from glass-windowed coffins at passersby. An older man gave Solomon a newspaper printed on the back of wallpaper. One rather skinny woman informed him that tea could be made from raspberry and blackberry leaves, that elderberry juice was good for making dye, and that speculators make heaps of money from the non-combatants selling food and other items on the black market. She cursed them in the same breath. A younger woman with three small children in tow explained that china berries could be used to make soap and that mule meat was better than pea meal bread. As he was making cartridges for the army, one elderly man talked to Solomon. He informed Solomon many civilians made the decision to remain in Vicksburg instead of evacuating before Grant instituted the siege. This elderly man told Solomon that he was born and raised in the South, in Mississippi, and proud of it—so proud he would stand and fight for his homeland and his rights.

Solomon, still hearing the din of the Union assault in the distance, could see smoke and dust rising into the air in a general cloud from the area of the fiercest fighting. He could see the Confederate flag flying atop the courthouse just a bit to the left of the black and gray smoke source in the distance. In his mind's eyes and ears he recalled the happy spirit and the martial music sending the volunteers off to war in spring of 1861 as he gazed at the courthouse Stars and Bars flag, jauntily floating in the wind juxapositioned with the smoke and noise of the desperate assault with its wounded, dead, and dying in the middle of chaos nearby. He thought he could hear the sounds of the battle—the booming of the cannons, the crack of rifle and musket fire, the screaming of artillery shells and their explosions on and above the ground, the intimidation of the sometimes inhuman aspect of the Rebel yell, the barking of orders, the whistling and whir of bullets and minie balls, the cries of the wounded, and the gasps and groans of the dying.

A tremendous explosion nearby jolted Solomon back to his time and place in Vicksburg, his reality in the war, and his mission. Now, as he walked the maimed streets, he carefully observed the buildings. A few had burned to the ground. Most had some type of damage from the Union cannonading from the mortar boats and land artillery. It seemed as though almost every home and business had destruction marks of some sort or to some degree. The streets, pockmarked with holes from exploded shells and barricaded ever so often with man-made obstacles, were just barely passable for the most part. Now another big explosion occurred in the immediate area. Those people who were out and about, conducting daily chores and other business, now began to disappear in anticipation of sustained shelling in the neighborhood. The people were walking briskly or running to shelter as they looked upward into the sky to spot rounds or the smoke trail of burning fuses to calculate the trajectory of the incoming missiles. More and more smoke trails crisscrossed the blue sky, and more and more explosions threw up dirt and debris or smashed through homes and threw out broken wooden planks, pieces of brick, and remnants of furniture and evidence of everyday living. Once or twice Solomon heard cries of anguish and pain. But he kept moving in the open areas and streets because he felt lucky; he knew he would not be a victim here of Union gunfire. His eyes searched the residences and other buildings for those serving as hospitals. He could help some of the wounded. He walked onward as he looked up at the sky for incoming shells.

Those wounded from the Union assault began arriving at the outdoor surgical area on all kinds of wagons and stretchers and make-shift litters. Some of the wounded walked there, helped by those with less-serious wounds and civilians as well as soldiers designated to transport wounded. One officer directed the wounded to be placed first in an open area around a small flagpole from which fluttered a Confederate battle flag and the Bonnie Blue Flag. This space was to hold the newcomers until a doctor did a quick examination to determine where they would go next. The severity and nature of the wound dictated whether the wounded soldier would be moved to what area—non-life-threatening wait placement, immediate surgery move, or nothing-can-be-done station. A few of the wounded benefited from the shade of some trees, but most of the soldiers lay out in the open, direct sun. At first, twenty or so wounded soldiers, awaiting quick diagnosis, were arranged in neat rows. Then the number swelled to fifty or more, now in somewhat irregular rows. As more and more wounded filled the area, a crescendo of groans and moans from the pain floated upon the air. That human suffering noise became punctuated by loud, crisp orders from the examining physician about where to move the men next.

The doctor, making the determination moved quickly among the new wounded brought in, looked at the wounds with his trained and experienced eye, and barked out the orders. "This man and this one, too, to the surgeons! That man and that man to the nurse care area." The physician pointed and commanded as he moved among the wounded. "This soldier and that man to the home over there!" He pointed with reluctance to the nearby house that would be the final earthly home to those with mortal wounds. "Take care when y'all move them, orderly! Be kind!"

Turning a corner, Solomon found himself at the edge of the area for initial placement of the incoming wounded soldiers. He watched the doctor walking among the disabled soldiers and heard him sharply bark out his orders as to where each individual was to be moved to next. The wind gusted a bit, and the flag caught Solomon's eye. He fixed his gaze on the flag until he heard a directive to the nurse care area, and his eyes followed stretcher bearers carrying one soldier there. Through a doorway he caught sight of one nurse, motioning them to bring the soldier inside. They disappeared from his line of sight. Solomon's eyes glanced back at the doctor making the preliminary decisions as to the next location of the wounded would be. His ears caught the word "home" in the doctor's directive. Now two stretcher bearers loaded one man rather mechanically on the stretcher and carried him quickly to the residence now being used for the last stop in life's journey for the men mortally wounded and about to die. Solomon followed the two stretcher bearers into the residence that was called "home" by the doctor. He realized this euphemism was used to disguise the inevitable for these unfortunate soldiers. He followed the stretcher up the steps and into the home and watched through the doorway as the stretcher bearers found an empty spot on the floor for the soldier. Solomon made his way over to the soldier just brought in, stood by him, and looked him in his wistful eyes. Unexpectedly, the soldier groaned loudly as his body shuttered with pain. The soldier jerked his body once more and opened his eyes wide to focus on Solomon. The soldier attempted to say something but could not. Saliva and blood gushed briefly from the corner of his mouth. An eerie feeling engulfed Solomon. He felt the presence of the Grim Reaper. This man was about to die. Solomon kneeled next to the mortally wounded man and reached for and grabbed his hand. The wounded man's hand tightened in Solomon's grasp. As he felt the dying man tighten his grip on his hand, Solomon also felt a pool of warm blood forming around his knees.

"Easy there, brother," came the words soft as silk from Solomon's mouth. "Go easy now." Solomon heard the death rattle in the man's throat and felt his hand relax and go limp. The man's labored breathing ceased, and his body was at peace. "The war is finished for you, my friend." Continuing to kneel there next to the deceased soldier, Solomon prayed for the man's soul.

"Is he dead?" inquired a female voice.

Solomon stood, turned toward the voice, and quietly said, "Yes."

"Thank yew for bein' with him. At least, he wasn't alone at his last time on this earth," the female nurse replied. She paused. Stretcher bearers entering the house made both the nurse and Solomon direct their attention to the entranceway. The nurse pointed to an open area on the floor next to the east window. "Put him there," came her words crisply. They followed her orders, and then she said to them, "Now please move that deceased man to the morgue area in the next house!" A groan from the next room caused the nurse to follow its sound and disappear from Solomon's sight.

Solomon now slowly walked out of the home. The diagnosing doctor outside shouted, "This soldier to the surgeons now!" Solomon watched other stretcher bearers lift the wounded man and convey him to the outdoor surgical area. Two doctors amputated limbs at this station. One of the surgeons, covered with blood and holding a surgical knife in his teeth, was Major Herrington. The doctor worked at a pace that belied his recent escape from death himself. The other doctor, also covered in blood, was sawing the bone just below the knee of a soldier who was moaning in a low tone while biting on a piece of wood stuck between his

124

teeth. The sound of the saw, ripping away at human bone, was anathema to Solomon's ears; it grated on his soul; it stirred his empathy for the men on the make-shift tables and especially for those lying in line for amputations needed by each. He looked at each of the men waiting in line as he walked among them. A strange queasiness filled his stomach as he gazed directly into the faces of the wounded. He saw what the minie ball could do because of its flattening as it made its way through a soldier's body. He had seen it before when he engaged in battle, but he had never had the time really to look at a wound for any length of time. Now he could see, almost feel, the damage inflicted. This man possessed two shattered legs, one that would be amputated below the knee and one that would be amputated above the knee. The next soldier's right arm appeared to be only a mangled mess of human flesh and bone with little to identify it as an arm just below his bicep. The next man's left hand had been completely blown away. His wrist, crudely wrapped in cloth, was a bloody nub. The soldier on Solomon's right was delirious and cursing the Yankees as he flapped what was left of his mangled and bloody right arm. The next soldier eyed the surgeons, both now grinding surgical saws that resembled carpenter's saws across the bones of the wounded on the operating tables. Some soldiers asked for anesthesia, and others pleaded to be knocked unconscious before they faced the knife and the saw. The sound of the saw Solomon would never forget—and he would never forget the look in the eyes of the wounded soldiers awaiting their turn. He wondered what state of mind he would be in if he were in that line. Now his ears were filled by the scream of one of the men under the knife. The soldier's scream of pain subsided but was replaced by the scream of an incoming artillery shell. Solomon and the others looked up and beheld a trail of burning fuse smoke from across the river. Solomon heard someone's voice yelling, "Get down!" Instinctively he flopped his body between the rows of the wounded. As he hit the ground, he heard that same voice screaming, "No, not here!" The explosion occurred somewhere between the flagpole and the area where the two surgeons were working on the wounded soldiers.

"... to the nurses. This man to the surgeons! Quickly now!" bellowed a loud voice. Solomon felt himself being lifted and moved. His head hurt severely and his ears could not distinguish all the words he heard. His eyes saw only blurs. His ears reverberated with a ringing that made him think he was inside a bell tower with continuous clanging of all the bells therein. His eyelids drooped themselves shut. In this confusion Solomon attempted to regain complete consciousness and command of his senses. He could not feel any part of his body except that he realized he had been lifted and that he could tell that rhythmic walking was moving him somewhere other than where he had been. His ears seemed to clear, and he heard the unmistakable, unforgettable horrible sound of a surgeon's saw ripping through human bone. Suddenly he felt himself being placed down. Now he could hear two saws cutting human bone. He gathered his wits about him, trying to remember how he got here. The sawing sounds drew his attention. He must be on the ground near the surgeons! He still could not feel his body or determine if he could move any of his limbs. He summoned inner strength to focus his mind on his situation.

"I am in line for the surgeons who are amputating limbs!" he vocalized. He focused his mind even more. He opened his eyes and could see that he was near the surgeons. "I wonder how bad off I am," he thought. He turned his head slightly and focused his blurry eyes. All he could see was a pile of human limbs, amputated by these surgeons. He could not feel his arms or his legs. "My God, are they going to cut off one of my arms or one of my legs?" he uttered aloud. He brought all his mental faculties into play. His sense of feeling slowly flowed from his head to his body and then to his extremities. His head and his body ached as never before. But his head was clearing and not paining him as it had been doing. He moved his arms and his legs. He moved his fingers on his right hand and then his fingers on his left hand. He wiggled the toes on both of his feet. He thought he felt everything move and work as normal. He tried to raise up but could not do so at the moment.

"Check that man over there near the doctors!"

Solomon now raised his upper body almost to a sitting position. He looked at his legs and arms. He could see no visible damage. He let himself back down to lie still for a time. His mind cleared itself more.

"Jist lay still," said a voice. "Yew in the wrong place."

Solomon felt himself being lifted and transported up a few steps into a nearby house. Solomon now relaxed and could feel a general heaviness over his entire body and a great sense of tiredness engulfed him. His eyes closed. But going up the steps, he faintly heard a male nurse's voice say to him, "Peace be with you, Brother." Solomon lost consciousness once again

A deep, full voice melodiously belted out the words to the song, "Bonnie Blue Flag." These sung words filled Solomon's ears when he next awoke. Solomon thought the voice familiar. It was the same voice that he last heard as he was carried up the steps into the house. Other voices of the wounded and the nursing staff joined in the song and carried the tune briskly. Words blurred for Solomon. But the catchy tune made him add his voice to the chorus. His voice got louder, and his spirits lifted. He knew the lead voice. He recognized that the deep melodious voice leading the jaunty song belonged to Xenophones, the New Orleans street preacher!

Solomon closed his eyes as the song ended. He focused on gathering his wits about him and summoning his strength. He felt better. Opening his eyes, he glanced about the room to find Xeno. Solomon, raising himself to a sitting position, swept the room again with his eyes. No Xeno. The soldier next to Solomon was awake and sitting upright as well. Solomon turned to him and asked, "Who was the man leading the singing? Is he still here?"

The other man replied, "That crazy feller is the one up from Nawlins. I never learnt his name. Naw, he ain't heah rat now. He done moved on to the next medical ward to sing theah to cheer soldiers up wit singin' peppy tunes. Some times he hep wit some of us wounded. All'n us soldiers lak 'im. Why, I even seed him on the line at the outer works a'fightin' them damn Yankees as he allus calls 'em.

"Well, I need to find that gentleman and talk to him about a time in New Orleans," uttered Solomon. He stood up, at first a bit unsure of his stance, but his head stopped swimming. The only female nurse in the room noticed him and rushed over to him. She grabbed his arm to steady him.

"Sir, be careful. Be slow. Where are yew injured?" the nurse said.

"That incoming shell explosion must have knocked me unconscious for a time. I am better now. I need to find that man!"

"But, sir, yew may need a doctor's attention. Wait for a couple of minutes. Let me look at yore head to see if there is a scalp injury. Yore eyes may tell me something, too. Sit here." She examined his scalp and found nothing. She then cleaned the dirt and grime from his face, ears, and neck. She washed his hands and forearms. His shirt, unbuttoned at the top, revealed more grime on his lower neck and upper chest. She used the wet cloth to wipe his lower neck and then said, "What is this? This bit of red just inside yore shirt?" She reached just under the open shirt front and pulled out a snatch of red material. She held it up for both of them to see. It was a bit of red cloth, burnt on three sides and a little in the middle and unraveling on the other side. She pulled some of the loose strings, and they detached from the snatch of red material that was about as big as the nurse's small hand. Five or six of the loose red strings fell from her fingers. They floated gently to the floor. Solomon removed the snatch of red material from the nurse's hand and put it in his pocket. He

128

knew the small red piece of material was from the Confederate battle flag at the hospital bomb explosion site. He would keep it for luck. Then the nurse used her soft hands to turn his head to look into his eyes. She was silent for a moment. Solomon returned her gaze, and the nurse seemed mesmerized momentarily.

Solomon broke the silence between them by saying, "Thank you, Miss. You have a gentle touch about you. I'm glad one of those big men nurses did not see me before you did." Solomon smiled that intriguing smile of his at her. "Can I go now?"

"Uh, ah, well, yes," the young nurse replied. She grinned a dreamy grin up at Solomon when he had stood tall from his seat next to her.

"So very kind of you to help me," said Solomon. He turned to leave the building. He wondered how long he had been out. It was night now, and the cannonading continued. He glanced up at the night sky ever so often to watch for incoming artillery or mortar rounds. Each soldier he encountered he asked about where to find Captain Sawyer Dundee. Finally one private told him that Captain Dundee and his unit were rotated to the outer works this night and the next. Solomon was directed to the unit's city dwelling. Surroundings looked familiar to him now, even at night. He found his cousin's cot and collapsed on it, fast asleep in seconds.

"Solomon. Cousin. Solomon Witcher. Wake yoreself. Yew have that meeting with General Pemberton in two hours," warned Sawyer. He pushed and shook his cousin. "Solomon!"

Solomon raised up on the cot. His head was foggy and hurt a little. "I'm awake, Saw."

"It's time for some mule meat and pea meal bread. The food's so good that there won't be much of it left if yew don't hurry up."

Solomon stood and said, "Give me a minute. I need to splash my face and wash my mouth out before I taste that fine cuisine."

"I will be out front. Come on out."

In a few minutes Sawyer and Solomon were briskly walking to the cooking area nearest them. "What is that delicate aroma whiffing its way to us?" asked Solomon with a grin on his face.

"It's the finest fare of Hotel de Vicksburgh!"

The cousins laughed out loud. They had their food smacked onto their tin plates and moved to an area in which many soldiers were sitting on the ground while eating. They threaded their way among the soldiers to go to the open area toward the river. They sat by a group of soldiers that were speaking English and Cajun French. As they sat, the soldiers saluted Sawyer Dundee. Solomon, who outranked them but wore civilian clothes, received head nods and grins.

"Where are you soldiers from?" asked Solomon.

"From Louisianne," replied one. The others ceased their conversation and looked at the two cousins.

"What area? What parish?" continued Solomon.

"Mocksville. In Avoyelles Parish," answered another soldier.

Surprising the soldiers, Solomon said, "I played a few hands of poker for several nights at the Bell Tavern in Marksville. I ate some of that spicy Cajun food there as well. Man, was it good!"

"Yew been to Mocksville, *mon cher*? Yew been to dat place?" asked another soldier.

"Did yew go to a *cochin de lait*, one of dose pig roasts? It be a lots better dan dis mule roast!"

All the men laughed uproarishly.

130

"My name is Captain Sawyer Dundee. This man in civilian clothes is my cousin Solomon Witcher. He is a soldier like us, but he is a courier for the brass hats and all them other big dogs. Today is his first time to eat our special delicacy, mule meat!" At that Solomon grimaced and gagged much to the delight of the soldiers around him. "Too bad we don't have one of those Hotel de Vicksburgh bills of fare for him to see what other gourmet food servings can be adapted with mule meat!" Solomon got wide-eyed at this comment and showed off for the men to see. The men roared laughing again.

Now Sawyer became serious and asked the soldiers their names. He added, "What's y'all's unit?"

"All us tree be in de First Louisianne Heavy Artill'ry companies," said one soldier who identified himself as Paul Avery as he pointed to the men on each side of him.

"I'm Lewis Lemoine."

"Me, Alcide Scallan," said the next soldier.

"And the two of us be in de Louisianne Light Artill'ry batt'ries," said a soldier sitting beside Alcide Scallan. "My name is Pierre Couvillon."

The soldier next to him gave his name, "Ferdinand Moreau, Sir." He added, "And dat fella is jist a pore lil' plain soldier of de trenches." All laughed and looked at the last soldier.

"My name, likewise, is Pierre. Pierre C. Lemoine," offered the last man of the group. "Yew tole dat yew been in Mocksville, *bon ami*. Me, *mon cher*, am a direct descendant of de founder of Mocksville, Marc Eliche." His face brightened as he made the remark.

"Yeah, dat an' a Yankee coin gets yew some more mule stew up in heah!" quickly teased Ferdinand.

All guffawed loudly, and Pierre Couvillon shouted, "Ahiee!" Ferdinand patted Pierre Lemoine on the back.

Sawyer now asked, "Lost many friends while here at or fightin' around Vicksburg?"

"Most died from the sicknesses goin' 'round de camps," put in Paul Avery. "Hilaire Ducote, Alexandre Dufour, uh, and Jean Baptist Dufour, and . . . "

Pierre Couvillon added names, "Joachim Dupuy and Ambroise Guillot be two mo."

"Dat be de ones we know'd 'bout," continued Alcide Scallan. "Sum others been shot; sum missin' and may be dead." All went silent for a few seconds.

Now Solomon injected himself into the conversation with the question, "A few years before this war began when I was in Marksville I heard a story about a redheaded healer woman in those parts. Do any of you know anything about that?"

Pierre Lemoine answered first, "No, *mon cher*, but my cousin done tole us 'bout dat redneck dat—how yew speak dat in Anglish?—man done stole him new-birthed baby frum dat angel of death on de stormy night. My cuz said dat de lightnin' showed no life in de infant and dat de stranger pulled de life back into de baby. He cheated death. He is a marked man." Pierre Lemoine spoke all these words in a deadly serious manner.

"Us soldiers in dis command needs dat redneck to pull some life back into all us," added Alcide. "Shore wish he be heah in Vicksburg."

Solomon quickly said, "No, I never heard of anybody doing what you said. But do any of you others know anything about that redheaded woman healer I hcard about down there?"

Ferdinand Moreau answered Solomon, "My twin brother Ferrier

and me heard dat rumor about dat redhead healing de poor. She demand no money but took whatever a person could give, if anything. We hear she even accep' a Bowie knife. Dat make her dangerous!" He paused a moment. "But she done left de healing place wit out tellin' de folks around dere. Me an' Ferrier scouted dat place one Sunday afternoon after she be gone. De people done placed lots of flowers at the base of de big shade tree. And—quaint t'ing—dere be lots of red strings tied to de branches of dat big cypress tree. She gone. Dat's all."

It was at this time that Sawyer checked his pocket watch and said, "Solomon, the general is expecting yew in jist a short time. We, unfortunately, must end this conversation and go over to Willis House." Sawyer stood as did Solomon. All the soldiers stood as well.

One of the soldiers, Pierre Lemoine, said, "I almost forgot dat dis war be goin' whilst talkin' wit yew two rednecks. Yew two cuzzins be like home kin to dose of us heah from Avoyelles. Yew two visit Mocksville after dis here war be over and done wit, an' I be buyin' yew a drink at dat Bell Tavern. Ferdinand, yew and Ferrier, show up for dat drink. Maybe's we kin go over to Mansura to find my cuzzins who roast dat pig real good. Makes dat a deal, yeah, *mon cher*!"

"Let's do jist that," replied Sawyer.

"It is a deal," answered Solomon.

"*C'est bon!*" added Pierre Lemoine.

The men saluted the cousins and then shook hands. "Godspeed, my friends," added Sawyer. The two cousins turned and put up their plates and utensils near the food line. They hurried to Pemberton's headquarters, the Willis House on Crawford Street.

There the general called them in immediately and shook hands with both cousins after salutes. Sawyer was allowed to stay. The meeting lasted for but a few minutes with General Pemberton finally handing

133

Solomon a small courier's pouch with a belt attached that could be worn under his clothes. "These are important. It is imperative that each set of papers reach the correct commanders. You cross the lines tonight at the same location. Captain Dundee will send you on your way. The location is the same as when you came in. It is where his unit is in rotation tonight. May God guide you through safely," said the general. Sawyer and Solomon saluted and turned to leave. They strode out of the house and onto the street.

"I don't what yew do for the Confederate States of America—what yore mission is—but I pray for yew. Now let's go back to my billeting area for yew to git some rest before yore departure tonight," said Sawyer. As they walked back, the cousins talked of their adventures as young boys in Natchez. When they reached their destination and before Solomon went in to try to sleep, Sawyer remarked, "No cannonading now. I wonder if it will stay that way for yew tonight."

Solomon responded, "Saw, I assure you that will happen, and I will get through the lines unnoticed again. I cross at midnight."

"I suppose that will be yore good luck rearing its beautiful head," replied Sawyer.

In a low voice that Sawyer did not hear, Solomon said, "Good luck and planning."

Darkness enveloped Vicksburg, the siege lines, and all of the people inside and outside those lines. Sawyer was accompanied by an Irish sergeant named Conlen, who roused Solomon, telling him he had two hours until midnight. The three of them walked slowly but surely toward the crossing point from the Confederate side of the siege line outer works.

"Here is the area yew came across from the other night. Orders have been issued for no shooting until an hour after midnight unless there is a general charge of many men from the other side. Remain here with Sergeant Conlen until I return. The sergeant is an interesting man. He will keep yew amused for a bit," Sawyer said to his cousin. "And if yew want a real fightin' man by yore side, Sergeant Brendan Conlen is the man! Why, this Irishman can use any weapon yew place in his hands—pistol, musket, carbine, bayonet, knife, or even a rock!" Sawyer left quickly.

"Holy crow!" uttered Conlen. "That Captain Sawyer makes me into some war machine. That's a fret, me friend! I rather be at home sipping some Irish whiskey and squeezing me Bridget anywhere beyont." Solomon just nodded his head and sat on a fascine behind the earthworks.

Conlen grinned, "But it kin be donkey's years fore that happen. Them Yankees git closer inch by inch, foot by foot, each day the sun crosses the sky here. Yanks are mining 'neath ourn defenses day and night. Den boom. God's earth jist heaves itself up and den down. We Rebs hold off Grant's straight assaults on ourn lines. Those brave blue bellies some time jist seeming wants to be kilt one rat after anuther. That last big charge against us had so many kilt and fall on top of tuther jist put a sane man's heart crossways. That's a fret, too."

"Those Yankees are just doing what you on this side of the lines do; you do your duty when called on," replied Solomon.

"Sure look it," came back Conlen.

Both men peered out into the darkness beyond the rifle pits. They heard nothing but the sounds of the insects and frogs this night at this moment. Conlen somberly said, "Mr. Witcher, when it is time to cross that ravine and the open areas, don't yew go arseways and let some Billy Yank put a minie ball in yew. Yore cuzzin says good tings 'bout yew. This Southland be needin' good men after this war gits finished."

Solomon, remaining silent for a time, stood and took a couple of steps to examine one of the unfinished gabions that day-duty soldiers had worked on. "These things work?"

"Holy crow! Yeah! One of 'em stopped a Yankee minie ball afore it could cut through this here Irish heart of mine. Me Bridget must of been prayin' heavy fer me that mornin'."

Sergeant Conlen, looking beyond Solomon, saw Captain Dundee walking quickly toward them, said, "Sir, the captain is here. It must be time."

"Solomon, it is time for yew to cross over. Be safe, cousin. I don't know when we two will meet again. Our cause forever!" said Sawyer as he embraced his cousin. "Orders have been issued and double-checked about no shooting. Now go."

Solomon looked at Conlen and said in a solemn voice, "I will try not to go 'arseways,' my friend. You do the same." Conlen and Witcher shook hands.

Solomon turned to his cousin. "Just one more moment," advised Solomon, as he put his hand into his vest pocket. He pulled out the piece of red fabric that had once been part of the Confederate flag flying at the hospital where he had suffered the blackout from the bomb explosion. "Apparently this was lucky for me once. Now I want it to be lucky for both of us." As he talked, he ripped the piece of the flag into two parts. A couple of bits of red string floated momentarily on the air and were lifted upward a foot or two by a small gust of wind. "Here. This part is for you to keep. I will keep the other piece. These bits of the flag will help us both be lucky and remember the other. Take it and hold it dear!" Sawyer took the small piece of red cloth and smiled at his cousin. Solomon added, "The red string story, another time."

"Until we meet again!" replied Sawyer.

With a smile and a tip of his black hat to Sawyer and Conlen,

Solomon, dressed completely in black, slipped into the darkness to go to the nearest Confederate rifle pit about a hundred feet forward. At the pit were two Rebels who were expecting him. Pausing there for only a moment, Solomon stood up halfway and quickly made for the nearest scraggly clump of small trees.

Solomon knew the small ravine was coming up. As he made his way to its near edge, he felt inside his vest for the white rectangle of cloth he would have to hold up over his head when he approached the Union lines. The ravine in the dark seemed steeper than it really was. He awkwardly climbed down and slid some to the bottom of the ravine. He caught his breath and began the climb upward. About half way up the side of the ravine, Solomon halted and turned his body so that his feet had secure footing and his back was against the side of the steep incline. He paused to gaze upward at the stars in the almost clear sky. His eyes wandered among the stars, and he reflected on his stay in Vicksburg. He had not informed Sawyer about the red string nor had he told Sawyer that he had visited the Windsor house himself on May 1. He remembered the exact date because he had a conversation with a Union soldier who was sketching the house. The soldier's name was Henry Otis Dwight of the 20th Ohio Infantry, and he was finishing the sketch as they talked. Solomon watched him complete the drawing and write the date on the page. Solomon thought the sketch really captured the look and the essence of the Windsor house. The house was majestic. It rivaled the Surget's Clifton in Natchez in many ways. But the Windsor mansion presented itself in its own unique manner. When at Windsor, Solomon had some idle time on his hands so he decided to circle around the huge mansion to view it all.

Solomon walked to the front of the mansion. He stood about thirty yards directly before the decorative wrought-iron steps that formed a stairwell up to the front doorway to the home. The huge house, as well as he could remember from some college classes, seemed to be Greek revival style. The residential floors were the second and third floors with a basement serving as the first floor. The iron stairs led up to the second floor. He guessed each column to be from twenty-five to thirty feet tall with a supporting base about ten feet tall of paneled stucco plinths. Ornamental iron balustrade connected the columns, and some connected to the floors of the home. He wondered how many rooms there were in the home. An attic sat on top of the residential floors. He wanted to go up to the roof-top observatory to see what view it enabled one to see. All sides of the Windsor mansion projected wealth and magnificence. He thought this house and Clifton to be the epitome of riches and influence. He was envious. Solomon counted eight chimneys and twenty-nine columns as he walked around the home. It was not exactly square because an ell had been constructed on one side. Four sets of iron stairs, counting the front stairs, allowed access to the second floor.

Solomon did acquire permission to go atop the home to the observatory. Up there he could see the river and some Union gunboats. In the distance on land he thought he could make out a group of Union soldiers. He pulled his eyes back to look at the roof of the home. He saw some water tanks that supplied rainwater to the inhabitants of the Windsor mansion. He was impressed, to say the least. He saw some wounded soldiers outside in the shade of some trees. He saw other soldiers all around, hurrying from place to place. He looked at the tree where the Yankee soldier had sat beneath to sketch the Windsor mansion. He did not see the soldier artist, nor did he see the short piece of red string caught in a spider web near his feet.

Now Solomon reflected on the fighting in this area. Because the Union command had used Windsor house as a hospital, it probably would survive the siege if it ended soon with a Union victory. If the Rebels succeeded in lifting the siege and maneuvered any groups of soldiers and fought again near the house, it could be damaged by one side or the other or deliberately destroyed by the Union army. Solomon closed his eyes and thought about Windsor. He had not told his cousin Sawyer that when Sergeant Conlen awakened him he was dreaming about the Windsor house. In his dream he envisioned the house burning, going up in flames—flames that produced a giant bonfire with fingers of fire reaching for the heavens. The fire's heat seemed hotter than the proverbial fire in hell itself. The heat was intense; the light was intense; and the scene permanently burnt in his brain was intense. In his dream he was approaching the house, even though the heat burnt his skin and the intense light seared his eyes. But to him one of the plumes of red fire reminded him of Egiap's hair—his eyes showed him the illusion of her face with its beguiling smile. He stared at that plume and walked toward it. The fire began to exact its toll on him. He experienced exasperating pain at the moment Conlen roused him awake.

He opened his eyes briefly and saw the stars in the night sky and felt the coolness of the ground of the side of the ravine. He felt coolness all over and closed his eyes once more. In his mind he saw the house engulfed by flames with its stately columns sheathed in red hot cloaks of fire. He closed his eyes tighter, and now his vision of the future of the house revealed to him only a set of very wide stairs leading from the ground up to nothing but eerily sitting among the many columns not consumed by the flames. He heard the wind whistling through the intricately designed cast-iron capitals crowning the tall columns producing a rather intriguing yet eerie moaning sound. He stood on open ground with surviving naked columns in neat rows to his left and right, behind him, and in front of him. Some of the columns in one corner area of the mansion had not survived the fire and were only remnants of themselves, devoid of the majesty of survivor columns with their exquisite cast-iron Corinthian capitals atop the fluted columns. Here and there in the neat lines were other broken columns. A line of other columns extended out from one side.

A sound near Solomon made him open his eyes abruptly to look

139

left at his eye level. He saw a snake tail slither over a dry branch and into a clump of scraggly grass about four feet away. "One of those cottonmouth water moccasins," he said aloud. He raised his head and reclosed his eyes for a moment. He saw Windsor mansion again. Its appearance was that of its fresh, original visage once more.

He slowly opened his eyes to gaze upward at the starry sky and out into the universe. He smiled and turned to scramble out of the ravine to advance to the Union line.

Near the top Solomon readied the white cloth and remembered the words he was to say loudly to the sentries and the soldiers in the forward rifle pits on the Union side. A few trees clumped together here and there. He picked his way forward for about forty yards and slipped in among the trees in one of the clusters. He pulled out the white cloth, held it high over his head, and stepped out from the trees. He walked this way for about ten steps until he heard, "Halt! Identify yourself now or be shot dead!"

As he approached a rifle pit, he repeatedly said, "Orders are to dig another damn canal!"

He walked straight to the voice in the darkness that threatened to kill him. He made out one of the Union soldiers standing and pointing his rifle at him. Solomon kept repeating his identifying message. Now he heard one of the soldiers still lying prone in the rifle pit say, "He's the one expected. Take him in immediately. But keep yore rifle on him 'til we git into the light to be shore he is the one."

"Yew! This way," barked the soldier pointing the gun at Solomon. "Keep them hands of yores up all the way in."

"Captain Benjamin! Prisoner en route!" shouted the soldier still in the rifle pit as he stood and began to walk toward the Union main line. He gestured for Solomon to follow him. The two Yankee soldiers and Solomon now saw many Union soldiers manning the line with guns ready.

The three men climbed a small earthen work in front of a trench and went down a gradual incline into the trench.

The other soldier who had shouted for Captain Benjamin now added, "He repeated the password phrase. But we know yew must verify him, Captain."

A Union captain awaited them. Still holding his weapon pointed at the intruder to the Union lines, the initial soldier Solomon encountered spoke once more, "Captain, is this the man we wuz to watch fer?"

Captain Benjamin looked at Solomon and asked, "When will this war be over, Mister?"

Solomon answered, "Eight, eight, sixty-eight."

Captain Benjamin laughed out loud and said, "I hope you are wrong, Major Witcher. Very wrong, Sir!"

"I, too, want that date to be very wrong, Captain!"

"All of us hope and pray as well," replied Captain Benjamin. "May God have mercy on both sides!"

Solomon paused for a moment and turned to gaze into the darkness toward the Confederate lines and said, "Many brave men fill the trenches behind the earthworks on each side."

Captain Benjamin nodded his head in agreement. "This way to headquarters, Sir." He motioned for Solomon to follow him. Within an hour the Union bombardment of Vicksburg lit up the night sky again.

Solomon Witcher met with his superiors at headquarters and completed his report. When he was dismissed several hours later, he went to officers' quarters tents and found an empty cot to sleep for a time. At first he slept deeply and without dreaming, but soon he dreamed of his experiences inside Vicksburg with the soldiers and the civilians. His dreams transformed into nightmares about the surgeon's amputation saw with its accompanying horrific sounds of the cutting of human bone and about the wounded soldiers being burned alive in the hell of the fiery hospital ward after the exploded artillery round. Then his dreams turned pleasant. This beautiful young woman in a wedding dress walked slowly toward him with guests at a wedding reception all around them. She stopped only an arm's length away from him and smiled. Suddenly she brought her right arm upward and pointed at his face a derringer—his derringer—with a red string tied around the barrel. Her smile changed into an ugly frown as her skin became deep red with blisters and pustules popping out from what once was a creamy white complexion. She now turned the gun on herself. He looked deep into her brown eyes and yelled, "Dodie! No!"

He jerked upright on the cot where he had been sleeping. His face and body were drenched in cold sweat. The vision of Dodie lingered in his mind's eye. He shook his head back and forth from side to side as if to deny his nightmare and its slowly fading image of the grown-up and yet still sick Dodie. He thought positively and out loud said, "I will dance at that girl's wedding." He smiled to himself.

It was the middle of the night, and most of the cots were filled by sleeping officers. He looked around inside the large tent. No one else was awake. He lay back down fully and tried to sleep. He dozed on and off, not dreaming of anything. When awake, he thought of Egiap, the beautiful redhead.

At daybreak he resolved to find Egiap. His orders were to rest and recuperate for a couple of days and then report to the general for his next assignment. He had two full days to seek Egiap. He would begin asking questions at breakfast at the eating area. Perhaps someone had heard rumors or seen something or knew someone who could help him in his search. Fortune did not shine his way. He next thought of heading to a hospital area. He circulated among the less-seriously wounded and carefully asked questions intended to make soldiers think he was on official business. Luck was not with him here either.

Solomon left the hospital area and soon sat beneath a large cottonwood tree to think. The cannonading of the besieged Vicksburg continued with its noise and smoke from all the artillery batteries in play at the time. He could hear heavy mortars from the river gunboats. But he thought that the bombardment sounded different from this side of it as opposed to being in Vicksburg. At one point the steady roar of the Union cannon made him think of the steady chanting of the people for Egypt at the healing huts. He could see Zethro, standing tall with his arms outstretched.

"That's it," Solomon said aloud. "I should look for Zethro. I should look at the location where contrabands are detained."

Now Solomon asked soldiers where the contrabands were held for processing and assignments. He eventually asked a group of three officers who knew the area where the contrabands were assembled and had to wait for determination of assignment and location. One of the officers informed Solomon that the area was just about an hour's walk from where they were at the moment. Solomon struck off in that direction at a fast pace.

Within the hour Solomon topped a somewhat high ridge and began his walk downward to the contraband camp in the distance. Dirty white standard army tents studded his field of vision. Some tents were rectangular in shape with a pitched rooftop, and others reminded him of the Indian tepees he had read of and seen drawings of in school. There were a few drab brown and gray cabins constructed from roughly-hewn wood for sides, and the same drab hand-hewn wood was the shingles that topped the roof. These cabins looked like giant wooden crates large enough for a man to stand tall in and to lie down full length on the floor. Most of the cabins that dotted the field of tents were in the eastern side of the camp. Looking for the processing center, Solomon knew that he had quite a task in front of him in attempting to find Zethro. He noticed the Federal flag flying from a rather tall flagpole on the eastern side. He worked his way toward it. As he walked, he swept his eyes back and forth, looking at the teeming individuals along the way. He saw children, women, and old men but no young to middle-age able-bodied men. Either the able-bodied men were away at a work detail, or they were billeted elsewhere.

In several minutes he had walked up to the large main processing tent. He gave his rank and military unit and inquired about a contraband named Zethro. "Is there a last name that goes with that name?" asked a grizzled old sergeant who obviously was unhappy with his current assignment.

"Zethro is the only name I know," replied Solomon. "But I can describe him for you. That may . . . "

"All them contrabands look alike to me," interrupted the sergeant.

"Sergeant, listen to me. This Zethro is real big, real big. He is a giant to most of us—weighs over 300 pounds I'd say. He is a young contraband. He is slow in his ways."

"Yew mean he is lazy like the lot of them niggars."

"No, Sergeant, no. He does not seem to be very smart, but he is smart. He is just slow in figuring things out . . ."

"So he's a dumb one like the lot of them," interrupted the sergeant.

"Sergeant, would you stop interrupting me and listen to me carefully right now," said Solomon in a rather loud and irritated voice. "He is slow in figuring things out except when he needs to protect the redheaded white woman he accompanies. He would fight to the death for her." Major Witcher scowled at the sergeant.

144

"Well, why didn't yew tell me that before?" answered the old sergeant, obviously somewhat nervous and yet relieved that he could give the upset officer some information of value to him and get him to move on. "Most all of us here knows about that big young buck fightin' and screamin' for that redheaded woman. I hear tell that it took close to twenty soldiers to take down that big contraband when he was mad about being parted from her. He must have put five or six men in the hospital." The sergeant smiled up at Solomon.

"Where is he?" shot back Solomon.

"He was out of control. He was pickin' up soldiers and chunkin' 'em like rag dolls all over the place. They was gonna shoot him until that redheaded woman calmed him down afore she was taken away." The sergeant continued, "It wuz amazing—like Sampson out of the Bible."

Now it was Solomon's time to interrupt the sergeant. Solomon curtly asked, "Where is Zethro? Tell me now!"

"That Zethro of yorn is locked up in the military jail stockade over yonder about a mile from here. Story is that they put chains on him jist in case he became mad agin. They ain't taking no chances with that young bull. That there niggar is strong!"

"Which way is that again? Who is the ranking officer?"

"It be that way. This direction," the sergeant pointed. "The officer in charge is old Colonel Maunder."

Solomon, already walking in the direction indicated, heard the name of the colonel he had to talk with. He picked up his pace. A feeling of hope swept over him.

Egiap, Ann, and Zethro fled New Orleans just before the Union forces took control. One of the last steamboats out of New Orleans took them upriver to Natchez, and they lived in the cypress swamps along the old Natchez Trace, eventually working their way up to the Port Gibson

145

area where Egiap and Ann volunteered to assist the doctors with the sick and wounded.

Talk was that the Windsor mansion and its grounds served as an observation point atop the building and a hospital on the grounds and in certain rooms. Egiap, hoping to help the ill and wounded, led the others to the Windsor house and plantation. The three travelers from New Orleans stood at a distance in the front of the house and marveled at its size and design. The huge house faced the West.

"Mistress Egypt, all dat, dat big ole house be for jist one family?" asked Zethro in awe.

Ann commented, "Dem people be proud!"

Egiap then said, "Who really needs a mansion like that one?"

Again Ann commented, "Must be lots of folks 'round heer needs a big house. We seed enough 'round heer."

The three of them stood for a time longer just looking at the house. It was as if they were mesmerized by the sheer beauty and size of the home. But suddenly Egiap snapped them out of the pause by saying, "There must be some soldiers that need our help. Let's walk up to the house to ask someone on the grounds. It looks like a hospital area over to the side on the grounds near the home. Zethro, you must give me your Bowie knife while we are among the soldiers. It will be less dangerous for all of us because they will not trust you with that big knife. Let's place it in my haversack for safe keeping. Come on."

Zethro and Ann picked up their knapsacks and bedding and followed Egiap. Zethro handed his Bowie knife to his Mistress Egypt, who then placed it in her haversack as they walked. Egiap, who had held on to her belongings in a haversack, walked briskly up to the grounds of the house. She encountered a Confederate officer whom she asked about volunteering. He directed them over to the area where wounded were lying on the grounds. He pointed out a doctor for them to talk with. Soon all three were assisting the doctor and attending to the wounded.

The doctor, after several hours, called Egiap over to him to tell her that food was available on the opposite side of the Windsor house and for her and her two companions to stop what they were doing and partake of the food and drink for a well-deserved break. The doctor showed them a place on the grounds under a large tree to sleep for the night. He commended them for their assistance with the wounded. He was apologetic for the lack of better accommodations but told them he would try to locate something more comfortable than the ground for the next night. As he talked with the three unlikely companions, he thanked them and offered a single question to Egiap, "Suddenly I see a piece of red string fastened about the ankles of most of the soldiers treated here. I watched y'all care for the men and saw yew tie a piece of red string onto their ankles. What is that fer?"

"Doctor, that piece of red string is more than just a piece of red string. It is a token of good luck, of good fortune, of hope and strength. It is faith. It is a physical thing the soldiers can see and touch. It is something they can believe in. They see others with it, and that gives them strength and an inner peace. It helps heal. Even though we only see just a piece of red string," replied Egiap.

"Yew are a healer. Yew know how to prepare natural remedies. I noticed that yew sent out yore man and yore woman to gather herbs, other plants, and substances that y'all mixed to form poultices and plasters for the various wounded soldiers. I don't know what other magic yew work with the wounded, but I don't want yew to stop." He paused. He rose from where he sat and said to Egiap, "I will search about for more red string or thread to give to yew."

All three slept hard that night. Egiap awoke before the others and walked to the house and up the iron stairs. She walked lightly so as not

147

to awaken the slumber of others and not to arouse the notice or interest of those who were already up and working. She searched quietly for stairways on each floor that led upward to the roof and the observation post. She realized that she was actually close to the last stairs upward when she was accosted by a sentry. She smiled at him, flirted just enough to beguile him, asked him to show her the cupola observation post, and held his hand as he guided her upward. One other Confederate soldier was at the observation post, looking outward toward the Mississippi River with great interest. He diverted his attention to Egiap and her escort but quickly and quietly turned back to his watching for activity on the river when Egiap smilingly informed him that she was a recently arrived niece of the owner of Windsor, seeking sanctuary from the invading Yankee soldiers in the region. Egiap did a full circle to see the spectacular view from atop the Windsor mansion. She stepped over to several vantage points to look. She could see where she and her companions slept last night. She saw Zethro stand and stretch underneath the large tree where they had placed their bedding. She saw Ann sit upright. She knew it was time to get back to those two because soon they would visit the wounded. Noise like distant thunder caused the two soldiers and Egiap to look toward the northeast. Some smoke began to plume upward in the distance. One of the soldiers said aloud, "Fighting. Yankees are on the move." The two soldiers stared toward the smoke and noise. Meanwhile, Egiap removed a piece of red string from her pocket and tied it on one of the rail supports next to her. She turned and touched the soldier who had led her up to the top on the arm and indicated she was ready to leave. She smiled at him once again.

Back out on the grounds Egiap hurried to where Ann and Zethro were still waiting for her to be back under the large tree. She informed them of the fighting in the area and of the need to be at the hospital when the wounded were brought in.

By noon the wounded trickled in at first, and then more and more came in steady numbers. Zethro and Ann had gathered specified plants for Egiap that were mixed, crushed, and otherwise prepared in poultices before the first wounded had arrived. They were ready to assist the two doctors there at the house.

Zethro helped carry and move wounded soldiers to various locations on the grounds. Sometimes he assisted as a stretcher bearer, and other times he merely picked up carefully as he could and carried individual soldiers to the places indicated by the doctors. Ann cleaned wounds and did errands as needed. Egiap administered to wounded soldiers after the doctors examined them, decided what action to undertake, and completed the procedure or turned the soldier over to a nurse. One could tell which soldiers she had helped with because of the red strings.

One young Confederate soldier, probably no more than seventeen in Egiap's estimation, moaned in extreme pain from a minie ball wound in his right leg. The doctor said the minie ball had not done enough damage for an amputation but that the pain would be intense for a time. The young man begged for a painkiller, but everyone knew painkillers were in short supply and would be needed for those more badly wounded. Egiap hovered over him and quietly comforted him with her words and gentle touch. She motioned for Ann when Ann came near and then whispered in her ear for her to fetch a certain poultice from the place Egiap had laid them out on the ground for easy and quick pick up. The poultice in hand, Egiap placed it carefully and gently on the leg wound. The young soldier cried out in pain as he jerked his body. "Now, young man, this herbal poultice will draw out most of your pain in a timely manner if you will keep still for a few minutes as I talk with you." She mumbled some words under her breath that the soldier could not make out.

The young soldier looked Egiap directly in her blue-green eyes and drew a deep breath. He gazed at her with wonderment in his eyes and his voice as he said, "The poultice is working. I can stand the pain now. How can that be? Are you a healer? Did you use magic? What was that chant?" Egiap grabbed his hand and held it firmly in between her two hands. He smiled up at her.

Egiap simply said to the soldier, "I serve the Good Lord." She smiled back at him. "This red string I tie on your ankle is to help you focus on getting well. It is for luck."

He closed his eyes while saying, "Thank you." He slept.

In several days the Confederates had to abandon their positions around the Windsor mansion and reposition themselves closer to Vicksburg. The Confederate commanders issued warnings to the local population to expect Yankees to move in and confiscate slaves and other property and commandeer houses and other buildings for their use. The Confederate forces planned for an orderly withdrawal from the Windsor mansion and its immediate area but were surprised when Confederate messengers rode swiftly onto the Windsor grounds, yelling that the Yankees were sweeping through the area and would be there within an hour. The planned orderly withdrawal turned disorderly. Almost everybody and almost everything was suddenly uprooted and put into motion to withdraw. Much of value was taken. The ambulatory wounded moved out, but those more critically wounded remained without doctors. Some of those remaining were slowly and painfully dying. Egiap, Ann, and Zethro stayed there on the Windsor grounds for those who could not be moved. Egiap attempted to persuade Ann and Zethro to leave with the others, warning them that the three of them could get arrested and separated. Neither Ann nor Zethro would leave Egiap. Egiap and Ann did convince Zethro to bury his Bowie knife before the Yankees arrived.

Zethro left them for about thirty minutes and returned with dirty hands and face. "Its be done, Mistress Egypt."

Egiap replied to Zethro by saying, "Now stay close to me. Do as I say when the Yankees get here. Ann, you stay close as well. We do not know what to expect."

Both Ann and Zethro nodded their assent, and Egiap smiled at the both of them. "I could not ask for better friends," she said quietly yet firmly.

Egiap held the hand of one of the dying where six or seven of them had been placed together for their last hours. Zethro sat next to Egiap. Zethro made a low continuous hum as he prayed and waited for the different soldiers. Ann, nearby, wet cloths and placed them on the foreheads of several soldiers. She held her rosary and moved her fingers along the beads as she mechanically muttered prayers in between refreshing the cloths on the soldiers' foreheads. Egiap began an ancient Druid chant and rocked side to side.

Union soldiers burst from the tree line in the distance. They yelled out and ran toward the big house and the few remaining people there and on the immediate grounds. Officers barked out orders, and the Yankee swarm overtook the house and grounds. One old Union officer fired his pistol twice in the air to alarm the civilians and wounded soldiers who remained at the house. Those pistol discharges startled some of the wounded and Zethro and Ann. Both immediately ceased what they were doing and stood upright. Egiap, who had opened her eyes, but was not frightened by the noise and the gun shots, insisted that they sit back down and be calm. Both obeyed, but Egiap could see fear and uncertainty in their eyes. The Union soldiers were all about and pointed guns at the wounded soldiers as well as Egiap and her friends. They were ordered to stand and move away from the wounded as two Yankee soldiers walked among the wounded Confederates, prodding them unmercifully to test if they were really hurt or not.

A single shot rang out from the front entrance of the house. Shouts emanated from the front iron stairwell of the Windsor mansion.

Most of the Union soldiers now moved into and past the house to continue their advance. Only two remained, following the orders of an officer to detain the two civilians and the contraband until he returned in a few minutes. Both the soldiers pointed rifles menacingly at the two women and the former slave.

The Union soldier on the right facing Egiap looked at her and said, "Why, yew are right purdy, Miss Red Hair. And what is that shiny bangle pinned to yore dress? And is that a brass hair clasp of some sort shining in there in yore red locks?" The other soldier just stood there, pointing his gun.

The talkative soldier took a couple of steps toward Egiap. Zethro tensed himself to spring. Egiap held her hand up to motion Zethro to remain as he was. The soldier lowered his gun and took another step to place himself right beside Egiap. He reached out and grabbed her red hair just next to the brass hairpin. He jerked her toward him.

Zethro, even though the other soldier's gun was aimed at him could not contain himself any longer when he heard the slight squeal let out by his Mistress Egypt, leaped for the soldier who was pulling her hair. In the same instant that the other soldier adjusted his weapon and aim to hit the big black man, Ann threw herself in front of Zethro and cried out, "No, he's innocent!" In the very next second the soldier pulled the trigger to discharge his weapon. Now Egiap reacted to all going on about her. She reached up to her brass hairpin and pulled it from her red hair, drew it back, and plunged it into the left side of the neck of the soldier that held her hair in his grasp. That grasp weakened, and blood gushed from the struck artery in the soldier's neck. That soldier crumpled to the ground, holding his bleeding neck. The other soldier, who had fired his rifle, now dropped it to the ground with smoke emitting from its barrel. He froze in place for a brief instant and then turned to run. But it was too late for him. Zethro, in mounting anger, grabbed the soldier by the head and twisted his neck with a force he did not realize he possessed. The soldier's body went limp, and Zethro dumped him on the ground. He turned to see Ann, bleeding on the ground. Egiap had already dropped down beside her and lifted her head and shoulders to hold her close to her own body.

Egiap could feel the life oozing out of Ann's body as her blood oozed out from the wound in her chest. Egiap could feel the pumping of Ann's heart weaken and slow. Zethro knelt beside them. "Mistress Egypt, do sumpthin for Miss Ann. Do sumpthin. Her save me. Her save me." He looked at Egiap with pleading in his eyes. Egiap looked back at him with sadness in her own eyes and shook her head sideways.

Egiap looked at Ann whose eyes fluttered open and shut. Tears flowed down Egiap's cheeks and dropped onto Ann. "The bullet hit her heart. Too much damage," she said quietly to Zethro. "All I can do now is hold her close."

Ann now kept her eyes open for a time and spoke in a soft firm voice as she looked first at Zethro and then Egiap, "Zethro, my innocent one, yew *mon cher* be the innocent child I losts time back. Egypt, yew be the older sister I allus wanted. Tie me a piece of dat red string on my ankle."

Egiap felt Ann's strength and vitality ebb from her body and sensed the last beat of her heart. Egiap sobbed and said, "She's gone." Both Egiap and Zethro, stunned at the events of the last few minutes, froze in place. Egiap remained motionless, holding Ann's lifeless body and crying. Zethro, still enraged but motionless as well, seethed with anger inside his huge body.

153

It was Zethro who pulled Egiap from her sorrow when he stammered, "Mistress Egypt. Mistress Egypt, us'n needs to leave dis heah place rat now afore them other Yankees gits back heah. I carry Miss Ann. Yew gits ourn packs over dere wheres we put 'em. Please, Mistress Egypt. Please, dem soldiers be back afore we knowed it." He stood and reached his big hand down to Egiap. She looked up at him and gently placed Ann fully on the ground. Egiap pulled a piece of red string from her pocket and tied it just so around Ann's ankle. Egiap now placed her smaller hand inside the huge hand of Zethro and his strength easily pulled her up to a standing position. She turned and went to secure their nearby haversacks. Zethro carefully lifted Ann into his huge arms and stood there, waiting for his Mistress Egypt to return. Egiap looked back at the wounded soldiers and the Windsor mansion. They headed to the nearest woods that the Yankee soldiers had not come from or gone into. They disappeared into the trees.

"Wifey! Wifey!" shouted a Confederate corporal, strolling through the campground area. "Wifey! Wifey!" Soldiers resting crowded the open area and around the old shabby, dirty-looking tents. "Wifey! Wifey!"

"Yeah. Heah. Heah. Over heah," said a voice belonging to a Confederate private who was about six feet tall and rather skinny for his frame. "I'm heah." The private stood to get the full attention of the soldier calling out.

"Captain Sawyer Dundee wants yew to report to him," barked the corporal. "I'll take yew to him. Foller me. Yew are Flanders?"

The private responded, "Yeah. That is me." He moved quickly to accompany the corporal who had turned about and briskly picked his way between tents and groups of soldiers trying to forget the war for a brief few minutes.

The two soldiers approached a road, and Wifey walked faster and spurted up along side of the corporal. The corporal now looked at Flanders and asked, "Why they call yew Wifey?"

"How yew knowed my nickname?"

"When I talked with yore captain, he tole me where to seek yew and how to git yore attention quick. He said to call out 'Wifey' in the middle of the campground. Why they call yew Wifey?"

"My friends put that nickname on me when we furst git heer 'cuz they tole me that I talk about my wife all the day long and in the night, too," replied the private. "She is such a beautiful woman. She is intelligent more than yew kin imagine. She is a school teacher and learnt me much. She is a lot smarter than most men I know. She can cook so good. She is . . ."

"I git it. I understand," cut in the corporal. "Yore fellers got it rat, by golly. Yew are a hoot, Wifey." The corporal grinned over at the private as they continued to walk.

As they ambled on, Wifey asked, "What does yore Captain Dundee want wit me?"

Still walking briskly and not looking at Wifey, the corporal glibly answered, "I wuz not tole why yew are summoned. I ain't knowin' nuthin' 'bout why yew wanted—'cept'n I am to fetch yew to the Captain. Patience, Wifey, yew'll find out when yew need to know." They walked on for about twenty minutes with no conversation from the corporal and intermittent remarks uttered by Wifey about what his wife's views were about the war, the Yankee invasion, the evils of slavery, and his well-being in the military.

As they entered another camping site, the corporal said to himself under his breath, "Some adventure this fetchin' wuz."

Wifey, hearing something said but not understanding, asked, "What yew say, Corporal?"

"Nuthin'. It wuz nothin'. I jist said that I kin see Captain Dundee over yonder at that largest officers' tent."

"Yew know, my wife, would of volunteered to fight them Yankiees if'n she could. She ain't affeered o' nuthin' or nobody," related Wifey. "She be too beautiful to fight though."

"So beautiful, huh?" said the corporal as they neared Captain Dundee. "I wisht I could see yore woman, Wifey."

Captain Sawyer Dundee looked over at the two soldiers winding their way toward him as he completed his briefing with three officers. The corporal and Wifey now stood before him at attention and saluting. He returned their salute and asked, "Corporal, is this the man requested?"

"Yas, sur," replied the corporal. "This heah is Wifey, er, uh; I mean Private Flanders. Sorry, sur."

"'Wifey' you said?"

"Yus, sur. It's his nickname, sur . . ."

Sawyer cut in with, "Given by his comrades in arms I bet my last dollar." He smiled a knowing smile and continued, "I'll allow the private himself to tell me that story. Corporal, yew are dismissed. Thank yew." Sawyer saluted as the corporal did likewise and then turned to leave.

"Private Flanders, please sit here, and let's talk."

The private and the captain both sat. Sawyer looked extremely seriously at the private and solemnly said, "Wifey, huh? Tell me why Wifey." He broke into a broad grin.

Wifey, in a dead serious mood and wondering why he was summoned to a captain he did not know, now felt a bit relieved with

Sawyer's facial expression and question. Wifey now explained how he had acquired his nickname and how he was accustomed to his moniker as tagged by his fellow soldiers. He then asked Sawyer if he had a wife; and when Sawyer related that he was not married, proceeded to tell the captain about his own beautiful, intelligent wife. Sawyer listened politely for several minutes, not interrupting even once but smiling and nodding several times. Sawyer realized that Wifey's constant talk about his actual wife was how he handled the stress and the realities of the war.

Captain Dundee, knowing other information about the soldier called Wifey, knew that he had the right soldier for the task at hand. Two key bits of information about Wifey attested to the fact he would be perfect for the task—Wifey had proven battlefield courage, and Wifey had worked in Louisiana salt mines.

Dundee explained to Wifey that Union miners apparently were tunneling beneath the Third Louisiana Redan to place explosives there for detonation and an accompanying assault on the defensive line. Confederate soldiers could hear sounds from the earth below their position. They determined the sounds to be the noise of miners working with picks and shovels. Confederate command thought that its soldiers could dig a smaller one-man tunnel to intercept the Yankee tunnel. This countermine could be used to thwart the Union effort to demolish the Louisiana Redan or parts of it.

Dundee asked Wifey if he would volunteer for the underground detail. Wifey realized the urgency of the situation, agreed to volunteer, and asked, "When do I git down under? Where the digging?"

Captain Dundee answered that the tunneling had started yesterday. Several soldiers and one officer who worked in coal mines before the war began the countermine from an inside bank of the steep ravine along the defense perimeter. No danger would exist from Union artillery at the point of the dig because of the Union command not wanting any possible

157

problems with their tunneling and digging. Danger did exist from the very fact of tunneling and countermining as in all types of mining operations. The Captain did point out one other problem on the outside area of one approach to the manway of the Confederate tunnel—a Yankee sniper could fire into one section of the way to the tunnel works. The sniper had constructed a crude tower using railroad ties. Known as "Coonskin" on both sides of the siege works because of the raccoon fur cap he donned while shooting, the sniper proved deadly to the Confederates.

"Yew still want to volunteer?" asked Captain Dundee once more.

"I kin do it, Sir."

"I read reports and talked with yore fellow soldiers, and every single one of them praise yore bravery. It's outstanding. How do yew come by yore courage?"

Wifey replied, "I jist think of my relative I wuz tole 'bout frum the time I wuz a little boy. He fought the Mexicans at the Alamo. The Alamo defenders wuz outnumbered way more then us heer at Vicksburg. He and them tuthers fought for freedom—the way we are doin'."

Captain Dundee said reluctantly, "But those defenders died in the fight."

"Me," responded Wifey, "I ain't plannin' to die. I got me a beautiful wife to go home to. Now where be the diggin'?"

"So be it. I didn't want to make yew," said Dundee. "It had to be yore choice. Thank yew, Private." Dundee did not say what he was thinking—that the Alamo defenders did not plan to die either. He also did not say aloud that he thought of how brave the private was. He was inspiring to Sawyer. "I'll go there to the digging with yew now. Yore Captain knows that yew are with me and where yew are assigned."

Captain Dundee and Wifey made their way to the area approaching the Louisiana Redan within the Confederate lines. Wifey, uncharacteristically silent, observed the lay of the land, the way the ridges and hills formed, and the Rebel lines of fortification in general leading to the redan. He noticed a second line of defense being constructed behind the redan. At one point Captain Dundee cautioned, "About twenty yards ahead of us is the area that is a window of opportunity for Coonskin to shoot and kill us. See the whitewashed post with the broken rifle nailed to it. That is yore warning. When we reach the post, it is quite dangerous for us for about thirty yards or so. That is his main kill zone. He sometimes shoots at other points along the line, but this is the area that he is the deadliest shooting in. So be on guard and move quickly without stopping. Be aware that he can hit other places as well. Keep yore head down."

The two soldiers quickly and nimbly crossed the deadliest zone. They kept up their brisk pace for a short time until they came to the tunnel project opening. "This area here is not subject to the sniper's fire because of the angle of the ridge and hill," advised Captain Dundee.

"That's good," responded Wifey.

They approached several soldiers at the opening. Sawyer introduced Wifey, calling him Private Flanders, to the men and informed them that their new addition had salt mining experience and was fearless. Dundee shook hands with Wifey and said, "Remember the Alamo." Wifey grinned and nodded and turned to go to work with his crew of miners. Captain Dundee likewise turned to leave.

Several days passed with constant bombardment as usual. From his billeting area Sawyer Dundee about mid-afternoon on June 25, 1863, could hear gun and cannon fire all along the line near the Louisiana Redan. At one point he heard the sound of a huge explosion or explosions coming from the same area of the Confederate defense perimeter. The ground shook under his feet.

159

"It must be the Yankee tunnel explosions and a general assault by Grant's soldiers there at the Louisiana Redan," Sawyer said aloud to himself and others near him. He and other soldiers started running to their specified battle stations along the defense lines. He knew that a major assault was taking place at the Louisiana Redan but that his assigned section of the perimeter could come under attack as well. He and his unit would have to man their positions just in case. The noise grew in intensity from the Louisiana Redan direction. A black and gray smoky haze formed above the fighting.

Looking out across to the Union lines from his sector, Sawyer saw no indication of movement of soldiers on the other side. Then several thoughts tormented him, "Where was Wifey at the time of the big explosion? Was Wifey in a countermine at the time? Was the poor young man buried alive?"

Solomon headed for the military stockade in the indicated direction. He wondered if Zethro would still be held there. He thought that a trouble-maker could be transferred rather quickly. But if he could find Zethro, his odds of locating Egiap would be increased. He had a good feeling in his gut. As he walked, he started humming the song "Bonnie Blue Flag" that he remembered Xenophones' voice singing loudly in the hospital area when he was in Vicksburg and awakening from the effects of the explosion he had been near. Now he felt even more positive than before. He followed the wagon-rut road and walked as fast as he could.

Trees almost engulfed the pitiful road of ruts. Then abruptly Solomon encountered a sharp left curve in the road, walked about a dozen paces more, and broke through the tree line into open area. Ahead, about half a mile it seemed, he saw three wooden buildings grouped together. He walked even quicker and soon arrived at the cluster of buildings. Several small tents were pitched about twenty yards in front of the smallest of the three buildings. In among the tents was the Union flag on a short pole. A few soldiers, sitting and talking, were among the tents. Union soldiers were in guard positions all around the cluster of the buildings. All had rifles at the ready. Solomon walked over to the tents and inquired as to the whereabouts of the commanding officer, Colonel Maunder.

One of the soldiers replied that he had just seen Colonel Maunder leave the larger building and walk with another officer to the smaller wooden structure on the left behind the larger building. Solomon turned to walk that way. As he approached the smaller wooden building, two guards blocked the entrance. From the slightly opened door came angry shouts of three or four voices. One of the voices was that of Zethro.

"No entry!" barked one of the two guards who blocked the doorway. Solomon had to pause momentarily but heard the voices become even louder and angrier. The loudest voice was that of Zethro, who was lamenting the death of someone. Solomon's heart beat violently within his chest. His emotions rose to a height that he had never before experienced. He speculated wildly at who had died. Solomon, kept outside by the guards, knew not what to do. He stammered some words to the guards about his rank and unit and suddenly yelled at the top of his lungs, "Zethro! Zethro! Zethro!"

The guards looked at him weirdly and pointed their guns at him. The shouting from within ceased. Nobody said anything until Zethro's unbelieving voice cried out, "Massa Solomon? Is dat yew? Massa Witcher?" Then silence occupied the building.

The wooden door was thrown completely open by one of the officers on the inside. "Who in the hell is Massa Solomon?" asked the officer that had opened the door. He poked his head and shoulders out of the entrance with his eyes open wide, looking for Master Solomon. "At ease, sentries," he added. Now the officer occupied the entire doorway. He stared coldly at Solomon.

"Are yew this Massa Solomon?"

"I suppose I am, Sir. I am Major Solomon Witcher."

"Well, git yourself inside and tell us how in the blazes of the inferno did yew calm this here Negra down jist by yore calling the name Zethro. Yew did say Zethro, didn't yew? Colonel Maunder thought yew had yelled Jethro. Come on, which is it?"

"I did say Zethro."

"This way," the officer moved out of the doorway and motioned to Solomon to enter the jail building.

Solomon walked in and stood face-to-face with Colonel Maunder. "Who are you, and why are you here?" demanded the colonel. Everyone else was quiet, including Zethro, who had a big grin on his face. Zethro, in the smallest cell in the building, was standing manacled by heavy iron chains on his wrists and ankles. His wrists and ankles were bloody from the metal rubbing and cutting the skin. The opposite ends of the chains were attached to the heavy log walls with large iron spikes driven deep into the wood.

Solomon quickly related his name, unit, and other information, including that he knew Zethro from several years ago in New Orleans. He explained that he also knew Zethro was not a slave and was purchased by Egiap, a friend of them both.

"Oh, so, that is the Egypt this boy's been yelling for," said the officer.

"Her real name is Egiap, not Egypt. That is only a corruption of her name. She saved him from the New Orleans slave pens and a cruel master there," continued Solomon. "He became devoted to her. He chose to stay with her, even though he was a free man." He told them a bit more information about Egiap, but nothing about her healing and knowledge of magic.

"How did you calm this big fella down?" asked Colonel Maunder.

"The big guy is really a gentle giant unless he gets riled up," replied Solomon. "What did the soldiers do to him? To Egiap? To Ann?"

"Massa Solomon, dey done kilt Miss Ann! De soldiers kilt her dead at dat big Winds house when we'ns he'pin' dem dying soldiers dere," blurted out Zethro.

"Ann is dead? What about Egiap?" shot back Solomon. He looked at the Union soldiers and then Zethro, standing still with the chains binding his ankles and wrists.

"Mistress Egypt be fine," interjected Zethro before one of the officers could utter a word. "She gone. No Yankee gonna find her." Solomon let out a long breath of relief.

Now Colonel Maunder spoke, "We don't know nothing about this Egypt or Egiap you talk of. All we know is that we got this big hulking contraband who is angry most of the time and that we almost shot him just before you arrived here today. We have asked for him to be transferred north to Corinth at least, but we have not received any orders to do so yet."

Boldly Solomon said, "Let me take him. I can control him. You see that, don't you? I will be responsible for him and his actions. Just give me the proper papers to show to anyone who would question me about him. I can take him off your hands." He looked at Colonel Maunder and thought about focusing his attention on the colonel for persuasion sake.

But Colonel Maunder, recognizing an opportunity, spoke quickly himself, "You kin have this beast of a man. I will draw up the papers now. Follow me to my desk in the other building, Witcher." Colonel Maunder glanced at the other officers in the building and smiled. Under his breath, he said, "I hope you know what you have on your hands, Witcher." He was all smiles as they walked from one building to the next.

"Here you are, Major Witcher. The man you call Zethro is now in your hands and is your responsibility. We know that he had injured some soldiers, but we heard they will recover from their encounter with your beast. Good riddance!" said Colonel Maunder proudly. "Take this order back to the other building for his release, and then git the hell out of my compound!" He grinned at Solomon.

Solomon could hardly wait for the guards to release Zethro from the chains that shackled him in order to leave the area and then ask about Egiap. All the while that the guards attended to him, Zethro repeatedly said, "Thank yew, Massa Solomon. Thank yew, Massa Solomon." Solomon and Zethro were at the doorway to the building when Solomon turned to the guards to ask, "Did he have a haversack or something?" They stopped to look at the guards.

"Nuthin'," replied one of the guards.

Zethro said in a low voice that only Solomon could hear, "Mistress Egypt hab my sack o' belongins."

"Let's move," said Solomon. Solomon walked out of the door to the grounds followed by the grinning Zethro. They walked past the tents to leave the compound. All the Union soldiers stood and watched, amazed at the huge black man following the other man quite tamely. Neither Solomon nor Zethro looked back.

Solomon and Zethro remained silent as they walked a distance from the compound and eventually into the line of trees from where Solomon had emerged to see the three wooden buildings in the compound cluster and the tents close by. Just inside the trees Solomon turned to Zethro, smiled, and said, "Zethro, I am happy to have found you and even happier that I could get you released from the stockade. We must continue to walk to the area I am billeted for food and drink. I must somehow make arrangements for you now and especially when I am ordered away. But that can be handled a bit later. Now I want you to tell me what has happened to Egiap and you since I last saw you in New Orleans. Walk beside me and talk to me." The two men now continued their walk. The shade of the trees made for a more pleasant walk.

"Yas, sur, Massa Solomon, whats yew wants me to tells yew?"

"Tell me whatever you remember after we parted ways in New Orleans," instructed Solomon. Now Solomon would let Zethro talk with limited questions from him.

As they walked, Zethro, glad to be free from the stockade and eager to please Solomon, babbled away with various details of the time away from Solomon. He told Solomon that they had remained in New Orleans and that Egypt continued to heal people on the south side of the river where they had first seen Solomon. He then said that news of the war came and that Egypt seemed different and uneasy about everything after that news. Zethro informed him of the big boat ride on the big river up to Natchez. He told of living in the swamp lands for a while and then walking up to that big house to nurse the Confederate soldiers. Zethro said they tended the soldiers for days until the Yankees came.

It was at this point in his narrative that Zethro became angry and agitated as he talked. Tears welled up in his angry eyes, and his words came faster. "Dey kilt Miss Ann! Dem Yankee soldiers kilt Miss Ann!" He suddenly stopped in the middle of the narrow road, became silent, and tensed all the muscles in his body. "Aarrrh!" he screamed out. Before the last sound died in his throat, he collapsed to a sitting position on the ground. Solomon dropped to his knees by the huge Zethro and put his right hand on Zethro's left shoulder as he faced him.

"I know you are sad and angry, and your anger needs a voice; but I think that Ann would want you to continue to live your life to help Egypt

165

and others," Solomon paused and then said, "Don't you?" He looked at Zethro with pity in his heart. Now he noticed the bloody wrists and ankles on the big man. "We will tend to your injuries when we reach camp."

Zethro sat there, still seething with anger for a few moments. He then looked at his wrists and wiped them on his shirt. He felt the hem of his shirt, looked up at Solomon, and said, "Massa Solomon, I gots mines red stone that Mistress Egypt give us'n in Nawlins. I gots Miss Ann's red stone, too. Mistress Egypt done give it me back in de swamp afer I done tote Miss Ann's body dere when we's runnin' frum dem Yankees at dat Winds house. We put her to res' in de deep swamp. I's digged her grabe so's Mistress Egypt coulds fix up de body for de bural dere." He pulled up the hem of his long shirt to show Solomon. "Mistress Egypt done took de red stone frum dat necklice thin' fer mees."

Solomon could make out the shapes of two stones sewn into the hem. He noticed, too, that the hem was reinforced with the sewing of heavy red thread. "Why, yes. I see. Ann would be happy for you to keep her red cork stone," said Solomon comfortingly. "That is the perfect way for you to remember her—you can always reach your shirt hem to feel the red cork stones sewn inside."

"Yus, sur, Massa Solomon."

Zethro stood up, and the two men resumed their walk back to Solomon's billeting area. They walked on in silence for a few minutes until the cannonading of the besieged Vicksburg started once more.

Now Solomon posed to Zethro the burning question he had been holding for a long time, "Where is Egypt? What separated the two of you?"

Now Zethro, as Solomon listened intently, related the series of events from the moment he picked up Ann's lifeless form.

166

Carrying Ann's body, Zethro followed Egypt among the trees as she picked their way to evade the Yankee soldiers. Fearful of being discovered, Egiap attempted to observe in all directions and to listen for all sounds. At one point she turned to look at Zethro, put her finger on her lips to warn him not to talk, and crouched down behind a larger tree with Zethro doing the same close beside her. A Yankee patrol of several men made their way through the woods about fifty yards in front of them. The soldiers talked loudly, laughing loudly so often as well. Within minutes the Yankee patrol meandered out of sight, but Egiap still heard the voices for a time longer. Egiap and Zethro remained motionless and speechless for a few minutes more. Finally Egiap rose and motioned for Zethro to follow. For almost the rest of the daylight hours they trudged deeper into the woods, then through an open area, and then into a swamp where they meandered for a time until Egiap uttered, "This is it. This is where we want to be. This is the location in my dream last night. That is the cypress tree with the fairy circle of cypress knees revealed to me." She pointed out a large cypress tree surrounded by tall cypress knees. The water had receded, leaving the area dry and open except for the cypress knees. Zethro looked intently at the tree and its many knees as he stood, still holding the body of Ann. Egiap slowly walked over next to the trunk of the big tree and said to Zethro, "Place Ann here." She pointed, and Zethro gently put Ann's body where his mistress had indicated. "Now, Zethro, go search and gather me as many plants like these three that you can find close to our circle of cypress knees here. Hurry. It won't be light much longer."

Zethro had noticed that his Egypt had slowed and stopped briefly at several places in the swamp to pick some plants as they sought this location. These now were what he would seek nearby. "Yus, Mistress Egypt. I kin do dat fer yew." Zethro immediately set himself to his task.

When Zethro returned with two big handfuls of plants, a small fire was ablaze; and the darkness began to dominant the day. The sounds of

167

frogs, insects, and other natural swamp citizens resonated from outside the cypress knees fairy circle. Zethro sat and leaned upon a large cypress knee so he could watch Ann's body and his mistress. Soon he was asleep from the exhausting walk while carrying Ann's body. He did not dream as his Mistress Egypt would when she would sleep a few hours during the night after preparing Ann's body for burial. Egiap was glad that Zethro's deep sleep insulated him from the day's events. She welcomed her own slumber after midnight, hoping that additional guidance would be given to her as she slept there in the cypress swamp. Her brief dream gave no revelation of guidance; it was merely a remembrance of her first meeting with Ann.

Rays of sunlight penetrated the swamp. Awaken by the light, Zethro sat up and rubbed his eyes. "Morning," Egiap said. She held out her hand, offering Zethro some hardtack she had taken at the Windsor hospital area. "I have enough of this hardtack to keep us going for a time. You will have to trap or hunt or fish for us some other food," she said to him. "Do that later—after we say good-bye to our beloved friend Ann."

"Yus, Mistress," Zethro replied sadly as he ate the hardtack biscuit. Shortly Zethro rose and asked where to start digging the grave.

Egiap walked over to a spot just outside the large circle of cypress tree knees and said, "Here is where you dig."

Zethro looked about. Egiap now reached into her haversack to pluck out a knife for him to dig with. He set about his work with no other words.

When Zethro was finished, Egiap told him to lift Ann's shrouded body and lay it in the three- to four-foot grave dug for her. "Miss Ann smell good," said Zethro to Egiap. He placed her down into her final resting place.

"Thank you, Zethro," said Egiap. Now Egiap faced the direction of the sun, looked up into the sky, and chanted something Zethro could not understand. Then she turned to him and asked him to begin filling the grave. He obeyed, and she chanted out loud something different this time. She halted abruptly and started reciting words from the Bible. Zethro recognized "ashes to ashes" and "dust to dust" among others. Egiap stopped and wept silently.

Zethro looked at her and said firmly, "Now Miss Ann be wit Jesus, ain't her?"

"Yes, yes, my Zethro. She is," replied Egiap.

They heard the sound of some kind of cat meowing from their left, and from their right up in a tree they heard the cawing of some type of crow. A rustle from the bushes on their left caused them to look that way. Then the fluttering of wings from their right and directly above them captured their attention.

Egiap continued to weep now. Zethro walked over to her and said, "Nots to be sad. Her be wit Jesus now, Mistress Egypt." He hesitatingly put his hand on her shoulder. She looked up at him and smiled. "She be happy," added Zethro.

They hid for many days until a Confederate soldier came running through the swamp and went right through the cypress knees fairy ring and leaned up against the large tree to hide, just as he realized that Zethro and his mistress were camping there. The soldier looked at them with alarm and yelled, "A Yankee patrol is following me. They seen me about ten minutes ago and came after me. Yew better run, too." With those words he sprang from behind the tree and bolted away.

Alarmed, Egiap quickly instructed Zethro to look around them and remember the lone willow tree in the location, so he might come back to the place; then she began to gather their belongings. Zethro had just finished sweeping his vision around one time when he turned to look at Egiap as she shrieked, "There they are! Run!"

But it was too late. The Union soldiers had them surrounded. One of the soldiers shot up into the air. "Halt! Give yourselves up." Egiap and Zethro froze in place with rifles pointed at them.

"Keep calm, my Zethro," warned Egiap. Zethro heard and remained silent and still.

"What's the likes of the two of yew doin' out here in de swamp. Yew holding on to this here contraband, woman?" said the sergeant of the patrol. "This here man is free according to President Lincoln. He ain't yores no more now." He looked at the both of them and then at their haversacks, checking for weapons. Satisfied that there were no other weapons but the knife he removed, he ordered his patrol to escort the two of them to the contraband camp.

That evening right after dusk they reached the contraband camp near Vicksburg. Here both were instructed to bed down at the side of the entrance. Processing of the contraband would take place in the morning. Zethro slept soundly, even through the noise of the cannon and mortars firing during the night. Egiap had a more fitful sleep, worrying about the fate of Zethro when they would be separated and wondering what the Yankees would be doing with her. She would doze and then be jerked awake by the booming of cannon and then doze again. She did not dream.

Just after daybreak the sound of Yankee bugles awakened her, and she roused Zethro. One soldier brought them some food for breakfast and told them that someone would come for them soon. He pointed out several guards nearby and said not to try to leave. If they did, the guards had orders to shoot.

Most of the day had passed before an officer with two enlisted men holding rifles approached Egiap and Zethro. "Ma'm," addressed the officer, "we are taking this contraband and processing him into the camp. You will be taken to nearby officers' quarters for questioning. Do the both of you understand?"

Both of them did, especially Zethro. He said loudly, "Yew ain't takin' Mistress Egypt frum dis here place witout me!" He moved to place his big body in front of her.

Egiap quickly said, "My Zethro, be careful. You don't need to do this."

The soldiers leveled their guns, and the officer drew his pistol.

"Please do not shoot him. He is only trying to protect me," cried out Egiap.

"Don't shoot him unless I give the order to do so," responded the sergeant. He called out to other soldiers nearby. "Over here. Assist us with this big contraband." About thirty other soldiers who had been watching the action unfold quickly walked over to the area. The sergeant yelled, "Take the big buck down!"

Several soldiers yelled as they jumped toward Zethro. Others from all sides moved toward him menacingly. The first one to touch Zethro felt a big fist in his face and dropped straight down. Two reached Zethro at the same instant, and both were peeled off by the big man with ease. Now many came at the big man at once, and eventually brought Zethro down to his knees before Zethro shed two more and stood defiant. The Union soldiers kept coming at Zethro, producing a real donnybrook with one man by himself fighting many. Several soldiers once down on the ground remained there, moaning and holding a bruised or bleeding body part. More soldiers came over to help their cause. Finally Zethro was toppled flat on his back, held there by twenty or so Yankees. It was all they could do to hold him on the ground.

Egiap, ignoring flailing arms and legs, moved around to Zethro's head in between soldiers and said firmly to him, "Zethro, they are not going to hurt me the way Ann was hurt. Please stop fighting and do as they say before they decide to shoot you and me. Please."

Zethro heard and obeyed, fearing his mistress' being shot by the Yankees. His body suddenly relaxed completely, and the soldiers holding him released their grips in disbelief that the giant of a man could be stopped by the redheaded woman.

"Please let Zethro stand, and let me say something to him," pleaded Egiap.

"So be it. Let go of him and move back a step or two, men," ordered the sergeant.

The soldiers all stood after letting Zethro go and backed away a bit. Zethro stood tall and defiant. Egiap stepped to him and motioned for him to lean over for her to whisper in his ear. The towering giant quietly did as she asked him to do. Egiap whispered several sentences in his ear and smiled at him. He straightened upright and smiled back at her. She looked closely at him, especially his face. It was cut and bled in three or four places. She asked him to bend over so she could touch his face. He did so. She reached up with both of her hands to cup his smiling face and spoke some words that no one understood but him. She pulled her hands from his face and smiled at him again. He stood tall. Egiap turned to the sergeant and spoke, "He is peaceful now. He will do as he is told. He will stay docile until provoked. Please do not provoke him once I leave him. You may take him in to be processed." Then to Zethro she added, "Go with the soldiers, Zethro, and don't fight them."

Zethro went with the soldiers without a problem, uttering not a word.

172

The officer that initially talked with them now told Egiap, "Yew come with me. Two colonels are waiting to speak with yew. I am sure they will ask yew about this ruckus yore boy kicked up. This way." He motioned to Egiap, and she walked by his side to the officers' tent.

In the tent the two colonels introduced themselves as Colonel Shannon and Colonel Yount. Both quizzed her about the big fight to take down Zethro. Then they settled in to a rather routine series of questions that Egiap could tell they had asked many people many times. Then they asked about Zethro once more.

"Is that big boy your slave?" asked Colonel Shannon.

"No, he is not a slave. He is a free man."

"Where are his papers proving he is a free man?" asked Colonel Yount. "Do you have them? Does he have them?"

"No, the papers were lost somewhere between here and New Orleans. That is where I purchased him and set him free. I had both sets copied and filed in the Orleans Parish Courthouse at the time of the sale and the manumission."

"But we are not in New Orleans, Miss Egiap," said Colonel Yount curtly. "And we have no means of securing those papers immediately."

"That means that the big man is a contraband," added Colonel Shannon. "And since you have no proof, he is to stay in the contraband camp with the other contrabands until it is decided otherwise. He could be shipped out to other more permanent camps at any time."

"But Zethro is not a slave! He is a free man. I know. I bought him and then set him free! It is not fair. It is not fair."

"Don't worry about the big guy. You need to worry about yourself," injected Colonel Yount. "We think that you are a spy for the Confederates. You are, ain't you. Now admit it. Admit it!"

173

Egiap gave the officers an aggravated look and replied, "I am no spy. I do sympathize with the Rebels, but I am a nurse, a healer. I have helped both Yankees and Rebels."

"You are a traitorous spy fer sure," piped up Colonel Shannon. "We will detain you for additional questioning." The colonel looked at her and smiled smugly.

Now Colonel Yount called out, "Guard. Guard."

In came a single Yankee soldier with a rifle. "Take this spy over to General Muniz's headquarters tent and remain with her until a proper detainment escort can be assembled to transport her to the stockade. Watch her carefully, soldier."

"Yes, Sir," responded the young private. He pointed his rifle at the redheaded woman.

"We will be at the general's tent in a few minutes. Wait for us," ordered Colonel Shannon.

"Let's go," said the private smartly as he escorted her out of the tent and into the dim light of the camp at night. "Move it."

Egiap thought quickly. They walked for a couple of minutes among the many tents. She was hesitant in her gait, all the while observing the immediate way in front of them. At the section of ground between two large tents was the dimmest place she could determine. There she took a purposeful awkward step and fell to her knees; she cried out in false pain. No one but the soldier escort saw her. He dropped his rifle aim away from the woman, held the gun with his right hand, and dropped to one knee to reach for the redhead's arm to pull her back to her feet. Egiap meanwhile had reached into her dress pocket to retrieve the small soft leather pouch that held the last half pinch of aromatic powder that would be her only hope of escaping the Yankees and heading into the cypress swamp again to hide out and hopefully reunite with Zethro.

Egiap gasped again in fake pain when she felt the soldier first grab her arm to pull her upright. She made her body go limp and crumpled again to the ground. The soldier put his face closer to her as he gripped her arm tightly and said, "Git up, woman." Egiap moved quickly and managed to blow most of the powder into the face of the soldier. He tried to talk but could not. He fell to the ground—his body completely limp now.

Fortunately for Egiap the Yankees had not restrained her hands. Also, to her luck, no other soldier had noticed what had just happened. Egiap arose and walked swiftly toward the outer tents and the darkness beyond. The cannonading of Vicksburg began anew and drew attention to the night sky in the opposite direction. She ventured into the darkness and made it to a clump of trees without being challenged by any soldier. Now she looked into the sky to determine her position. She used the stars to gauge where she was in relation to the swamp where she desired to be this night. She left the clump of trees in a slightly different direction than the one she had been heading forward in. She knew that she would have to be on guard and extra careful when the night changed into day. But she worried about Zethro. He preyed upon her mind. She prayed as she picked her way through the trees and the dark moonless night.

Sawyer Dundee now peered into the darkness where his cousin Solomon Witcher had left his sight. "Well, Sergeant Conlen, I wonder when we will see him again," Sawyer said in a low voice.

Conlen replied, "I cain't never could predict the future, but I bet me blessed mother's thistle brooch that yore cousin wilt be luckier than a leprechaun's twin brother's shillelagh coming out of this here war smelling like a spring morning in the hills of me dear Emerald Isle."

Both men turned to go a bit further behind the exterior line of fortifications to an area that held several tents for officers. Conlen veered off to the right to return to the rear of his squad of soldiers on the line.

Sawyer decided to go to his duty tent to sit and think about his cousin's visit.

Sawyer Dundee reached the tent, sat on a rickety stool, and stared out the tent entrance. He held a blank stare until a nearby large, loud explosion jostled him off the stool. More explosions occurred and increased in number. It seemed that all around him there were multiple explosions from shells landing nearby. Debris from the blasts peppered his tent until a closer explosion's blast carried the tent away. He hugged the ground, waiting and praying that the barrage would stop or move on away from him. The rolling barrage finally moved on from his immediate area. He stood upright and surveyed the now unfamiliar surroundings with the bomb blast holes and dirt and debris strewn everywhere it seemed. He could not see very far. A couple of soldiers with lighted torches rushed into the area, providing dim light for him to be able to see more of the bomb blast results. He heard some moaning from his left. "See to the men there," he ordered as he pointed left. One of the soldiers with a torch moved quickly to three men still down.

"Sir, two are dead. One alive," the soldier said.

Now other soldiers came with lighted torches. More and more of the barrage destruction could be seen. The wounded were attended to when found in the body search.

Sawyer Dundee walked a few yards and surveyed the carnage left by the barrage. Here and there for the twenty yards or so he could see in the meager light lay bodies twisted in heaps. Some wounded soldiers sat up, still dazed by what had happened. One tall man stood completely upright and shook his fist in the direction of the river and yelled, "Yew damn Yankees ain't kilt me yet. Long as I got fight in me, yew ain't go run over me. Yew bastard Republicans cain't control me. Yew kin kill me, but yew'n cain't eat me!" He stood defiant for another minute and then sat on the ground and looked on both sides of him at bodies of the dead.

Dundee walked over to the defiant soldier and asked, "Are yew hurt?"

"Naw, nuthin' but my pride," replied the man, still sitting but looking up at Sawyer.

"Are yew sure?" continued Sawyer Dundee as he sat on the ground by the man. "What's yore name, soldier?"

"Folks jist call me Carpenter," answered the man. "Cuz I bilt and fixed things afore this heah war. And I still am afixin' things fer the army." He stood. "I must find my friend Pollard. He wuz right close to me. Where he be?"

"I was in a nearby tent, too, my friend, but that tent and other things are gone, blown away or apart by the explosions. I will hep yew find yore friend," said Sawyer as he stood and started looking among the bodies. "What does yore friend look like? Is he young or older? Short or tall?"

Carpenter now said, "He looked jist like a young'un, but he tweren't a tall." He looked at the dead near him and turned over bodies to see faces as he talked. Dundee heard Carpenter say in a questioning tone just after he turned a lifeless body over, "Pollard? Pollard? Oh, my dear Lord above! Pollard!"

The man knelt and picked up the body and held the deceased soldier in his arms. "Them damn Yankees and their Lincoln. Why don't they leave us be? Why did they invade ourn homeland?" He let out a guttural yell from deep within himself. Still holding his friend's mangled body, Carpenter fell to his knees. Dundee moved over to Carpenter and sat down in the dirt beside him. Dundee could see the pain in the grimace on the face of Carpenter. He listened as Carpenter now talked once more,

"Young Pollard done tole me that he wuz brung up by his grandpappy over there in Louisiana. When news that Lincoln called for Yankee volunteers to put down the rebellion got to them, both his grandpappy and him wanted to serve to defend their homeland from the Yankee invasion. But his mama would only agree to their fightin' if'n the two of 'em did not serve in the same unit. She did'n want to lose 'em both in one battle she sayed. Sos his grandpappy Valery Bordelon went wit Louisiana volunteers that would stay in the state, and Pollard comes over to Mississippi to sign up. Oh, his pore mama!" Carpenter paused for a few seconds as tears ran down his face. "They wuz jist poor farmers trying to live respectable-like. Pollard said they done all the farm work themselfs. They did't own no slaves. He tole me they twarn't fightin' fer slavery. Young Pollard tole me that nobody should own any other person. They fought against Northern aggression agin their rights at home. His whole family hated the politicians—the whole shebang, both Lincoln's Republican monsters and the rich Democrats, who controlled society in the South." Carpenter continued his lament for a few more minutes, as he held the body of his friend close in his arms. Sawyer Dundee now put his hand on Carpenter's left shoulder and felt a dampness from freshly shed blood.

"Yew are hurt. Yew must have been struck by some shrapnel or something," pointed out Sawyer. "Come along. That's an order, soldier. Come get tended by a nurse."

Carpenter gently let down to the ground the body of his friend and fellow soldier. He stood upright again and looked into the distance to see light from exploding shells and heard the rumble of anger of the explosions as well. He followed Dundee to find a hospital area. As they walked, Sawyer wondered about his cousin Solomon.

Back outside Vicksburg, Solomon listened to Zethro tell his story. When Zethro told of the actual separation, Solomon said aloud, "How can we find her? Who would know where she is?" He stared blankly at Zethro as he consumed hardtack biscuit after hardtack biscuit. Zethro, chewing one of the biscuits, uttered some words that Solomon did not understand.

"What did you say?"

"I say dat Tree wouldst hep us'n." Zethro swallowed hard. He repeated, "Tree."

"Tree. Did you say Tree?" asked Solomon.

"Yas, sur, Massa Solomon. I heered talk of dem Yankees whilst dey kep me chained up. Dem soldiers talked 'bout dis black woman who be blind but cud see things and knowed things 'bout sum of dem soldiers and other mens."

"A blind woman who could see?" uttered Solomon.

"Yus, sur. It be couple of dese black Yankee soldiers dat come in and furst talk of Tree. I lissen good whens dey don't tink I lissens. Dem black Yankees be like me—kinda affeered of dis Tree, buts I still lissen eben dough it be scary of sorts. Dem white men Yankee soldiers talks more 'bout dat Tree woman afer the black soldiers done left the stockade. I heered dem talk more. Sos I lissen to all dat talk."

"What did you hear, Zethro?"

"Wells, Massa Solomon, dat Tree mights be sompin likes Mistress Egypt. She mights have sum power of sum kind. Dere be all kinds of talkin' 'bout dat woman called Tree. I heered dem say she be blind but cud see where folks wuz and what dey doin'. I member all dere talks. Dey sayed Tree hads a he'per woman, a young one. Hers name be—how dey sayed it?—it sound like Tu-sun-dri-anna or de like. Tu-sun-dri-anna. Dis young woman hep her de way Miss Ann done fer Mistress Egypt I believes."

179

"Did anyone ever say where this Tree woman is? How is she found?"

"Dats one of de mysteries 'bout Tree dey sayed. Nobody ever finds Tree and Tusundrianna exceptin tru de stranger called—sorry, Massa Solomon—it be anuther name I cain't say rat neither. It sound like Ab, Abdolay. Sumthin like dat. Abdulay. I don'ts know how to say it frum my mouth. I ain't never heered sech a name exceptin one time down in Nawlins whens I heered 'bout a man servant from far off. He done had a differen religion dan our'n. His clothes be differen dan our'n, too. It be said dat when he walked out on de streets of Nawlins, alls de people stop what dey doin' and jist stare at hem—tills he gwine by dem. Sum sayed he walked abouts with a strange sword. It be curved or sumthin. Dat man dey called Abdul." continued Zethro.

"Abdul. A curved sword—a scimitar?" He paused momentarily and then said, "Zethro, you presented us a clue to follow. Let's find this Abdolay fellow and find Tree and then find your mistress!" Solomon, so excited now, said to Zethro, "Now we must put together a plan. Tomorrow we begin our search at the stockade."

"Massa Solomon. Massa Solomon."

"Yes, Zethro?"

"Anuther thin' 'bouts dat Abdolay man. I heards dat he be a tinkerer and go in and outs of de contraband camp as he pleases. He don't hab no curved sword. All he has be a push-cart of wares and fixins fer pots and pans dey say."

"What did you say?"

"He be a tinkerer to fix and trade goods in de contraband camp."

"Then we go to the contraband camp to seek our man! That is our plan for tomorrow morning after I check for orders."

180

The next morning Solomon Witcher reported to his superior for directives. In less than an hour he returned to his billeting area, looking for Zethro. A few minutes passed, and Zethro came lumbering quickly to the tent. "Massa Solomon! Massa Solomon! I gots sum news 'bout dat tinkerer man. A slave of one of dese Yankee officers done tole me dat de tinkerer man come to dis heer camp dis day! Dey says he go 'round to mo places, buts dis day he be heer. Dey say he allus come in 'bout noon at de east gate. We's gonna be dere to watch fer hem?"

"Good work, Zethro. That makes it rather easy for us. My orders will take me away in three days. We will have time to find this fellow, and then I will make arrangements for you while I am away for a few days," replied Solomon. "First, I must talk with Captain Ford about a horse and rations. You wait here for me. When I return, we will go to the east gate of the contraband camp." He smiled at Zethro and then walked away toward the quartermaster tent nearby.

Well before noonday, Solomon and Zethro had positioned themselves just outside the camp's east gate area. Zethro sat on the ground, looking eastward. Solomon paced back and forth, looking in all directions. The sun beat down upon the two who were not in any kind of shade, causing both to sweat profusely. Zethro constantly wiped his forehead with the back of his left hand. Solomon repeated his pacing. Finally Solomon sat beside Zethro, but he looked in the opposite direction. In the distance they heard big guns firing and saw smoke billowing upward from the besieged city of Vicksburg. One huge explosion that was extremely loud made both of the men jerk their heads to look in the distance beyond the contraband camp. As the noise died down, both men could hear the singing of a man's voice, the jingling of bells, and the gentle clanging of pots and pans against themselves and other items of metal. These sounds drew their attention and their gazes. "Massa Solomon, it be hem," said Zethro, unbelievingly.

A dark-skinned man pushing a homemade cart headed directly toward them. The cart sported a faded red coat of paint and a makeshift cloth sunshade hanging over it directly to fend off the bright rays of the sun. Fifteen to twenty various sized bells hung from the sunshade supports and jingled and jangled because of the motion of the cart and stronger breezes of the intermittent wind. Some of the bells reflected the sun brightly; whereas, others, dulled by weather, only showed a bronze hue. Larger bells hooked themselves to the sides and front of the pushcart. They, too, clanged their message out to the whole area. Different sized pots, pans, and other metallic objects, attached all around the cart, clinked and clanked their own announcements. Cubbyholes in the front of the pushcart brandished with metal objects held in them by homemade netting. The sides of the carts possessed several little drawers hiding tools and small treasures. The back of the cart, where the dark-skinned man pushed and controlled it from, opened somewhat at the bottom to allow the owner to walk comfortably as he pushed and directed the cart. In the center of the back was a larger drawer with a metallic knob. On the knob hung a small vial containing some type of liquid. The singing voice loudly proclaimed a feeling of joy to everyone along its path, even though the sung words could not be understood by anyone there. Most of the soldiers near the gate stopped what they were doing to gawk unapologetically at the man and his pushcart approaching the gate. The man, seemingly imperious to the stares, continued his singing and his brisk gait. The man, dressed in rather colorful clothes compared to the civilians and contrabands, wore fairly loose pants somewhat like that of Zouaves and a bright red small vest as well as a Union kepi cap and standard-issue Federal army shoes. He touted a faded yellow sash around his waist. He came nearer. Now Solomon Witcher arose and walked in his direction with Zethro following closely behind.

"Mr. Abdoulaye," hailed Solomon.

The man stopped as Solomon and Zethro walked toward him. The noise of the bells and pots and pans ceased. The man removed his cap to wipe the sweat from his brow. His coarse hair, closely cropped on the top of his head, contrasted with the full beard on his face. Now he said slowly and haltingly in a strange accent, "I, sir, am Abdoulaye, at your service." He looked Solomon directly in his eyes. "What needs fixin'?" He grinned mischievously.

All eyes of the many soldier and civilian bystanders still glued themselves on Abdoulaye. Solomon approached nearer, looked at Abdoulaye, and then scanned all those persons watching. He then said to the dark-skinned man, "Let's move over to the shade of that tree where we can talk without all these people hearing what we say." Solomon pointed to the shade of a large nearby tree away from the gate and the majority of the people.

Without talking, Abdoulaye, Zethro, and Solomon moved toward the tree shade. The pushcart sounded out its usual message of bells, pots, and pans. Now the observers began to go back to their business and not watch the three men. As they reached and entered the tree shade, Zethro immediately sat at the base of the trunk. Solomon stood by Zethro and motioned for Abdoulaye to come closer to the two of them. He did so and set down his cart to rest there in the shade of the cottonwood tree. He moved slightly to the left side of his cart and looked questioningly at Solomon.

Solomon now spoke to Abdoulaye, "I desire you to help me find a woman called Tree."

Abdoulaye took one step toward Solomon and gazed deep into his eyes for several seconds without speaking. "I do not speak English good," he answered slowly and in a halting manner as he had done before. "But I do understand good," he continued. "You think I be of hep to you?"

183

"I know you can be of help to us," replied Solomon emphatically as he looked into the dark brown eyes of Abdoulaye and began to focus all his consciousness on the man. A strong gust of wind caused the bells of the pushcart to jingle-jangle loudly for a couple of seconds. Abdoulaye's eyes opened wide as the noise seemed to startle him.

"Tree is friend," said Abdoulaye in a soft yet firm voice. "You intend her no harm?"

"All we want is to meet her in order that she, with the abilities she has, can help us locate a certain individual, a woman who set Zethro here free."

Here Zethro could not contain himself and said, "Mistress Egypt." Zethro looked at Abdoulaye with a longing expression of need. Abdoulaye had turned his attention to Zethro when he had spoken.

Abdoulaye firmly and convincingly said, "Tree see. Tree see much."

"That is what we understand," added Solomon. "Will you take us to her?" Solomon now concentrated all his thought processes on Abdoulaye.

"I can not," replied Abdoulaye as he looked intently at Solomon. Abdoulaye shuffled his feet, broke Solomon's gaze, and looked down at Zethro. Zethro frowned and sighed heavily. Now Abdoulaye said to the other two men, "I must pray before this conversation is carried further. I must pray." He stepped back to his cart, quickly located a small rug of bland colors, and walked briskly over to another nearby tree to place the rug on the grass in a certain position after looking up at the sun briefly. Solomon and Zethro, taken aback by the quick action and words of Abdoulaye, were literally dumbfounded and stood and sat respectively all the while watching Abdoulaye quite intently. He immediately knelt on the rug, seemed to chant in a language unknown to Solomon, and bowed

184

to place his face on the end of the rug. He continued this practice for several minutes. He paused in his actions, spoke in that same language, and then stood upright. He bent once more to gather his rug, walked over to his cart, and stowed it away. He now turned to Solomon and Zethro and spoke slowly and haltingly as he always did, "I can not take you to Tree. Only TaSondryana can do that. But I can take you to TaSondryana." He smiled at the two men but mostly at Zethro. Now Zethro stood and grinned a large toothy grin at Abdoulaye and Solomon.

"When?" asked Solomon.

"Tonight."

Zethro grinned even more.

"When and where do we meet you?" questioned Solomon.

"After the Yankee soldiers eat their meal. About dusk. Here at this gate," came the slow, halting answer from Abdoulaye. He smiled at Solomon while saying, "At your service, I am." He smiled again and said, "But there is a fee, a cost, my friends." Solomon looked quizzically at Abdoulaye but said nothing in reply to the comment. Solomon knew he would pay anything if he could locate Egiap.

Abdoulaye bowed slightly and turned to go to his cart. He lifted it off the wooden pole rests and began to push it toward the contraband camp gate. The bells and pots and pans began announcing his presence once again as he walked toward and through the gate. Contrabands began to crowd around him as he pushed onward to the center of the camp. His voice rose again in singing his song in his foreign language.

Zethro and Solomon watched Abdoulaye and his cart vanish into the throng of contrabands in the camp. They turned to look at one another. Solomon suggested that they attend to preparations for the meeting after supper. They made haste in leaving; both were anxious to meet TaSondryana, another step in locating Egiap.

At dusk Solomon and Zethro waited impatiently outside the gate of the contraband camp for Abdoulaye to return and make good his promise to lead them to TaSondryana. Soon they heard the pushcart's bells and metallic clanging and clanking coming toward the gate from inside of the camp. Abdoulaye did not sing aloud as he came through the camp and out from the gate. He saw Zethro and Solomon and said loudly, "My friends."

Abdoulaye turned his cart toward the road from the east that led to the camp, and Solomon and Zethro followed for a time and then took positions on each side of the pushcart. Solomon looked at Abdoulaye and said, "I have money. How much do you want?"

No answer came from Abdoulaye for several minutes as they walked up the road to a ridge top. Abdoulaye abruptly stopped pushing his cart; the bells, pans, and pots went silent; and then he spoke, "I require nothing. No payment from you. I want for nothing. I humbly request that no harm come to TaSondryana and Tree. The cost for you will be revealed in time. Be patient, my friends." With that statement, Abdoulaye resumed his pushing of his cart and said nothing. The cart did the talking, along with all the sounds of Mother Nature's night creatures. The men remained silent again for a time. Solomon considered Abdoulaye's words about the cost. He wondered what the actual cost would be.

Suddenly Abdoulaye halted again and spoke to Zethro and Solomon, "See, in the dark distance, a faint lantern light." He pointed ahead of them. "TaSondryana." He pushed the cart once more and said, "I must sing, or she not be there." He belted his other-language song outward into the darkness of the night as they walked the road toward the lantern light. They turned right off the rudimentary road into what seemed in the darkness to Solomon the outskirts of a marsh or swampy area. The light disappeared suddenly and then re-appeared. Abdoulaye kept walking, pushing his cart to a tree with a petite black woman beside it.

"No fear for any of us here," said Abdoulaye loud enough for all there to hear quite plainly. The pushcart formed ruts in the ground. Abdoulaye stopped his pushing of the cart and turned to Solomon and Zethro, saying, "This girl here is TaSondryana. She is Tree's hand maiden."

TaSondryana, a pretty young woman, was dressed in a plain brown skirt and a grayish loose blouse tied at the waist with a piece of red yarn. Her hair was up on the top of her head, encircled within a dull yellow length of cloth. She smiled at Abdoulaye, all the while touching or rubbing the left side of her head and face. Both Solomon and Zethro noticed her constant attention to that side of her head. Abdoulaye spoke to her quietly and directly so that Solomon could only make out a few words or phrases that meant nothing to him in the disconnected manner he heard them. He understood when TaSondryana replied to Abdoulaye, "I wills dew jist dat fore ya. I understands. I takes them to Miss Tree." The men again noticed her constant touching of her face and the same side of her head.

Abdoulaye and TaSondryana traded some items, and then Abdoulaye turned to Solomon and Zethro to say in his halting manner, "Here is where I leave you. TaSondryana now your guide to Tree." He solemnly said other words that only he understood and then said, "I not go." The woman extinguished the lantern and placed it by the cart.

TaSondryana placed the items she received from Abdoulaye in a sack she carried and slung it over her shoulder. She looked at Zethro and Solomon and directed, "Follows TaSondryana. Now. Be's quick. Couple of gators roams 'round heer." She walked away into the darkness without the lantern but with Solomon and Zethro following with quick steps.

A half-moon began rising in the night sky. Its reflected light enabled the three sojourners to travel a bit faster, especially Zethro and Solomon, who were not familiar with the path TaSondryana took them over. The three picked their way through the swampy area with care.

They could hear the sounds of the night, particularly the huge, loud bullfrogs bellowing out until the two men following the woman tread near them. TaSondryana moved quickly and adeptly through the quagmire with the two men following, struggling to keep pace with the young woman. As she led the men, TaSondryana continuously touched her face and the left side of her head. At one point she paused and placed both of her hands on the top left side of her scalp and rubbed furiously while saying lowly, but loud enough for Solomon to hear, "Dese creepy crawlees insides my head! Miss Tree, I needs yew." The pause was only a brief one, and she motioned for the men to continue to follow her.

"We's close to Miss Tree. Careful-like rat chere. Don'ts rouse dem gators dat we seen crawlin' and restin' rat ober dere at de water edge," TaSondryana said. All stepped delicately for a few yards. A small lean-to, illuminated by the light of scores of candles, came into view of the three. Someone was seated under the lean-to, and a man stood with watchful eyes over to the left side. Solomon and Zethro stopped to look more closely at the lean-to and its immediate surroundings as TaSondryana hurried over to an old black woman, wrinkled with age, to reach out to touch her hand as she called out, "Miss Tree. I be's back. Yew hab visitors send by Abdoulaye." TaSondryana sat on the right side of the old woman and held her rough, small, withered hand. It was at this moment that the old woman turned her head toward TaSondryana. Zethro and Solomon surveyed the surroundings of the lean-to. It sat up on the highest ground of the immediate area. From where they were standing the ground sloped upward for several feet to a patch of ground about twenty yards wide and ten or so yards in depth from front to back. The lean-to, situated approximately in the center of the high ground, fastened itself to a large cypress tree on the left side. The old woman, protected by the lean-to, now smiled at the touch of TaSondryana's hand. TaSondryana smiled as well. Solomon noticed that TaSondryana no longer touched the left side of her face and head. She had stopped that and seemed at peace there with Miss Tree.

The scores of lit candles cast an eerie light in the immediate area of the lean-to housing the old black woman called Miss Tree. TaSondryana there beside her kissed the hand of the old woman. The other individual standing to the left almost as rigid as a sentry for the old woman finally seemed to relax as the others did. Solomon and Zethro walked closer to the old woman until TaSondryana held her hand up to stop them. They, now close enough and with enough light to see fairly well, examined the old woman's face with their straining eyes. Miss Tree looked directly at them it seemed, but Solomon could tell that something was amiss concerning the old woman's line of sight. "The old woman is blind," thought Solomon to himself.

At that moment Miss Tree spoke in a crackly voice, "Yas, I be blind. But I senses thin's dat many folk wit good eyes misses. Yew two be seekin' a fair redheaded Irish woman." She paused.

Zethro said under his breath so that only Solomon could hear, "Massa, how her knowed dat?"

"I knows."

Zethro shuddered in disbelief that Miss Tree knew what she said and that she heard him whisper to Solomon.

"Sits, friends of Abdoulaye. Yew be friends of Miss Tree now."

Zethro sat immediately, and Solomon followed. Both devoted their full attention to Miss Tree.

But it was TaSondryana who spoke. "Miss Tree, even though blind, see much. Miss Tree sense much. Miss Tree hab powers gifted frum God Almighty above. Rids evil frum yore hearts afore yew ask of Miss Tree. Reflects on yoreselfs afore yew ask of Miss Tree." TaSondryana ceased talking, held up two willow twigs, and tossed them

189

to the two men. She held up two more willow sticks, handed one to Miss Tree, and began to chew on one herself as Miss Tree did likewise. "Friends, chews de willow. Ease of pain come to de body and de minds."

Zethro had already picked up his willow stick and had chewed as indicated. Solomon, a lot slower, nibbled a bit and then followed Zethro's lead. Solomon admitted to himself that he thought some of his fatigue was easing, but he did not speak it aloud. The four people stared at each other for a time with the flickering candle light projecting strange shadows behind each set of two persons. Zethro, somewhat frightened, remained by Solomon and also stayed silent. The sounds of the swamp rose to a crescendo.

Miss Tree started to chant, "Tree see. Tree see. Tree see." Momentarily TaSondryana and the other individual, a black man with a deep voice and dressed in drab brown trousers and a gray shirt, picked up the chant as well.

All three repeated, "Tree see. Tree see. Tree see." They kept repeating for a few minutes until Miss Tree ceased the chant, causing the other two to stop as well when they noticed Miss Tree had stopped.

Now Miss Tree turned her head toward Zethro and said, "Boy, Miss Tree know yore name be Zethro. Miss Tree know by yore name and yore actions and talks dat yore tru to de meanin' of yore name. Yew be trulys dat birthed innocent one told in olden stories fer away in de islands. Miss Tree trust yew pure intents."

Zethro, wide-eyed in disbelief once again, turned to look at Solomon, but he did not say anything.

Miss Tree now addressed Solomon, "Witcher Man. Voodoo mon sums tink. Miss Tree know, can feel yore gifts. Sum yew knows—and sum yew not knows. Yew struggles wit dat yew knowed and dat yew still cain't knows yet. Heer de words of de Good Book: In dat night didst God appear unto Solomon, an' sayed unto him, Ask wat dat I shall giveth thee . . . An' God sayed to Solomon . . . Wisdom an' knowledge be granted unto thee." Miss Tree stared blindly at Solomon Witcher as Solomon in amazement soaked in what she preached at him. At her silence, as if on cue, the swamp creatures croaked, groaned, and screamed out their cacophony of sounds that blended into a symphony of disharmony like the one of Solomon's conflicting thoughts and doubts and dreams. The swamp sounds now blotted out even his thinking process.

Finally, Miss Tree began again with her blind stare at Solomon and her preaching aimed at him, "Tree see. Tree see de reason yew be heer ats my feets de way yew wuz at old Elnora's. The Good Book tell all and guide all. Yew be heer to asks as de words of de Song of Solomon sets forth: 'Wither is thy beloved gone . . . ?' Yew seeks Egypt! An' Egypt seek Solomon not!" Her voice ended in a high shrill tone.

Solomon, speechless, nodded in disbelief—Egiap not looking to find him. He could not remove his eyes from Miss Tree. The old black woman continued quite somber but with a firm voice, "The Good Book speak to yew likes de Solomon ob old: An' Solomon had hosses brung outs of Egypt, an' linen yarn: de king's merchants receive de linen yarn ats a price." All there—the black man servant, TaSondryana, Zethro, and Solomon—concentrated on the voice and words of Miss Tree. Miss Tree mesmerized all four of them. They had not noticed the gentle breeze that gained a bit of strength and now rustled the leaves and limbs of the trees about them. Miss Tree paused. Suddenly she shouted as loud as her old voice could, "An' dis be de yarn yew seek!"

At that instant the strong breeze gusted and snuffed out all of the candles providing the flickering light for the encampment. Miss Tree held her right arm up in the air and kept it still. TaSondryana and the black man servant, recovering from the shock of the moment, hurried to light candles again. At first Zethro and Solomon looked at the points of light that TaSondryana and her fellow servant lit around the edges of the encampment. The two moved to light candles nearer to Miss Tree. Now everyone could see what Miss Tree held in her hand above her head. It was a piece of bright red yarn, fluttering in the slight breeze!

Solomon's and Zethro's eyes fixed themselves on the bright piece of red yarn lifted upward to the night sky. No sounds came from the swamp creatures all around them. The silence stifled all there. Only the words now uttered by Miss Tree commanded the quiet night. Miss Tree spoke once again after most of the candles had been re-lit. She emitted her words slowly and deliberately and in a strong yet caring voice, "What Tree see be of mighty interest to youse dat sets rat heer afore Tree. Tree see dat weepin' willow surround by dyin' cypress knees; a beautiful, smilin', young woman in a white weddin' dress a'dancin' wit de undertaker; and dis bigs black burd wit de gray head feaders flyin' most fastest in de urly mornin' light frum outs ob a grabeyard."

Miss Tree paused for a brief moment and let out a terrifying scream and then lamented aloud, "Naw, naw, naw. Gud Lord, lets dat nots happens." Miss Tree, now along with all there in the middle of the swamp, sat paralyzed in place.

Abruptly Zethro and TaSondryana both fell flat on the ground, engulfed in spasms. Before Solomon and the black man-servant could move, Miss Tree spoke, "Leave dem be! Lissen ta me. Tree see dat Xeno know." Now Miss Tree collapsed onto the ground from her sitting position. No spasms controlled her; she lay still, breathing heavily. This act seemed to liberate and invigorate the night sounds of the swamp. Solomon looked all about him, and his ears filled with the excessive noise of the night. He glanced at Zethro and TaSondryana; both now resembled corpses long still.

Solomon bent over to Zethro, motioned to the man-servant to go to TaSondryana, and called Zethro's name several times as he placed his hands on Zethro's warm face. Zethro opened his eyes, saying, "Massa Solomon, wheres I been? Dere be Mistress Egypt at de weepy willow tree; dere be dis undertaker man callin' out sumtin likes Dodie gurl whens allus dat dancin' music play; and dere be mees aflyin' likes a burd frum dat Nawlins cemetery place we wuz at. An' den I's sees dat Xeno man. Ands, Massa Solomon, Mistress Egypt and dat Dodie gurl, and mees as dat burd, and Xeno—allus hab a piece of red string tied on us'n. Wheres I been?"

At this time TaSondryana sat up, helped by the man-servant. She flailed at him at first and then calmed down. She cried softly. She looked over at Miss Tree and immediately arose to check on the old black woman. Some of her tears fell upon Miss Tree's face, and she opened her eyes weakly. Her eyelids fluttered, and she said simply, "Rest. I's needs rest." With those words, she reclined with TaSondryana's help and immediately fell into a deep sleep.

Now TaSondryana called the man-servant by name saying, "Ezra, covers Miss Tree wit hers blanket." He did so quickly but with an obvious practiced care. "Nows we'ns leave her be fer a time."

Ezra stood up straight and motioned for Zethro and Solomon to follow him as he walked gingerly to another high spot about fifteen yards to the north of the large tree with the lean-to. He lit several candles and an old rusty lantern, which gave off surprisingly much light. TaSondryana joined them momentarily and sat on the dry ground next to where Ezra sat. Zethro and Solomon sat as well. Initially they all stared at each other until Solomon broke the silence by saying, "What just happened?"

No one said anything for a long pause. Finally, TaSondryana spoke against the background of the natural sounds of the swamp. "Ezra and me seen Miss Tree do dis riddle foretellin' afore now. She's done dis ting afore dis heer war done start. Fore dat, Miss Tree onlys foretells simple tings. Miss Tree see if'n a gurl get married or if'n a husband be

193

cheatin' or if'n a sickly child get ober de ill times. De time 'fore dis heer war dat Miss Tree do dis same big foretellin' wit hers needin' rest be de time dat her tells of de fightin' atween dem Yankees and dese white folk alls in de South. Miss Tree done tells us'n all 'bout de biggest war we'd ever, ever seed dat comin' down to allus peoples heer. Allus done figures outs her riddling foretellin' onlyest after de shootin' done start." TaSondryana took a rather deep breath and then clawed at the side of her head.

"Is Miss Tree all right?" asked Solomon.

"Yus, sur, Miss Tree be good afer she done sleeps fer a time."

"Massa Solomon, how do Miss Tree know dose tings her be tellin' allus?"

"I am still pondering, thinking about what she said that we know is true and still wondering about what she said about your mistress at the weeping willow tree, the dancing undertaker, and that crow flying. And, Zethro, what you said when you came out of the seizure that you had at the same time as TaSondryana."

"Miss TaSondryana done whats I dids?" questioned Zethro.

"Yes. Both of you had a sort of fit at the same time."

None of the four people said anything for a few seconds; they just sat and let the swamp sounds fill their ears.

"TaSondryana, did you dream or envision things during your black-out time?" asked Solomon.

"I's dream of a cat dat be shot by a Yankee soldier. Ands den dis here big ole crow done flied down to de ground by dat little cat. Dat big old burd seem to cry fer de cat. I goes ober to de burd an' holds my hands out to dat crow burd. He done fly up to dese hands and lands rat in dem. He den cawed so louds de sounds done hurts my ears," she replied. "De cawing wakes me up." She reached up to touch her face and pressed on it gently.

In the distance of the swamp the four heard the screech of a swamp cat, immediately followed by the flapping of large wings overhead and the cawing of a large crow. All were startled. "Massa Solomon, yew heered dat—dose sounds we be talkin' 'bout?" asked Zethro in amazement.

"Yes."

Ezra finally spoke, "I goes by Miss Tree." Rising, he walked carefully to where Miss Tree slept. He sat some five feet away from her at an angle he could see her face.

"Tell us about Miss Tree," said Solomon to TaSondryana. "How did the two of you get together? Was she always blind? How did she get the name Miss Tree? Was she a contraband?"

TaSondryana scratched her scalp, looked at Solomon and Zethro, and replied, "Naw, sur, Miss Tree nevers been a contrabands. Her says de contrabands camp 'most like a prison to her. Her says her not gonna die in dat camp. Dem Yankees don't cares 'bout de old peoples and dose cripple in sum way. Alls dey wants is de mens to dig holes and die in shooting at de Rebels. Her says de feber and de Yellow Jack runs in dose camps. Her sees too many ob her peoples done died in camps."

Solomon added, "Miss Tree may be right about the illness that runs through the camps."

"Me and Miss Tree? Miss Tree tooks me in to care fer when I be little gurl. I be put out on de side of de road sout of Vicksburg. Dey say I wander alone fer days 'til Miss Tree tooks me off de road and intos de swamp ways away frum dose peoples dat says my scratchin' and rubbin' my head and face be frum de devil heself. Dey says I be evil. Buts not Miss Tree. Her seed me and tought I be blessed child loved by de dear

195

Lord above us'n all. It be one day 'bouts ten year back dat I furst seed sumthin' wrongs 'bout Miss Tree's eyes. She be wakin' up frum a night's fitful sleep and habe dis sort of green, crusty mess on boat of her eyes. We treats dem wit a poultice I be tole to mix. Miss Tree be blind from de next days on. But we see dat her lost hers eyesight but gained sumden else frum de Good Lord. Her be a foreteller. Her cud scc bits ob de future eben dough her be blind. De Good Lord done took hers sight, but He gives her greater sight. Ans when I be's next to her and touches her eber so often, dis infernal itch and creepy crawlin' feelin' be reliefed. I goes some ways away frum Tree, ands de infernal itchin' start 'gin. I's hab to be closer to Miss Tree. Likes now, I start de scratch agin. I too far frum Miss Tree. It likes God want us be close."

Zethro and Solomon listened carefully and in amazement to TaSondryana. She continued to answer the questions that Solomon posed to her. "Miss Tree get her name from hers granmammy when she be furst birthed. Miss Tree mamma name her Treannakeio, but de granmammy, old and some deaf, jist call her Tree cuz her say her dose not understand de real name. De old woman cud probly only heer de part da say sound likes Tree. De name Tree be what allus de family call her. It stuck on her. So's her be Tree to all peoples dere on de plantation."

"Massa Solomon, who be dis Dodie gurl I seed?" asked Zethro.

"She is a sick girl in Vicksburg I met," answered Solomon in a dismissive manner. "We must get back to that world of war out there." He pointed his hand. "TaSondryana, can you take us back out? Will Miss Tree be waking up soon?"

TaSondryana, scratching her head, stood and replied, "Miss Tree sleep long time. Ezra watch her. I kin git yew backs to da road wheres we meets Abdoulaye." Solomon, first to rise from his sitting position, reached his hand down to Zethro. The big man smiled and clasped Solomon's helping hand. Zethro's huge hand engulfed Solomon's hand,

and Solomon had to strain a bit as he helped big Zethro up from the ground. Solomon thought about the power and strength of Zethro and smiled back at him.

"Let's go," proclaimed Solomon. TaSondryana led the way past the lean-to where Miss Tree slept and onward through the swamp back to the road where they had first met. All the while, TaSondryana scratched and rubbed the side of her head and face. Solomon pondered the anguish felt by the young black woman as she endured the constant agitation of her skin and scalp. He thought that it was good that TaSondryana had made the connection with Miss Tree. TaSondryana and Miss Tree were good for each other. Ezra helped and benefited as well. "But what would happen to them in the middle of this war?" Solomon asked to himself.

Solomon recognized the road area as they came out of the thickets of trees that bounded the swamp on the side they had entered when they left Abdoulaye earlier in the night. The three trudged up the slight incline and noticed the first light of the new day coming from the east. All were tired from the experience of the night coupled with no sleep. They reached the road and stopped as Zethro, the last in line, stepped onto the narrow road.

TaSondryana turned to look at Zethro and Solomon. She said to them, "Please not tells where Miss Tree be. I's be affeered of the soldiers—boat Yankees and Rebels. Miss Tree be hard to move frum one place to anuther. Please." She reached her hand up to rub her face and scalp. She scratched her scalp hard.

Solomon replied to her comments, "We won't give up the location. Zethro and I swear it. You and Miss Tree helped us."

Zethro quickly interjected, "I's swears it, Miss TaSondryana." He looked at her with genuineness in his eyes. He continued to look at her and now said, "Miss TaSondryana, yew be bleedin' on de side of yore head. Be yew scratchs it toos hard?"

Solomon said, "TaSondryana, you must not scratch too hard and too much." He looked closely at the side of her head where the blood was gently oozing down. "Allow me to see for a moment please." He placed his hand gently on her chin and turned it slowly in order to see the bleeding spot on the side of her head. He touched the spot with two of his fingers, looked at the small amount of blood on them, and pressed his entire hand on her scalp while saying, "Put a little pressure here for a time, and the bleeding should stop. Ask Miss Tree for help in mixing a poultice or something to place on the spot when you get back to her." He removed his hands from her head and stepped backward. He looked at her again and said, "Thanks for taking us to Miss Tree. Thanks for everything. I will remember Miss Tree's words and attempt to answer the riddles and enigmas in them. I think that we will find the person we seek because of what Miss Tree told us."

TaSondryana nodded her head. Then she looked at Zethro. She said to him, "Maybes de big ole crow we'ns dream ob be a good sign." She smiled at him and reached over to put her hand on his. Zethro grinned a big toothy smile at her as he nodded his head in agreement with her. "Good-bye, Zethro." Now she turned to Solomon and said, "Good-bye, Massa Witcher." She reached into a pocket of her shabby brown skirt and pulled out something that she placed in Solomon's hand. It was the piece of red yarn that Miss Tree had held up. Now she turned and stepped off the road in the increasing light of morning.

"Farewell," said Solomon. He glanced down at his hand and the red yarn it held. Zethro waved to her as she looked back a few yards away.

The two men now followed the road to return to the Yankee camp near Vicksburg. As Zethro hummed, Solomon reflected upon the words and warning from Miss Tree.

TaSondryana reflected, too, but not upon the words Miss Tree had uttered in the swamp, but instead on the sudden realization that she was not scratching or rubbing her face or scalp. She raised her hand to touch the place that had bled. She could not find a raw open sore with her hand. Now she recollected some words that Miss Tree had spoken to Solomon. She remembered that Miss Tree had addressed Solomon as "voodoo mon" at one point. She felt for the open sore again and still found nothing at the place it had been on her scalp. She halted in place for a moment. No itch on her face or scalp. No creepies on her skin. She wondered how long it would last. She again walked, and now she hummed an old church hymn that Miss Tree had taught her. TaSondryana, while humming, thought about Zethro as she continued her way back to Miss Tree.

The cannonading now seemed never to cease in and around Vicksburg. Sawyer Dundee went through the regular rotations in the front siege lines daily. The Union General Grant determined that frontal assaults now would rarely occur; instead, the cannons and mortars could fire until the barrels became too hot for safe shooting. But to Sawyer it seemed that very few of the Union guns remained silent for any length of time.

This particular evening near dusk Sawyer Dundee sat and attempted to eat the meager food before him. The pea meal bread and the pea soup and the peas themselves quickly became tasteless after no variety of other foods. He sat and thought about his cousin and whether he had made it through the lines safely and pondered as to what was Solomon's real job in the military and how going from one side of the siege lines to the other would serve what purpose. He was deep in thought when he heard, "How yew?"

Captain Dundee looked up. "How yew?" said the deep voice once again. Two soldiers stood before him; and when he glanced up, the other said, "How yew, Cap'n?"

The other soldier said, "Want sum comp'ny, Cap'n? Yew look wrapt up in thought."

199

"Yes, welcome to supper heah in the Vicksburg Hotel, men."

As they ate and talked, Sawyer thought that these were his kind of people—plain, simple, ordinary farmers and workers—just like those Cajuns Solomon and he had conversation with. They talked of the weather, the Yankees, going home after the war, and lost comrades for a time. They laughed and joked with one another, poking fun at officers, including Captain Dundee, good-naturedly. They all were wondering aloud about what the future would hold—what the outcome of the war and its aftermath would be, even if the Union would ultimately force the seceded states back into the Union.

It was at this point in their conversation that another voice became an interloper at this supper meal. A man, who was standing nearby and eating, ambled up to them and said to them in a firm theatrical voice, "If you can look into the seeds of time/And say which grain will grow and which will not,/Speak, then, to me, who neither beg nor fear/Your favors nor your hate." He abruptly stopped and just stood before them, smiling.

The three men looked up at him. Solomon spoke with a question, "Those lines from?"

"Shakespeare's *Macbeth*, Captain, Sir," quickly put in the man.

"Come, sit with us. Yew will be an interesting addition to our conversations. Here. Sit here," directed Sawyer.

"Yeah. How yew?" said the first soldier. "I be Malachi."

The second soldier looked at the man and said, "How yew? I am Zebedee, but I answer to Zeb mostly."

"I am Sawyer Dundee."

"My name is Xenophones, but call me Xeno," added the stranger.

Xeno sat on the ground by the others. "Ye hail frum whereabouts?" asked Zebedee. All the men looked at Xeno.

"New Orleans, until them damn Yankees overtook it," answered Xeno. "My family lived there; that is, until the city politicians and so-called business leaders hid the Yellow Jack epidemic from the masses of the citizens. Thousands died who could have been saved if they had been told early on." Bitterness showed on Xeno's face and in his voice. He hung his head momentarily. "But those memories only haunt me some of the time." He went silent.

"We be frum the hill country in north Louisiana," put in Malachi. "We think them damn Yankees be wrong to invade our homeland. We jist want to farm our lands and raise our families in peace."

Sawyer Dundee now added, "Me. I am from jist down the river there at Natchez. My daddy owned a sawmill and a few slaves. I worked in the mill from the time I was old enough to gather scrap pieces of wood. When old enough and grown enough, I trained to be a sawyer jist like my name. It was destiny I suppose."

Sawyer halted his talking and looked into the fatigued faces of his fellows there in the besieged Confederate stronghold. "I, too, am tired already of this war, especially of this siege tightening around us. I can see the weariness in each of yore faces. But I see conviction to see it to the end—no matter what the outcome."

Zebedee put in, "We'ns don't care 'bout what dem damn Yankees do 'bout dem slaves. We never did own none and never would. Free 'em all. No niggar ever bothered me, and I don't mess wit 'em either. Jist leave us be. But don't come heah shootin' and killin' and invadin' this land."

"Jist leave us be," agreed Malachi. "Let them Yankee politicians free all them Negras and let us alone." All shook their heads affirmatively. Malachi added, "This be a rich man's war and a poor man's fight."

Sawyer now spoke, "What are yew doing up here in Vicksburg, Xeno? Yew are some kind of actor or singer, ain't yew?"

"I am an educated man," answered Xeno. "My dear mother made sure of that. I am literate in many areas and am trained in the theatrical arts. My family had money, much money; but that money did not save them from the yellow fever. I was the only one in my family to survive the epidemic. I spent and gave away my inheritance and roamed the New Orleans streets and alleys. A Catholic priest Father Ones pulled me from the streets, and I was a single vow away from committing my life to the priesthood. I took to the New Orleans *Vieux Carre* as a street preacher and holier-than-thou individual who felt sorry for himself for a long time. But I had an epiphany. One night in the Girod Street Cemetery—that is when it was. That night I realized, I knew, I felt the true power of the Lord God Almighty." He reached into his pocket and held out a piece of red cork. "I picked this beautiful stone from a bizarre grave marker memorial that projected a skull, a Death Head, outward for all to see at the cemetery entrance. This beautiful stone is my constant reminder of my personal epiphany. It was then that I became an instrument of good, someone to assist others. I now help those around me however I can. I have some skill in nursing the ill and the wounded. I have some skill in acting and singing."

Sawyer interrupted by saying, "That's where I have seen yew. Yew sing in the hospital area among the sick and wounded to build up their spirits. It does help. Many of the wounded have told me so. They remember yew."

"I hope I do raise spirits of those wounded and ill," said Xeno. He paused; his face displayed a compassionate and perplexing countenance. "I am truly apologetic, gentlemen, for my personal outpouring of grief and confession, but, but the three of you, here in this setting—your conversation and openness that I overheard before I came to join you and the dialogue we had, just somehow make me open up to you. I hope you accept my apologies for burdening you with my story."

Just as Xeno said that, a series of explosions began about three hundred yards away and marched toward the food preparation and eating area. One shell exploded some fifty feet away from the talking soldiers. Sawyer now yelled, "Gentlemen, nice to visit with all of yew. Pray we meet again. Back to yore stations." Malachi and Zebedee ran one way. Solomon and Xeno ran another. These two ran around a nearby house and parted ways.

Just before they split, Xenophones yelled at Sawyer, "Those who can look into the seeds of time are often fantastical!" Then Xeno ran rapidly into the darkness. Xeno apparently had halted for a moment more to shout out to Sawyer, "But those who hope in the Lord will renew their strength. They will soar on wings of eagles; they will run and not grow weary; they will walk and not be faint." His words from the Book of Isaiah floated ominously on the night air between the sounds of two immense explosions nearby.

Outside Vicksburg, Solomon wondered if he would find Egiap. He reflected again on Miss Tree's words, especially those about his seeking Egiap and those about her not seeking him. Troubled by those words and others of Miss Tree, Solomon remembered that Ann had told him that Egiap loved him and of Egiap's dismay at the fact he did not wear a red string about one ankle. He thought Egiap to be an enigma, but one worth pursuing. He remained steadfast in his hope and his resolve to re-connect with her.

He knew that the siege of Vicksburg was winding down and that the Confederates must soon surrender the city to General Grant. He would suggest that the area needed canvasing for contrabands not already in Union hands and that he would volunteer to lead and direct the effort because he had been told he would not be involved in any specific assault or surrender negotiations due to the clandestine nature of his duties. He knew he could persuade his superior. That very evening he discussed the suggestion with his commanding officer and received permission to carry out his plan for three days.

The next morning he directed two patrols as to where to look and how to search each day. He would search swamp areas. Each patrol would meet him back at camp in the evening and report. He, along with Zethro, would travel and search in civilian clothes.

The first day proved a futile search for Solomon and Zethro. Solomon hoped that Zethro would recognize some natural landmark that would help them in locating Egiap. He and Zethro sought willow trees as foretold in Tree's visions.

The second day found the two men sitting on a fallen tree trunk at high noon as they ate army rations. A bird's high-pitched screech caught their attention, and both men looked to the direction from where it seemed to originate. The wind gusted just a bit. Zethro, almost yelling at the top of his lungs, pointed and said, "Massa Solomon, looks at dat! See dat. See dat bit of red string." The flutter of a bird taking wing caused them to look up at a crow flying upward and away.

The men dropped their food, picked up their belongings, and quickly made their way to the small tree that had a red string tied to a waist-high branch. Zethro hurried to the tree and broke the small branch with the red string. He held it out to Solomon Witcher. "Mistress Egypt be's heer. She wuz rat heer."

"Yes. Yes," said Solomon. He took the small branch in his hand and twirled it between his fingers.

"Looks, Massa Solomon. Dere's anuther red string ways ober dere!" Zethro ran over to another small tree. He broke that branch off and, returning, handed it to Solomon.

"Stand here and look that way, the way deeper into the swamp, for more red string," directed Solomon. The men scanned about 180 degrees with their eyes. They saw nothing. "Take a few steps in that direction, and I will do the same in this slightly different way," said Solomon. Now both men moved a few steps.

Zethro became more excited and yelled, "Ober dere!"

Solomon walked to where Zethro was and looked to see what Zethro was excited about. It was another piece of red string tied on a low bush.

Solomon glanced back to where the other bit of string had been, figured a quick angle and direction in his head, and said firmly, "This way. Walk this way." He and Zethro began to walk briskly but carefully in the swampy area. They found another piece of red string and another and another as they walked. Each small piece of red string was tied on a tree or bush approximately twenty to thirty feet from the next one. Both men felt a rush of excitement and anxiety as they made their way deeper into the swamp.

Solomon spied a rather tall weeping willow tree and picked up his pace, striding toward it with abandon. Zethro followed just as quickly as Solomon moved. They came to an open space around the willow tree and knew it was the place where Egiap and Zethro had buried Anne's body that time in the deep swamp. It was the location that Miss Tree had described.

Zethro, almost jumping up and down, affirmed that this was the camp site and burial site. A closer look yielded even more proof—a small bit of red string was tied to almost all of the cypress knees that practically circled the willow tree. Solomon surveyed the area as Zethro slowly walked over to a nearby spot. He arrested Solomon's attention when he said, "Dis be wheres pore Miss Ann be put." Solomon looked over at the big black man and saw a heavy tear run down on his cheek.

"I am sorry, Zethro," responded Solomon.

"De Yankees kilt Miss Ann! She save me frum de bullet," Zethro's voice grew weak. He dropped down to the ground and sat, rocking back and forth. He prayed.

Now Solomon glanced around the area once more. He looked more closely at the willow tree's trunk. As he perused the trunk from the roots upward with his eyes, he thought about Miss Tree's use of the willow sticks and her seeing the willow tree in her vision. He could hear Zethro muttering prayers in the background. He turned to look at Zethro and then turned back to view the willow again. The wind gusted now.

A ray of sunshine found its way through the branches and leaves of the willow and for a brief moment reflected off the trunk. "What was that?" asked Solomon aloud. Zethro did not look up from his praying. But Solomon had to go closer to the willow tree trunk just to see if his eyes played a trick on him. As he stepped nearer to the tree trunk, he saw nothing in among the hanging branches of the weeping willow. He, disappointed in seeing nothing, nevertheless approached even closer, wanting in his heart and mind and soul to find a clue or something about Egiap. Still he saw nothing that could have reflected a bit of a ray of the sunlight that filtered through the branches and leaves. He stood only a couple of feet away from the weeping willow tree trunk. He sent his eyes down at the bottom of the trunk once more—the last look he thought—and lifted his eyes upward in a final desperate search for something, anything. He thought now positively that his eyes had tricked him, that his strong desire for a clue to find Egiap had influenced his eyes and mind to see something that was not really there. His face fell literally as he dropped his head down forward. But then, he spotted something unnatural about the tree trunk. He looked more closely at a spot on the tree trunk about two feet from the ground. It seemed to be a bit of metal stuck into the trunk. He bent down to examine it with his eyes and then reached out to touch it. He could not believe his eyes once more. It was a piece of metal, something like a large, long, thin nail that had something pinned to the trunk. He pulled on the metal object and removed it from the tree trunk. Along with it came a small leather pouch, almost the identical color of the tree trunk. The long piece of metal that had reflected a bit of a sunray that caught his attention was a polished brass hairpin! It was Egiap's pin that she used in her red hair and on her cloak! He pulled the long part of the metal hair pin from the small leather pouch and opened the pouch. A small piece of paper was inside, and it was tied with a short piece of red string. Carefully he pulled the string and unfolded the paper.

Solomon read these words from the paper: "Wither is thy beloved gone? Sing I the Song of Solomon."

Solomon froze in stance and place and time. He thought to himself that Miss Tree had uttered words similar to what was written. His mind reeled with wild phantasmagorial thoughts. Slowly he regained control of this thinking and brought himself back to the place in the Mississippi swamp. He folded the paper and placed it back into the small leather pouch. His fingers felt a slight roughness to one side of the pouch. He stepped out into an area of bright sun between the trees and examined the side of the small pouch. Something was scratched or etched into the leather. He looked more closely. It was some sort of design that he did not know what it was. "What is Egiap saying to me? What is her message?"

Again Solomon froze in position. He wondered where Egiap was and what had happened to her. He wondered where the war would take him next and what would happen around him and to him. He placed the pouch and its contents into his pocket. He put the hair pin in his boot. He did not know his fate.

Yankee cannon and mortars made life unbearable for the people of Vicksburg and its Confederate defenders. During the siege, the Vicksburg residents, who called themselves "rats," and soldiers had been forced to eat mule and horse meat, and when that was scarce, they ate rats, birds, and other small animals. They all knew the taste of pea meal and pea meal bread.

General Grant's army was ever tightening the stranglehold on Vicksburg and its defenders. The constant bombardment and intermittent assaults at several points along the Confederate lines kept the pressure on General Pemberton and his men. Things were becoming grim. The Confederate defenders needed relief, but none was available. General Pemberton was feeling desperate, and an air of despair and gloom was about in every staff officers' meeting.

On July 2, 1863, General Pemberton met in a hastily called afternoon senior officers' meeting. Pemberton looked particularly worn and distressed. The officers gathered with only a few words exchanged among themselves. No one spoke directly to General Pemberton, and he did not speak directly to any other officer either. He was preoccupied. Each officer knew that the end of the ordeal at Vicksburg was at hand, but none wanted to say anything about it. Sawyer had noticed a change in General Pemberton since Solomon had talked with him. It had been a gradual change, but it was one of drastic proportion he could see now.

"Gentlemen," General Pemberton broke the heavy silence," I have decided that the time has come for me to meet with my adversary, General Grant. I must surrender Vicksburg because of the hopelessness of our situation. Citizens of Vicksburg and our soldiers of the Confederate army have shown the utmost courage and valor while suffering severe hardships. I feel I must capitulate upon the best attainable terms." He paused to look at his officers. No one spoke. "Colonel Branigan, Major Dodd, and Captain Dundee, you three officers will please make arrangements for me to meet with General Grant tomorrow afternoon." He paused once again. He looked intently at his officers. "Thank you, gentlemen. You will be informed of the meeting as soon as I return. You are dismissed." The Confederate staff officers left the room, leaving General Pemberton sitting at his desk.

On the afternoon of July 3, General Pemberton and three officers met with Union General Ulysses S. Grant to discuss terms of surrender for the Confederate forces at Vicksburg. Grant had five of his officers at the meeting. Grant's terms were simple and blunt. He wanted unconditional surrender. Pemberton refused. The discussion bogged down. The meeting ended. The subordinate officers of Pemberton's staff had said nothing during the meeting's actual discussion. Only General Pemberton spoke for the Confederates. The four Confederates rode slowly and silently back into Vicksburg's defenses. General Pemberton went to his headquarters room and closed the door.

Later that afternoon Sawyer was alerted that three Yankee officers under a flag of truce were coming through the lines to General Pemberton's headquarters. He hurried there when summoned. Major Dodd and Colonel Branigan were there, also.

In General Pemberton's chamber the Union spokesman Colonel Wagner stated that his commander General Grant had modified his terms for surrender. "General Grant, sir, sends his regards along with us. He has thought about your statements and considered your requests." He pulled out a sheet of paper from his coat pocket. He read, "Soldiers must sign parole agreements not to engage in fighting again until exchanged as prisoners of war. They will be released upon signing the agreement. Officers may keep their sidearms and a mount, if horses are available in sufficient number in your hands at the present." He stopped, stepped forward, and handed the paper to General Pemberton. "General Grant stated that he is anxious to see an end to the hardship on your soldiers and the inhabitants of Vicksburg. I await your reply, sir. It does have to be in writing at this time, sir."

General Pemberton silently re-read the paper that had previously been read aloud to him. He looked around at his Confederate officers and then at the Union ones. He cleared his throat, paused momentarily in deep thought, and in a tired voice said, "Tell your General Grant that I accept his terms. When does he wish the formalities?"

"Tomorrow morning at 10 a.m., Sir," replied Colonel Wagner crisply.

"Agreed," stated Pemberton in a sad tone.

The Yankee officers saluted.

General Pemberton said, "Colonel Branigan and Major Dodd, accompany these gentlemen to their headquarters to work out the details. When you return, report to me at once."

"Yes, Sir," said both at the same time.

The Union officers and the two Confederates filed from the room.

"Captain Dundee, you are to assist me in preparation for tomorrow."

"Yes, Sir, at your service, Sir," said Sawyer.

They worked for an hour, sending out the sad orders for the Confederate defenders. An air of gloom permeated every action. Work slacked off. Confirmation of the receipt of the surrender order came slowly back from the various commands along the Confederate defensive lines. In several hours Major Dodd and Colonel Branigan returned from Grant's headquarters. They informed the general, and he immediately called an officers' meeting to discuss the next day's proceedings.

At the end of the meeting, General Pemberton dismissed his officers to go back to their men. "Captain Dundee, a moment please." The others exited the room. Only Sawyer and the general remained. "Captain, I need a minute or two of your time. I realize something that upsets me terribly above and beyond the fact that I surrender Vicksburg. It is what day tomorrow is. Do you realize tomorrow's date is July 4, 1863? It's Yankee Independence Day. The South will never forgive me for surrendering Vicksburg formally on July fourth. But I am doing so because I thought I could get more generous terms than if I held out longer." He stopped talking and sat at his desk, his head in his hands. He quietly said, "You are dismissed, Captain Dundee. I wish to be alone."

Sawyer left the room, closing the door as he did. He, too, was stinging from the fact of surrender on the Fourth of July. He, too, was hurting for his general. But he understood the general's thinking.

The next morning after a peaceful night of no bombardment the Confederates surrendered Vicksburg to Grant. Weapons were stacked and counted. Soldiers in gray marched out from Vicksburg, and soldiers in blue marched in.

Anguish sat heavily in Confederate troops' hearts and minds. Most participated in the surrender activities in somber silence. The Third Louisiana Infantry could not hold in their torment and cursed in loud preponderance. Some soldiers hit trees with their rifles and strew ammunition all around. Many Louisiana soldiers ripped their own flags into small pieces and shreds; soldiers took flag pieces as remembrances of the siege and their fellows. Many of the soldiers picked up threads and scraps of the mutilated flags that they had heretofore proudly fought under and for. They really did not want to be part nor parcel of the surrender. Captain Dundee witnessed the true anguish of the Louisiana soldiers; and, after the unit had moved on from the area, he himself walked over to scoop up shreds and threads from the leftovers of the flags. Reaching down with one hand to gather his own remembrance of the day, he gathered small pieces of blue and white and red material plus bits of blue and white and red string. He plucked one small length of red string from his hand and thought about his cousin Solomon's comment about the red string. He

211

looked at it intently—what had once been part of a symbol was now just a piece of red string. He twirled the small section of red string between his fingers and thought that all the significance of the flags would soon be only a part of history.

The parole agreement process began for soldiers who were not officers. Federal rations were given to the Confederate soldiers and civilians. Rebel officers would be the last in the parole process. Sawyer himself would be the last of the last. He was still in Vicksburg with General Pemberton when news came that Port Hudson had surrendered five days after Vicksburg. Now the Union had control of the Mississippi River. The Confederacy had been severed.

Sawyer did not know how long he was to remain in Vicksburg. When most officers had been processed, he was informed that officers of General Pemberton's staff would be detained for a period of time. Rumor indicated that some would be sent to New Orleans for a time and that some would be sent to Memphis. He did not know his fate.

To Be Continued . . .

212

Made in the USA
Lexington, KY
18 May 2019